"You and I don't have anything in common anymore,"

Elizabeth said, vowing not to cry.

"Just eighteen years of marriage," Donovan snapped.

"And we don't talk at all."

"Only every morning and every evening."

"It's time to end it now, while we still care about each other."

"A great way to show how you care." Donovan didn't look at her.

"Oh, Donovan. You've got to try and understand. I've been a wife and mother for so long that I'm not sure who else I am. I want to find out if I'm something more."

"Of course you're more than a wife and mother. Don't be a fool."

Elizabeth looked straight into his eyes. "What else am I, Donovan? You tell me."

Dear Reader,

Once again, we're bringing you a month of books that have us excited and, we think, will excite you, too. First up is the final book in Lucy Hamilton's Dodd Memorial Hospital Trilogy, *Heartbeats*. Nurse Vanessa Rice and Detective Clay Williams made their debuts in the first book of the trilogy, and two less-likely lovers could hardly be found. But in this book they learn that differences can be exciting as they fight for a future together.

Another special book is Lee Magner's *Mustang Man*. Lee has published a number of romances in the past, but we think she's really come into her own with her first novel for Silhouette Books. *Mustang Man* combines adventure, suspense and, of course, a strong dose of high-voltage romance to come up with a reading experience you won't soon forget.

Dallas Schulze is back with *Donovan's Promise*, a deeply emotional look at a once-married couple who are destined to get back together again, and Heather Graham Pozzessere visits her home state of Florida in *Angel of Mercy*, an Everglades adventure with a romance that sizzles.

Next month, as a special treat, look for *From Glowing Embers*, the first of a new miniseries from popular author Emilie Richards. Of course, Emilie will be in good company next month and in the months to come, when you can expect to see books from new discoveries like Andrea Parnell and old favorites like Parris Afton Bonds, Kathleen Eagle and Nora Roberts, to name only a few. As always, when you're looking for romance, you can count on Silhouette Intimate Moments.

Leslie J. Wainger
Senior Editor

Dallas Schulze

Donovan's Promise

Silhouette Intimate Moments

Published by Silhouette Books New York

America's Publisher of Contemporary Romance

SILHOUETTE BOOKS
300 East 42nd St., New York, N.Y. 10017

ISBN: 0-373-07247-3

First Silhouette Books printing July 1988

Printed in the U.S.A.

Books by Dallas Schulze

Silhouette Intimate Moments

Moment to Moment #170
Donovan's Promise #247

DALLAS SCHULZE

loves books, old movies, her husband and her cat, not
necessarily in that order. A sucker for a happy ending, she says her writing has given her an outlet for her
imagination, and she hopes that readers have half as
much fun with her books as she does! Dallas has more
hobbies than there is space to list them, but is cur-
rently working on a doll collection.

Prologue

I want a divorce."

The words were spoken without fanfare. The tone was even, emotionless. She could just as well have asked for the sugar bowl or commented that it looked as though it might rain.

But Elizabeth Sinclair had just requested an end to her marriage of eighteen years.

Having shattered her world, she pulled her gaze away from the window and looked at the man seated across the table. For a few, tense moments, there was no reaction. He didn't lift his head from the stack of papers he'd been studying during breakfast, he didn't gasp or choke or sputter. When he set his coffee cup down, his hand wasn't trembling.

If she hadn't known him so well, she might have thought he hadn't heard her. But she knew Donovan as well as it was possible to know another human being. He was digesting what she'd said.

She looked at him, feeling as if she was seeing him from a great distance. At thirty-eight he was a strikingly good-looking man—even more attractive than he'd been when they'd met. The gray that painted silver streaks at his temples only emphasized the inky blackness of his hair. His features were still even, but now they carried the added weight of maturity—hardening his jaw, leaving creases around his eyes.

He looked like exactly what he was: a successful man who was approaching forty without fears, who was tanned, fit, sure of himself and his life. There had been a time when Elizabeth had felt herself a part of that life. But that time was gone, drifting away so quietly she wasn't even sure when it had disappeared.

He lifted his head slowly, his gaze meeting hers. Donovan's eyes had always reflected his emotions. They'd turn warm green when he was happy and almost pure gold when he was angry. Now, they were blank.

"What?"

Elizabeth felt vaguely guilty. Even though she hadn't planned on saying anything at that particular moment, she'd had some time to form a decision, to brace herself to say the words. To Donovan, it must have seemed as if they were coming out of the blue.

"If this is a joke, it's not very funny." Irritation rumbled in the husky words.

"I'm not joking. I want a divorce, Donovan."

Panic flickered in his eyes. "What brought this on? If it's because I forgot to pick up the dry cleaning, I think you're overreacting a bit." His smile wavered uncertainly.

"It's got nothing to do with the dry cleaning."

"Then what the hell is this about?"

She ignored the snap in his words, knowing fear more than anger had put it there.

"I'm not happy." She said the words simply.

Donovan stared at her, clearly at a loss. "You're not happy. What do you mean? Why aren't you happy? And why haven't you said something or done something?"

She picked up her teacup and stared into the amber liquid. It was easier than looking into his eyes. His eyes demanded answers that she couldn't give. She couldn't even answer her own questions. How could she explain that somewhere along the line she'd lost herself. She'd lost her identity.

"What should I have said or done?"

"Why didn't you tell me you weren't happy?"

"Why should I? It wasn't your problem."

"Not my problem? Elizabeth, you're my wife. You've just announced that you want a divorce because you're not happy. I think that makes it my problem."

"Not really." She set her teacup down, but she still couldn't look at him.

He ran his fingers through his hair, tousling it into heavy, black waves. "Elizabeth, what's wrong? Is it something I've done? Something I've said? Do you think I'm having an affair or embezzling money or something?"

"Of course not!"

"Then what is it? You don't end eighteen years of marriage over nothing."

"Donovan, it hasn't anything to do with you. I'm just not happy."

She needed to do something so she got up and started to clear the table. She'd known this wasn't going to be easy, but somehow she hadn't expected his pain to hurt her.

She set the plates in the sink. When she turned, he was standing in front of her. She leaned against the counter, tilting her head back until she could meet his eyes. It was a mistake. The turmoil she saw there almost made her change her mind, almost made her tell him that she hadn't meant a word she'd said. Almost.

"Elizabeth. Beth. Talk to me."

The old diminutive gave her an unexpected stab of pain. It had been so long since he'd called her Beth. She drew in a deep breath and stared over his shoulder.

"We've grown apart, Donovan. We don't have anything to say to each other anymore. We hardly even see each other."

"What are you talking about? I'm home every night. We have breakfast together most mornings."

"But you're not here *with* me. You come home at night and you work in the study. In the morning you've always got a stack of papers beside you."

"If you didn't like my working at home, why didn't you just say so?"

"It's not just your working at home, Donovan. We've grown apart. Maybe you haven't noticed, but I have."

He again thrust his fingers through his hair, frustrated. "Why is it that women think you have to spend every minute of every day together to be close? I can't run a business without spending time at it."

"I know that."

"Then what's the big problem? You're not making any sense."

She stared at him, trying to think of a way to make him see what she was trying to say. "Donovan, what was the last thing that you and I did together? Just the two of us. Something that didn't revolve around Michael?''

The silence stretched out while he stared at her. Elizabeth waited for a minute and then edged by him to pick up the drinking glasses left on the table. He didn't move to stop her. He just continued to stand next to the counter, his expression hard and tight. She set the glasses in the sink.

''All right, so maybe we haven't been spending a lot of time together, but that could be changed.''

''I don't think so.''

''Stop saying that!'' His hand closed around her upper arm, jerking her around to face him. ''You can't just throw eighteen years of marriage out the window because we haven't been spending enough time together. What about Michael? How are you going to explain this to him?''

''Michael is old enough to understand.''

''Understand? How the hell do you expect an eighteen-year-old kid to understand when it doesn't make any sense to me?''

''Donovan—''

''What the hell are you thinking of, Beth? You can't do this.''

''Donovan, I don't want to hurt you. That's the last thing I want.''

''Well, you're doing a damn fine job of it.'' His fingers dug into her arm, but she knew he wasn't even aware of the pressure. She could feel her nerves stretching tighter. In a minute she was going to start screaming, and she was afraid she'd never stop.

''Donovan, when was the last time we made love? Can you remember?''

He stared at her, stunned. His fingers loosened, and she knew he was trying to remember, appalled by the time that had slipped by unnoticed.

He drew a quick, hard breath, his hand again tightening on her arm, pulling her closer. "If that's what this is about, it's easily remedied."

Elizabeth tried to draw back, but he held her in place, his free hand cupping the back of her neck, tilting her head. She didn't struggle as his mouth came down on hers. She knew he wouldn't hurt her—at least not physically. The pain she felt was lodged deep inside.

She could taste his desperation, could feel it in the taut muscles of his body. But that was all she felt. She could remember a time when just the touch of his mouth had lit a fire inside her where now she felt nothing but emptiness and regret.

The fire was gone. Not even an ember remained. Only a pile of cold ashes, gray and worn, without life.

She remained passive in his hold, sensing that this would convince him as perhaps nothing else could. A tear slipped from beneath her closed lids, losing itself in the golden-blond hair at her temple.

Donovan raised his head slowly and took his hands away from her, but not before she felt the tremor in his fingers. His breathing was harsh in the quiet room. She opened her eyes, seeing him through a blur of tears. Was it possible for a person to age in a matter of minutes? He suddenly looked every one of his thirty-eight years.

"I'm sorry, Donovan. I just don't love you anymore."

Chapter 1

THEN - NINETEEN YEARS AGO

I love you, Donovan. I'll love you forever." Beth's voice shook with the force of her emotions. At sixteen, she was sure of her feelings. Nothing would ever change the way she felt about the young man who lay next to her.

Donovan smoothed golden-blond hair back off her forehead and smiled. With only two more years behind him he was immeasurably older than the girl lying beside him.

"I love you too, Beth, but we've got to be sensible."

"I don't want to be sensible." She walked her fingers up his chest, feeling the way his heartbeat accelerated beneath the light touch. "I'm sixteen. That's old enough to make up my own mind."

Donovan caught her fingers in his. "Beth, we can't get married now. You're too young. And even if you weren't, your father would never give us permission. He doesn't like me. I've seen the way he looks at me."

"Daddy just doesn't know you, that's all. He thinks you're bad for me, but if he got to know you, he'd see how wonderful you are."

His mouth twisted. "I doubt it. And he's right. You deserve someone a lot better than I am. You could date any guy in school." She tugged her fingers loose and put them over his mouth.

"Stop it. I don't want to date any guy in school. I love you, Donovan. I love you so much."

"I can't offer you anything. A beat-up motorcycle, a job in a garage . . ."

"You're going to be an architect. The best architect in the whole world. Someday, you'll be rich and famous."

He felt her belief in him like a gentle hand stroking across his soul. In all his life, no one had ever had such complete faith, such boundless belief, in him. Looking into her clear blue eyes, he could almost see his dreams reflected there, whole and shining, polished by the light of her love.

"Oh, Beth. What did I ever do without you?"

"Much worse, I'm sure." Her fingers slid into the thick blackness of his hair. It fell in waves to just past his shoulders. Beth thought it made him look like a young Greek god, but she'd never have said so to Donovan. She was old enough to know the compliment would embarrass him.

Donovan leaned over her, his palm resting against her waist, left bare by low hip-huggers and a shirt tied under her breasts. Beth shivered beneath the look in his eyes. They'd been lovers for almost three months, but she didn't think she'd ever get used to the way he made her feel. She knew that after three months or thirty years, Donovan Sinclair would always be able to melt her bones with a look.

She closed her eyes against the intensity of his look, her mouth softening in anticipation of his kiss. His mouth was firm and warm, coaxing her lips to open to his. His hand slid around her waist, his fingers splayed against her spine, arching her into his body. Beth's hands tightened against his shoulders, clinging to him as his tongue explored her mouth.

A hot September sun blazed down around them, denying that summer was over. The grass smelled sweet and green with memories of summer. In the distance a group of small children were playing, but their shouts and laughter seemed very far away.

All that mattered was Beth and Donovan, lying beneath a huge, old willow in the warm, sweet grass. The dying summer didn't matter. Her father's disapproval didn't matter. All that mattered was Donovan's mouth on hers, his hands warm on her bare back.

He dragged his mouth away from hers, his breathing ragged. She could feel the pressure of his arousal against her thigh. She slipped her hands inside his chambray shirt, feeling his sweat-dampened skin. It excited her to know that he wanted her so much. Her fingers explored the hard muscles under the light dusting of hair that covered his chest.

Donovan was not like the boys she went to school with. At eighteen he was hard and firm, muscled from years of working after school and on weekends. When she'd first met him, all her girlfriends had warned her about him. He was older, he rode a motorcycle, he wore a black leather jacket. Everything about him spelled Danger.

Everyone in Remembrance, Indiana, knew about Donovan Sinclair. Boys like him never came to any good. His father was a drunk who'd never done an honest day's labor in his life. His mother had been a good woman who'd worked herself to death trying to support her husband and her son. Donovan himself was clearly destined for no good. No one could explain why this was so clear—maybe it was the way he looked. He was too handsome, too tough, too sure of himself. Maybe it was the way he dressed. Rebellion might have become a symbol of youth in the rest of the country, but in Remembrance there were still only two kinds of kids: good ones and bad ones.

The good ones played football or were cheerleaders, according to their sex. The bad ones wore black leather jackets, jeans that were a little too tight and hair that was a little too long. There were a few people who took note of the fact that Donovan Sinclair had never been known to take a drink and had held a steady job since he was sixteen. But most folks saw the insolent twist of his mouth and the way his eyes could seem to look right through a person, and they knew exactly what to label him.

Trouble.

Beth Martin had known Donovan most of her life— or, at least, she'd known *of* him. In a town as small as Remembrance, everybody knew just about everybody else, at least by sight. She'd never thought much about him one way or another until six months ago. She'd had a fight with her boyfriend, and Donovan had offered her a ride home on his motorcycle. Ordinarily she would have refused, but she was just mad enough at Brad to accept the offer.

During the course of that ride her entire world had changed. There was an electricity between the two of them that couldn't be denied. She knew Donovan felt it, too. Brad and the other boys on the football team suddenly seemed callow and boring. But Donovan knew what it would do to a girl's reputation to be seen with him, and he'd dropped her off at her house without saying a word about seeing her again.

For the first time in her life, Beth was the one doing the pursuing. It had taken her almost a month to wear down Donovan's resistance and convince him that she wasn't going to go away.

"Stop it, Beth." Donovan's voice dragged her out of her thoughts. His hand caught hers, pressing her palm flat against his chest, halting her sensuous exploration. She lifted her gaze to his and then looked away quickly. It still half frightened her to see how much he wanted her.

Donovan saw her uncertainty and his eyes softened. Sometimes he felt aeons older than Beth. She'd lived such a sheltered life. She'd never had to wonder where her next meal was coming from, never had to worry about having enough heat in the winter. Her mother had died when she was just a baby, but her father had done everything he could to see that his only child never lacked for anything, whether it was love or material things.

Donovan ran his fingers through her silky hair, contrasting its golden blond with his own tanned, work-roughened hands. She was so full of light, both inside and out. Everybody said he was no good, and he more than half believed it himself. How could she possibly love someone like him? But she did love him, impossible though it seemed, and Donovan was careful to do nothing that would frighten her, nothing that would show her just how unworthy he was of that love.

"You're so beautiful, Beth. What did I ever do to deserve you?" Beth smiled up at him, unaware of the underlying ache in his voice.

"I guess you just got lucky."

"I guess I did." His mouth touched hers again, feeling her body arch into his. He groaned low in his throat, rolling to press his full length against hers. The sweet scent of crushed grass rose around them. His hand slid upward, easing beneath the edge of her shirt to cup her breast. Beth stiffened for a moment and then seemed to melt beneath him.

Somewhere in the distance a dog barked, reminding Donovan that they were hardly alone. The hanging branches of the old willow provided a fragile privacy at best. He dragged his hand away from temptation and slowly broke the kiss, ignoring her murmur of protest.

"Beth, in a minute we're going to get arrested for indecent exposure."

"So what?" Her hands slipped reluctantly off his shoulders as he sat up.

"So I don't think you'd like jail, and I don't think your father would like bailing you out. I know he's not all that happy that you're seeing me anyway."

Beth felt the color rise in her cheeks, and she was glad that his back was to her. "Guilt" must be written in scarlet letters across her forehead.

"Daddy trusts my judgment. Besides, I'm sixteen, not six. He knows he can't tell me what to do anymore."

She hoped she sounded more confident than she felt. Less than a week ago, her father had strictly forbidden her to see Donovan again. He said people were beginning to talk. Beth didn't care what people said. She loved Donovan, and nothing was going to keep her from him. Not even her father.

Donovan stood up. "I'd better get you home. I'm due at work in an hour, and you've probably got homework to finish before school tomorrow."

Beth let him pull her up, sliding her arms around his waist and leaning into the lean strength of his body. "You work too hard."

"If I'm going to start college in January, I need all the money I can get. I won't be able to work as many hours."

"You'll probably have even less time for me then."

He slid his fingers into her long hair, cupping the back of her head and tilting her face upward. "I'll always have time for you."

Her mock pout faded into a smile that made his heart pound. Sometimes he wondered if Beth knew just how she affected him. She was so beautiful. He bent his head to taste her smile, as if he could drink in her warmth and light and banish some of the dark corners in his soul.

"How's Donovan?"

Beth swirled the straw in her glass of iced tea and glanced across the table at her companion. Carol Montgomery had been her best friend since kindergarten. They'd shared every big moment in each other's lives, from first boyfriends to bras. Looking into Carol's curious face, Beth found herself oddly reluctant to discuss Donovan. It wasn't that she was afraid Carol couldn't keep a secret, because in all their years of friendship, neither had ever betrayed a confidence.

Beth couldn't put her finger on what it was. Somehow, her relationship with Donovan was private. It was something she didn't want to share with anyone—not even her best friend.

She shrugged. "He's fine."

"Does your dad know you're still seeing him?"

"No. And Donovan doesn't know Daddy told me not to see him anymore."

Carol reached for another pack of sugar and stirred it into her tea. She was blessed with a metabolism that allowed her to eat anything and never gain an ounce. For once Beth didn't feel envious of her friend's genetic luck. The tea tasted funny. In fact, she was sorry they'd come to Danny's at all. The smell of baking pizza made her feel vaguely queasy. On the jukebox the Rolling Stones were screaming "Jumpin' Jack Flash," and the sound intensified the headache that had been plaguing her all day.

"What are you going to do if your father finds out you're still seeing Donovan?"

Beth pushed her tea away. "I don't know. I don't understand why Daddy's being so unreasonable about this. Donovan's never been in trouble."

"It's because he looks like he has been or will be at any minute." Carol leaned back as the waiter set their pizza in the middle of the table. "Boy, does that look terrific." Beth swallowed hard and closed her eyes against the smell of cheese and tomato sauce. "Aren't you going to have some?"

She opened her eyes and smiled at Carol. "In a minute." The queasiness was fading.

Carol bit into a slice of pizza oozing cheese, her expression indicative of absolute bliss. "The thing you've got to remember is that all parents automatically dislike anyone their children like." Carol delivered this piece of philosophy between bites.

"Daddy's never been like that."

"That makes it worse. All that pent-up feeling is just now coming out. He'll be adamant about Donovan. When you argue he'll say things like, 'Beth, I've never been unreasonable about your friends, have I? You'll just have to trust my judgment on this one.'"

Despite the seriousness of the situation, Carol's accurate imitation of her father's words drew a halfhearted laugh out of Beth. She reached for the smallest slice of pizza and set it on her plate.

"I'm *not* going to trust his judgment on this one. I love Donovan and he loves me, and I'm not going to give him up—not for anything in the world."

"Good for you. Personally, I think Donovan Sinclair is gorgeous."

"He is, isn't he?" Beth pushed a mushroom around the rim of her plate, the expression in her eyes dreamy.

Carol looked at her friend, her thin features envious. "Beth, I'm your best friend, aren't I?"

Beth looked up, dragging her mind away from Donovan. "Of course. Why do you ask?"

"What's it like when you and Donovan...when you...you know?"

Beth did know, and she felt the color come up in her cheeks until she was sure they were as red as the vinyl booth. "It's none of your business."

Carol sat back in her seat, her face as flushed as Beth's. "I'm sorry, Beth. I shouldn't have asked. It's just that you and Donovan look so happy together. I just wondered."

"It's okay." Beth looked anywhere but at her friend.

Carol reached for another slice of pizza. "I just hope you know what you're doing. I mean, I hope you're being careful."

"Careful about what?"

"Babies." Carol bit into her pizza, leaving Beth to flush even darker.

"Donovan takes care of that."

Carol nodded sagely. "That's what Betty Durbin's boyfriend told her, and she had to leave school."

"Donovan is very careful!" The words came out with more of a snap than she'd intended, and she looked around the big room, hoping that no one was close enough to hear what they were saying. Trust Carol to start a conversation like this in public.

She shifted, uneasy with the topic. Staring down at her pizza, she remembered one time when they hadn't been careful and how angry Donovan had been with himself. Still, one time couldn't be dangerous. Could it?

"Beth, you're going to be late for school." In answer to her father's call, Beth took one last look in the mirror and snatched up her books before hurrying out of her bedroom. She rushed downstairs, where her father was waiting impatiently by the door. His expression softened, as it always did when looking at his daughter.

Patrick Martin still found it hard to believe that this beautiful, vital young woman was his little girl. It seemed like such a short time ago that he'd been struggling to take care of a baby, juggling his work and fatherhood.

"Isn't that skirt a little short?"

Beth glanced down at the white denim miniskirt that ended several inches above her knee and then gave her father the exasperated look that all teenagers perfect early on.

"This is longer than the skirts a lot of the girls are wearing, Daddy."

"I'm not worried about a lot of the girls." But he didn't press the issue. He had to admit that the style suited her. How had those pudgy toddler's legs slimmed into this?

He picked up his hard hat and briefcase and followed his daughter out the door, giving a cursory check to the lock. There was no crime to speak of in Remembrance. Locks were more of a token gesture than a necessity.

Father and daughter climbed into the Chevy pickup that sat in the driveway. By a long-standing agreement, the radio stayed off. Since Beth wanted to listen to rock and roll and her father wanted to listen to the morning business report, they'd agreed that they wouldn't listen to anything at all.

Patrick started the truck and backed out of the driveway. "If they've fixed the light on Main Street, I should be able to get you to school before the first bell."

Beth nodded. The silence continued for several blocks. Patrick glanced at his daughter but her eyes were turned to the front, her expression pensive.

"Beth? Something wrong?"

She glanced at him and shook her head. "No."

The silence went on.

"Are you still upset with me over the Sinclair boy? I know you think I'm being unreasonable, but I haven't forbidden you much over the years. You'll just have to trust my judgment on this one, honey."

"I was just thinking about what kind of dress I want for the Homecoming Dance. Carol and I are going shopping tomorrow."

If he had been watching his daughter instead of watching the road, Patrick might have seen the guilty flush in her cheeks and the way her fingers clenched around the books in her lap. He might also have thought it was a little odd that she'd argued so passionately when he forbade her to see Donovan and now she seemed to have accepted his decision. But he wasn't looking at her, and he was relieved that she seemed to be taking it so well so he didn't probe.

"Who are you going with this year?"

Beth shrugged, not looking at him. "I don't know yet."

He slowed the truck for the turn into the school and pulled to a stop near the main entrance. "Well, I'm sure you'll have all kinds of offers."

Beth scrambled out of the truck without answering.

"See you tonight."

Beth lifted her hand in answer to his wave. The dark blue truck pulled into traffic, passing several parents who were getting their progeny to school even later than Beth.

Beth watched him go, blinking back tears. She'd never expected to feel so guilty about lying to her father. Since her mother's death when she was a few months old, it had always been her and her father against the world. He'd been her friend as well as her parent.

How could she tell him that she knew exactly who she was going to the Homecoming Dance with? Donovan had promised to take her more than a month ago. Her father would find out, she couldn't hide her relationship with Donovan forever. Once he understood how much she loved Donovan, he'd see how wrong he'd been.

The final bell rang, startling her out of her thoughts. She turned and sprinted for the entrance. She was going to be late for homeroom, after all.

"I don't think this is such a good idea, Beth. Your father wouldn't like the idea of your having me in the house when he's not home."

"Daddy will never know. He's not going to be back from Indianapolis until tomorrow afternoon at the earliest. Come on, Donovan. I want you to see my dress." Beth pulled on his hand, tugging him over the threshold into her bedroom.

Donovan stepped onto the thick, shag carpeting, hoping he didn't have any grease from the garage on his shoes. The carpet was the palest of pinks. It matched the ruffled curtains and bedspread. The furniture was painted with white enamel. Shelves along one wall held stuffed toys and books. Everything about the room was feminine and spoke of comfort.

Donovan felt as out of place as a buffalo at a wedding. He shoved his hands into the pockets of his jeans. He didn't belong in this room. This room spoke of too many things he'd never known: home, family, money.

"Don't you think it's beautiful?"

Donovan looked at the dress Beth held up, but he couldn't have said anything about it. About all that registered was that it was peach colored. What caught his eye was the excitement in Beth's face. She was so beautiful. What could she possibly see in him?

"It's...really nice." He hoped he'd said the right thing. Beth seemed content. She hung the dress back up and shut the closet door.

"I can't wait till the dance. I bet you look gorgeous in a suit." She sat on the bed and patted the spot next to her.

"I'll bet I look like an idiot." Donovan reluctantly took the place beside her. Beth snuggled against his side and he put his arm around her shoulders. "Don't you think we should leave now?"

She put her hand on his chest, working it inside the open front of his shirt, feeling the catch in his breathing when she touched him.

"Don't you like my room?"

"It's...it's beautiful." He slid his hand into her hair, tilting her head back until their eyes met. "You're beautiful. I just don't want to get you in trouble." His mouth touched hers, lingering in a slow kiss.

"I told you, Daddy won't be home until tomorrow."

His hand slid inside the neck of her peasant blouse, feeling the satiny skin of her shoulders, tracing the delicate line of her collarbone.

"What about the neighbors?"

"They aren't home." She lifted her mouth to his, feeling her bones melt like butter left out in the sun. He was everything she'd ever dreamed of, everything she'd ever want. His hands slid across her back as he leaned forward, lowering her slowly.

The mattress yielded beneath their combined weight. Donovan pushed the loose neckline down and let his lips trace the satiny skin of her shoulders. Beth closed her eyes, shutting out the familiar bedroom walls, shutting out everything but the feel of him against her.

He felt so right.

"Do you love me, Donovan?"

"Always." The word ghosted out against her breast. Beth's fingers slid into the silky, black hair at the nape of his neck, pulling him closer. "I'll love you always, Beth."

And she didn't doubt that it was true.

The late-September sun blazed down, but there was a melancholy feeling in the air that bespoke the end of summer. The leaves on the maple trees were turning colors, the brilliant green fading. It wouldn't be long until winter.

Beth felt as if winter had already arrived. There was a cold, heavy lump in her chest. She shut the door of Dr. Morrison's office behind her with a careful click and turned to walk blindly down the street.

At ten o'clock in the morning on a weekday, Remembrance was quiet. Inside the brick and wood buildings, people were doing business, but the streets were quiet. Beth wouldn't have noticed if a parade had been marching down Main. She walked without thought, her mind a blank.

It wasn't until she stumbled over a curb that she noticed her surroundings. The park was completely empty, the wrought-iron benches gathering the last of summer's sun as if preparing for winter's onslaught. Beth sat down. Her eyes were focused on the lake, but she wasn't seeing the cool water.

Pregnant. The word echoed in her mind. Pregnant. She couldn't get beyond that single fact. She was carrying Donovan's baby. She wrapped her arms around her waist, closing her eyes. It just didn't seem real. She couldn't be pregnant. Not from just one mistake. They'd always been so careful.

What was Donovan going to say? And her father? Oh God, how could she tell her father? She bit her lip to stop a whimper.

What was she going to do?

She stood up. She couldn't stay here. There was too much chance of seeing someone she knew. There would be questions to answer, and she couldn't deal with questions.

She turned toward home but stopped after taking a few steps. She couldn't go home. Her father wouldn't be there, but if one of the neighbors saw her they would want to know what was wrong. They'd ask if she was sick. A hysterical laugh threatened to escape. Sick? If only it was that simple.

She turned in the opposite direction, her feet moving automatically. She would go to Donovan's. He would be at work, but he'd shown her a way to climb in the window of his rented room.

It took her ten minutes to reach the little back street and Donovan's worn-down building. She slipped off her shoes and jammed them in her suede purse. The tree was just where it had always been, and it was the work of only a few minutes to climb to the branch that reached Donovan's window. She slid onto the warped floorboards, feeling as if she'd reached a sanctuary.

Donovan had only brought her here twice. He'd never said as much but Beth knew that he was ashamed of the place. She stood in the middle of the room for a long moment, just breathing. No one would find her here. No one was expecting her anywhere until after the school day ended, and she'd told her father she might be going home with Carol, so that gave her even more time.

And she needed the time. She needed every second. She set her purse down in the corner. Today Donovan worked until midafternoon. That gave her a few hours

until he'd be home. She'd have a little time to decide
what she was going to say to him.

What could she say? She was pregnant. Right now
she couldn't get beyond that one, blinding fact. She was
going to have Donovan's baby. She sat down on the
bed, feeling the mattress sag beneath her. They'd never
talked about children. She loved Donovan, she wanted
to marry him. In her world, love and marriage generally
added up to children. But not like this. Never like this.

This kind of thing happened to other girls. Girls no
one talked about. This didn't happen to Beth Martin.
It just didn't. She wrapped her arms around her stomach and leaned forward, closing her eyes. It didn't
matter how hard she tried, she couldn't make it real.

Tears welled up. She tried to blink them back, but
they wouldn't be denied. The dingy, little room swam
in front of her, and a harsh sob escaped. What was
Donovan going to say? Would he hate her? She could
bear anything but that.

She lay down, her arms still wrapped around herself,
her face buried in Donovan's pillow. Donovan would
know what to do. He always knew what to do for her.
She had to believe that this time wouldn't be any different.

Chapter 2

It was late afternoon when Beth heard Donovan's footsteps on the stairs. She sat up, brushing trembling hands over her hair, rubbing her fingers under her eyes, hoping she didn't have mascara streaking down her face. She hadn't spent a lot of time on tears. The situation seemed to have gone beyond that.

Her heartbeat picked up speed with every second that passed. What was he going to say when he saw her? How was she going to tell him? It had been foolish to come here. Their lives would be changed forever. She wasn't ready to see him yet. She couldn't tell him.

She was halfway to the window with some half-baked idea of escape, when he opened the door. She froze, then turned toward him. She couldn't tell him. Not now. Not yet. She pinned a smile on her face. She would just pretend that nothing was wrong and leave as soon as possible.

Donovan shoved open the door, his eyes on the mail that Mrs. Hill had given him. Junk, as usual. She always gave him anything addressed to "occupant." Maybe she thought it made him feel more at home. He caught a whiff of Beth's scent. He'd given her that perfume for the one-month anniversary of their first date, and she always wore it. She said it made her feel close to him even when they weren't together.

His head jerked up. She was standing between the window and the bed, her stockinged feet poised as if to run, her slim body tense. His eyes fell on her face. Her smile was bright and beautiful, but her face was pale and her eyes were filled with a frightening mixture of despair and panic.

The envelopes scattered to the floor with soft, whispering sounds, and he stepped toward her, his arms opening.

"My God, Beth, what's wrong?"

Beth saw the loving concern in Donovan's face, the strong arms held out to her. With a sob she rushed forward, burying her face in his chest, her arms locking around his waist. It was a safe haven after hours of emotional pain. Donovan was here for her. He'd always be here.

Donovan kicked the door shut and lifted Beth in his arms, carrying her to the bed and sitting down with her in his lap. She was shaking but not crying, her slim body trembling against him. He stroked her hair, his mind racing with each disastrous possibility.

"What's wrong, Beth? Is it your father? Has something happened to him? Something at school? Did someone say something to upset you? Something about us?"

She shook her head to each possibility, her face buried in his shirt. Donovan held her, reining in his fears, waiting for the trembling to ease. When she pushed away, he eased his arms from around her, letting her get up. She backed away without looking at him, her eyes on the scuffed floor. Donovan stood up, bracing himself.

"I've got to tell you something." Her voice was hardly more than a whisper.

"You can tell me anything, Beth. You know that." He waited, barely breathing. What if she said she didn't want to see him anymore? How could he bear it if he lost her?

"I . . . I went to the doctor this morning. I'm pregnant."

The words came out louder than she'd intended. They seemed to echo in the small room, growing louder and louder until they almost shouted back at them from the chipped wallpaper. Pregnant. Pregnant.

Donovan felt the words slam into him, knocking the breath from his lungs, leaving him gasping. Pregnant. A baby. Beth was carrying his baby. No! It wasn't fair. It just wasn't fair. There had only been that one time. One stinking time. It couldn't happen.

"Are you sure?" His voice sounded strange—hoarse. Not his at all.

She nodded without lifting her head. "Dr. Morrison says there's no doubt. I'm going to have a baby." Her voice broke on the last word.

"It's all right." Donovan spoke automatically. "It's going to be all right, Beth. Don't worry." He reached out, taking hold of her shoulders and pulling her into his arms. She was stiff in his hold for a moment, and then she went limp, letting him support her weight.

"What are we going to do, Donovan? It's all my fault. I'm so sorry."

"Stop it!" He shook her slightly, cutting off the flow of words. "It's not your fault. We got carried away and I should have known better. I *did* know better." There was a wealth of self-anger in the words.

"What are we going to do? I've thought and I've thought and I don't know what to do. I can't have an... I can't get rid of it. I don't even know how to find someone who'd... I just can't do that. I'm sorry. I can't, I can't."

Donovan shook her again, harder this time, breaking off the hysteria that threatened in her voice. He held her away from him until she met his eyes. "Stop it, Beth. I don't want you to get rid of this baby. Don't even think about it."

Beth blinked, responding to the authority in his tone. "What are we going to do?"

"It's going to be fine." Donovan pushed his own panic aside. "We didn't plan it this way, but we'll work it out. We'll just get married right away. I'm making pretty good money at the garage, and I've got some money put aside. We'll get by. I'll take care of the baby. I'll take care of you."

Beth leaned into him, drawing on his strength, feeling the panic leave her. If Donovan said he'd take care of her, she believed him. The room was silent while each of them tried to come to grips with the momentous changes a baby was going to make in their lives. In the end, it was too much to grasp.

"When is the baby due?" Donovan had to clear his throat to get the question out. It made it seem almost real. Permanent.

"The end of April, I guess. I'm sorry, Donovan."
Her voice shattered on the words, his name leaving her
on a sob. He eased her down on the bed and she began
to cry—not the quiet tears she'd shed earlier, but harsh,
sobbing tears that left her choked and breathless. "I'm
so sorry."

"Stop it, Beth." Donovan closed his arms around
her, drawing her against his chest and holding her
tightly, telling her over and over again that it was going
to be all right. Above her golden head, his eyes were
bleak. He could reassure Beth, but the words rang hollow in his ears.

He let her cry out all her fears, her tears soaking his
worn shirt. His hand stroked her hair, offering comfort and reassurance. When the tears at last faded into
an occasional choked breath, he eased her back down
on the pillows and stood up. Beth was too exhausted to
protest, though her hand clutched at his shirttail.

"I'm just going to get a wet cloth." He was back in a
moment with a damp washcloth, and Beth lay passive
as he wiped the cool fabric over her hot face.

"I'm sorry, Donovan." A convulsive sob broke his
name in half.

"Stop saying that. It was my responsibility."

"What are we going to do?" Her eyes looked up at
him with such faith that Donovan felt a momentary
flash of panic. She shouldn't depend on him so. Hadn't
he already proved that he wasn't worthy of her trust?
She wouldn't be in this mess if he hadn't let things get
out of control. He swallowed hard and forced a half
smile, his eyes showing more confidence than he felt.

"We'll get married, and I'll take care of you and the
baby."

"I'll have to quit school, won't I?"

"I...probably." Donovan took her hands and wiped the cloth over them. It hurt him to see her in pain. She was so young. This was his fault and his alone. It wasn't fair that she should suffer, too.

"What will we do for money?"

"Don't worry about it. I'm making pretty good money at the garage, and I think Dave will give me more hours if I ask him to. And I've got some money saved up."

"But that's your college money. You're going to be an architect."

Donovan's mouth twisted. He'd long ago learned the pain of broken dreams. He wouldn't have thought it would still hurt. All chances for getting his education were fading rapidly into the distance. But along with broken dreams, he'd also learned that you took responsibility for your own actions without whining about it. Beth needed him to be strong for her.

"I'll go to college later. Lots of people do."

Beth's eyes searched his, but she was too frightened herself to question his strength. She needed it too much.

"I'm scared, Donovan." In that moment, she looked so young and vulnerable that his heart ached.

"I know. But I'll take care of you. I promise. I love you, Beth. I won't let anything hurt you."

"I love you, too." She sat up and put her arms around his neck, resting her face against his shoulder. "I love you so much. At least we'll be together."

Donovan stroked her back, letting himself believe that everything would work out.

They held each other for a long time, not saying anything, not thinking anything—drawing strength from being together. Donovan had no idea how much time had passed until he heard the big clock in the hall downstairs start to chime. He counted each strike of the hammer. Five o'clock—and he'd left the garage at four. His whole life had changed in the space of an hour. Irrevocably altered. Never to be the same.

"Beth?" Her arms tightened around him, and he knew she was resisting a return to reality. "Beth, it's getting late. Your father will be worried about you." He felt the shudder that ran up her spine. "I know, love, I know. But he's got to be told. I think we should get married as soon as possible."

She let her arms slip away reluctantly, her eyes downcast. Donovan cupped her face in his hands, tilting it upward until her eyes met his. "I said I'd take care of you, Beth, and I meant it."

"I know. It's just that my father is going to be so angry."

"We'll face him together. He loves you. Let me change out of this greasy shirt, and we'll go see him."

Beth watched as he stripped his shirt off, her mind still only half functioning. She felt as though she was in the middle of some terrible nightmare. Any minute now she would wake up and find out that none of this was real, that her world hadn't tilted on its axis.

"I think I should talk to Daddy alone." She wasn't aware of thinking the words until they were said. Donovan turned from the tiny closet in one corner of the room, halfway into a clean shirt.

"I don't think that's such a good idea, Beth. We should face him together."

She shook her head. "I'll go alone. I didn't tell you that he forbid me to see you. I think I need to pave the way a bit before I tell him about the...about my...about me."

Beth stood up, smoothing her hands over her miniskirt and tugging the neckline of her peasant blouse into place. She ran her fingers through her long, straight hair.

"I think I should go with you."

"No. Really. It will be better if I do it alone. I'll call you and tell you what happened."

Donovan wanted to argue further, but he could see that her mind was made up. He didn't know Patrick Martin. Maybe Beth was right, maybe he would take it better this way.

"Let me at least give you a ride home."

"No, I'll walk." Her smile was strained. "I need some time to think."

He opened the door for her, his hand on her arm holding her for a moment. "Just remember that I love you."

Beth swallowed hard. "I know. I love you."

"Don't look so scared. Everything's going to be fine. We'll work it out."

Donovan shut the door and leaned back against it, listening to her footsteps on the stairs. His shoulders slumped. Now that she was gone, his confident facade crumbled.

He ran his hand over his face, aware that his fingers were shaking. For the first time in his life he wanted a drink. All the years he'd watched his old man drink himself into oblivion, he'd never understood why he didn't fight instead of hiding in a bottle. Now he had at least a partial understanding.

He pushed himself from the door and stumbled over to the bed, feeling centuries older than his eighteen years. The bed creaked beneath his weight, the sound loud in the quiet room. He didn't know how long he sat there, staring at nothing, letting everything sink in, trying not to think too much. Outside, people went about their business. Husbands were coming home from work, sitting down to dinner. Everything went on just as if disaster hadn't struck.

Beth was going to have his baby. He buried his head in his hands, swallowing hard on the sob that threatened to escape. It wasn't fair. It just wasn't fair. Like an echo he heard his mother's hoarse voice, cracked by hard work and too many cigarettes. "Who the hell ever told you that life was supposed to be fair, boy? You roll with the punches and hope the good Lord don't deal you nothin' you can't handle."

"I don't know if I can handle this, Mom. I don't know if I can," he said out loud.

But he knew he had to. For Beth's sake—and the baby's—he had to be strong. He loved her too much to let her down. Beth was the best thing to ever happen to him. He had to take care of her, and it had to start now. He should never have let her go home alone. He should be there when she talked to her father.

"Daddy? I'm sorry." Beth swallowed hard against the lump that threatened to choke her. She hadn't expected it to hurt so much when she told her father. There hadn't been time to think beyond what this was going to do to her life and Donovan's. "I'm sorry, Daddy."

Patrick Martin slumped in the big easy chair, his eyes focused on nothing in particular, his face old and worn. Silence stretched between them until Beth thought she'd break out screaming. The pain in her father's face hurt her, frightened her. What would she do if he threw her

out? Her father had been the center of her life, someone she could always depend on to be there for her.

She knelt by his chair, her face white. "Daddy, I love
you. I'm sorry. I'm sorry."

Patrick's eyes slowly refocused on her pale features,
and he saw the panic in her eyes. Beth had been his life
since her mother died. He couldn't remember a time
when he hadn't worried about her, fussed over her,
loved her. He'd watched her grow from a chubby toddler to a graceful young woman who sometimes seemed
frighteningly adult. He'd wanted so much for her, had
so many dreams. Now they were all in pieces. But she
still needed him.

"It's okay, pumpkin." His hand was shaking as he
lifted it to smooth her hair. With a sob, Beth bent and
put her forehead against his knee. For a moment, she
was a child again, able to believe that her father could
make everything right.

"I'm so scared, Daddy."

"I know, Beth, I know. But I'll take care of you.
Don't cry, honey. Come on, sit over here. We need to
talk, and tears aren't going to do any good."

Beth sat on the hassock in front of him, wiping her
eyes with the back of her hand. Patrick handed her a
handkerchief, and she blew her nose. They sat in silence for a few minutes—father and daughter—not
looking at each other, not speaking, each aware that
nothing could ever be the same again. Patrick cleared
his throat.

"Did Dr. Morrison say anything about your health?
Are you okay?"

Beth nodded, twisting the handkerchief in her fingers. "I'm fine."

"Good. Good." The silence stretched again. "I don't want you to worry about anything, Beth. I'll take care of you, just like I always have. There's room for a baby here, probably liven the place up a bit. I don't want this to be the end of your life, either. You'll have to drop out of school now, but we'll get you into night school or a correspondence course or something. You're still going to get your education. We'll find someone who can take care of the baby while you're studying. You'll see. Everything will work out."

"Donovan and I want to get married."

Patrick shifted abruptly in his chair, just the mention of Donovan's name enough to remind him of how impossible the situation was.

"I don't think so, pumpkin. You shouldn't compound one mistake by making another. You're too young to get married."

"Donovan wants to take care of me and the baby."

It was an effort to keep his voice level. "Donovan is just a boy. How could he possibly take care of a wife and a baby? The two of you would just be making a bigger mistake than you already have."

"I don't want my child to grow up without a father, Mr. Martin."

Patrick's head jerked toward the door, angry color rising in his face. He opened his mouth to order Donovan out, to harangue him for what he'd done to Beth.

"Donovan!" Beth was in Donovan's arms before Patrick could stand up. Donovan's dark head bent over Beth's fair hair as his arms closed around her.

"I shouldn't have let you come alone, Beth. I should have been with you."

Patrick wanted to rush across the room and tear Beth away from the boy. How dare he come here to this house? Hadn't he done enough damage already? But Beth clung to him, her arms around his waist, her face buried in his shoulder, holding him as if he were the most important thing in the world.

Patrick looked away, swallowing his paternal rage, trying to think calmly. No matter how much it hurt, he had to face the fact that this situation was also Beth's doing. He looked back at the young couple. They were so young.

Donovan lifted his head and looked at her father. His eyes met Patrick's without flinching, his expression calm and too old for his years.

"You'd better come in and sit down, both of you."

Donovan kept his arm around Beth as they sat on the sofa opposite her father.

"This must have been a shock to you, Mr. Martin. I'm very sorry."

"I think it's been a bit of a shock to all of us."

"I want to marry Beth, Mr. Martin."

Patrick tried to gather his thoughts. How did he explain to this serious young man that marriage was going to be just the beginning of their problems?

"Marriage is a serious commitment. You're both very young—"

Beth interrupted. "We're old enough to know that we love each other, Daddy. I wanted to marry Donovan even before...this happened." Beth's hands tightened around Donovan's arm as if she were afraid her father would try to drag them apart. Patrick looked at her helplessly. She was his little girl, his baby. He had always tried to protect her, to shield her from hurt.

"Mr. Martin." Donovan's quiet voice drew Patrick's attention to him. "I know this isn't what you wanted for Beth. It isn't what I wanted, either. But it's happened, and we can't change that. If Beth and I get married, it will at least give the baby a name. I love Beth. I'd take care of her and the baby. I'd do my best to make her happy.''

"Just how do you plan to support a wife and child?" Patrick saw the boy's jaw tighten, and he regretted his sarcastic tone.

"I have a good job at Sam's garage. I know they'd give me more hours if I asked. I also have some money saved. I had...other plans for it, but they can wait. It's not much, but it would get Beth and me started."

"Please, Daddy. Please say yes." Beth's mouth quivered with the intensity of the plea. Donovan put his arm around her, holding her protectively.

Patrick leaned back in his chair; suddenly he felt incredibly old. They were so pathetically young and so much in love. They didn't have any idea of what they were facing. Patrick studied Donovan's face, the eyes too old for his years and the jaw that already spoke of determination and will. The boy knew what they were up against, which made it all the more commendable that he wanted to take responsibility.

But that wasn't going to make it any easier. And Beth. His lovely Beth. She couldn't possibly understand what she was facing by undertaking motherhood and marriage. Either was a difficult adjustment, but to take on both at once... He loved his daughter, but he didn't know if she was up to the challenge.

On the other hand, if he refused to let them marry it would mean that his first grandchild would be illegitimate. While the rest of the country might be stirring and changing and saying "love child" instead of "bastard," Remembrance wasn't going to change anytime soon. A child born out of wedlock was going to have a rough time.

He closed his eyes, shutting out the young couple across from him. The burden of their future weighed on him. The decision he made now would affect both their lives as well as the baby's. It was important that he make the right choice.

He opened his eyes slowly and looked at them. Beth's face was pressed against Donovan's shoulder, her hands wrapped around his arm. Donovan bent over her, his hand stroking her hair, his expression tender. Patrick swallowed against a sudden pain in his chest. Beth wasn't his little girl anymore. She had other loyalties, other loves.

"I won't stand in the way of your marriage—on one condition."

Beth and Donovan looked at him, Beth's eyes bright with relief, Donovan's wary. He'd learned a long time ago that "conditions" were rarely pleasant.

"I think you'll agree that it's going to be very difficult for you to make ends meet on your salary alone."

"We'll manage."

"Beth is pregnant. That's not a good time to 'manage.' You can marry my daughter, but I want the two of you to agree to live in the apartment over our garage. We could have it cleaned out and fixed up in less than a week. It would save you rent money and let me keep an eye on Beth."

"Once Beth and I are married, she'll be my responsibility. I can take care of her." Pride bristled in the words.

"Swallow your pride, boy." Patrick felt unutterably weary. "It's going to be hard enough to manage all the expenses that go with a family. Beth is going to need some extra pampering now and, once the baby is here, you're going to need help with that. Think of what's best for Beth.''

Donovan stared at him, stubbornness in the set of his jaw, his eyes flaring. Beth said nothing. It was clear to her that the decision lay between the two males.

After a long moment, Donovan nodded, the movement stiff, as if it hurt to make it. "Fine. Thank you, Mr. Martin. I only want what's best for Beth.''

A week later, Beth and Donovan were married in a quiet ceremony in a judge's office on the outskirts of town. The proper words were said, and Donovan slipped a narrow gold band on her finger. Beth knew that the ring had belonged to his mother, the only thing she'd given him except her stubborn determination. The only guests were Beth's father and the judge's wife.

Afterward, Patrick drove them to a neighboring town for a wedding supper so they didn't have to worry about the sideways looks and whispered comments that were already beginning to follow them in Remembrance. Beth had dropped out of school, and no one had to ask why. There was only one reason why a girl left school. The fact that Donovan was the boy involved only added to the juiciness of the story. Everyone was able to say how they had always known that Donovan Sinclair was no good. His father had been no good, and blood will tell. It was just too bad that he'd ruined sweet, little Beth Martin.

It was a quiet supper. Beth picked at her food, speaking only when spoken to. Donovan ate with dogged determination, as if to prove that nothing was bothering him. Patrick barely noticed what he was putting in his mouth. The one question that ran over and

over in his mind was, Had he done the right thing in
letting them marry?

The drive back to Remembrance was short and silent. Beth sat between her father and Donovan, twisting the wedding band on her finger. Donovan stared out
the side window, his shoulders rigid. Patrick concen-
trated on his driving as if they were on a four-lane
highway instead of a two-lane country road.

When the truck was stopped in front of the Martin
home, no one moved for a long moment. They stared
at the garage in front of them, all thinking about the
pleasant little apartment above it. Each knew that their
lives were forever changed. Donovan opened his door
first, stepping out of the truck and onto the gravel
driveway before turning back to lift Beth down.

Patrick got out, and the three of them met in front of
the shiny hood. It was almost dark. Beth's hair caught
the last of the sunlight, seeming to glow with a life of its
own. She stood next to Donovan, his arm around her
waist. Patrick swallowed hard. A few hours ago, he'd
given her in marriage, but he felt as if this was the real
parting. She was a married woman now and soon to be
a mother.

He leaned down to drop a kiss on her forehead, glad
the light was too dim to show the dampness in his eyes.
''Be happy, pumpkin.''

''I will, Daddy.''

Donovan and Beth watched as the older man turned
and walked into the house, shutting the door behind
him without looking back. They silently walked up the
flight of stairs that led to their new home. Donovan
pulled out the key and unlocked the door. Then they
stood on the small landing, not quite looking at each
other, not quite looking at anything else.

After a long moment, Donovan pushed open the door and then looked at Beth. "Welcome home, Mrs. Sinclair."

He lifted her in his arms and stepped across the threshold with her. They'd left a light on, so the room was bathed in a soft glow. During the past week, Donovan had spent every moment he wasn't working or sleeping in fixing the apartment up. Beth's father contributed some furniture, and Beth hung curtains. It wasn't fancy, but it was cheerful and clean—not an altogether bad place in which to start married life.

Donovan set her down on the worn, wooden floor. Beth said nothing, but she continued to twist her wedding band.

Donovan cleared his throat. "It's pretty late. I guess we ought to get to bed. I ... I'm sorry I couldn't take time off to give you a honeymoon, Beth. We're going to need all the money I can scrape together before the ... in the next few months." It was funny how difficult it was to say the word. As if actually saying "baby" would make the situation real.

Beth shrugged. "It's okay. A honeymoon seems a little silly anyway."

"If you'd like to use the bathroom first, I'll just watch the news or something."

"Fine." She moved away without looking at him, and Donovan watched her go. She was so young. The bathroom door shut behind her, and he thrust his fingers through his hair, letting his calm facade slip. He had to be strong for her sake. He knew that he couldn't let Beth down, but it didn't seem to still the aching pressure in his gut.

He realized far better than she did just how rough life could get. Beth had never wanted for anything. His salary could provide the necessities, but there would be nothing left over for the things that Beth didn't even think of as luxuries. Much as it hurt his pride, he admitted to himself that being able to live rent-free was going to make life a lot easier.

He heard the bathroom door open and he turned, his face reflecting none of his tortured thinking. Whatever problems lay ahead, he would keep them away from Beth as much as possible. It was his fault she was in this situation; the burdens would be his.

All thoughts of burdens and future problems flew out the window when he saw his bride. He'd never seen her look so beautiful. She stopped, obviously wanting his approval, but Donovan couldn't find the words. The pure white negligee draped and flowed to the floor, hinting at curves, suggesting bare skin, without revealing anything at all. A pale peach lace ruffle decorated the bottom of the sleeves, the hem and stood up in a ruff around her neck. When she moved, the front of the negligee parted to show a matching white nightgown with an Empire waist.

She looked pure and innocent. Provocative and sensual. She was every dream he'd ever had. With her hair brushed out and flowing over her shoulders, he thought that surely she was the most beautiful woman in the world.

"Beth." Her name was all he could manage.

She turned her head away, and she smoothed her hand over the front of the negligee, her fingers shaking. "Do you like it?"

"Like it? Oh, Beth, you look . . . you look beautiful. I've never seen anybody as beautiful as you." His voice shook, and it was only through willpower that he prevented it from breaking, something it hadn't done since he was fifteen.

"Thank you."

Donovan stepped toward her, his hands touching her shoulders gently as if he expected her to disappear like a princess in a fairy tale.

"It's going to be okay, Beth. I'll take care of you. I promise."

She buried her face in her hands, her slim shoulders shaking with sobs. "Nothing is going to be the same again. None of my friends will speak to me. You can't go to college. We have to live in this stupid, little apartment. I'm going to get fat and ugly. You'll hate me sooner or later. I know you will. I don't want a baby." The words ended on a wail, her voice shattered into sobs.

Donovan pulled her into his arms, his chest aching. "Beth, listen to me. It *is* going to work. You'll see. It may take a while for your friends to come around, but they will. This place isn't so bad. We'll fix it up some more, and it'll be real nice. I'll go to school one of these days." He stopped, swallowing hard. He knew better than she ever could how unlikely that was. When he continued, his voice reflected nothing but optimism and reassurance. "And you're not going to be fat and ugly. My mom always said that a woman was most beautiful when she was pregnant."

Her sobs continued and he cupped one hand under her chin and lifted her head until she was forced to look him in his eyes. "You could never be ugly to me, Beth. Never. And I could never hate you. I love you. I'll love you always."

Her eyes clung to his, her mouth quivering. "Promise?"

"I promise. Nothing in the world could make me stop loving you."

He reached around her to pull a tissue out of the box on the tiny breakfast bar and wiped her tears away. "It's late and you need to get your rest."

He picked her up and she lay against his chest trustingly. If Donovan said he would love her forever, she'd believe him. Right now, she desperately needed to believe him. He carried her into the apartment's bedroom and set her on the bed, easing down beside her.

"I'll stay with you until you go to sleep."

"Don't you . . . shouldn't we . . . It's our wedding night . . ." She trailed off, her face flushed with embarrassment.

"We've got the rest of our lives." He brushed the hair back from her damp forehead. "Go to sleep."

She closed her eyes, her head resting on his shoulder. Donovan lay still, listening to her breathing gradually deepen and slow. The light spilled in from the living room and he stared at the bright path it left on the floor. He felt as if the weight of the world rested on his shoulders.

He rested his head against the headboard as he let the full burden of his responsibilities sink in. He squeezed his eyes together, but nothing could stop the slow tears that crept out, winding down his lean cheeks. With a shaky breath, he bent to lay his cheek against Beth's hair.

Chapter 3

The following two weeks were a confusing and difficult time for the newlyweds. There was so much they had to come to terms with, so many adjustments to be made. Marriage itself was difficult enough, but there was also the problem of Beth's pregnancy, which made its presence known with a vengeance.

Donovan held her while she was sick, held her while she cried, and held her sanity together. Beth didn't know which was worse, the morning sickness or the long hours when there was nothing to do but think. Donovan took on extra hours at the garage and, for the first time in her life, Beth found herself with only her own company day in and day out.

At first it was a novel experience. She was young enough to enjoy the vaguely sinful feeling of being at home when everyone else was at school or work. The novelty wore off quickly, and she found herself think-

ing about where she'd be if she was still in school, and
wondering what her former classmates were doing.

Desperation drove her to find something to fill her
time. There was an old, treadle sewing machine in one
corner of the apartment. It had belonged to her grand-
mother and, out of curiosity, Beth opened it up, dusted
it off and found that it still worked quite well. With
some fabric she bought on sale, she made a new set of
curtains for her father's kitchen. Donovan was duly
impressed when she showed him her creation. Her father proudly hung the blue-and-white check fabric
across the windows and then went out and bought her
the new sewing machine, which was the cause of her
first fight with Donovan.

"Dammit, Beth, if you wanted a sewing machine,
why didn't you tell *me*? I'm your husband. It's my responsibility to take care of you." Donovan thrust his
fingers through his dark hair, his mouth tight with anger.

"I didn't ask Daddy for a sewing machine. He was
worried about me using that old treadle machine so he
bought me a new one."

"Give it back to him."

"What?"

"I said, give it back to him."

"No."

They glared at each other, the little room seemed to
quiver with tension. Anger filled Beth's eyes. She'd
been so excited by the present, and he was ruining
everything.

Donovan's chin set in a hard line. She was his wife,
he would buy her anything she needed.

"We don't need your father's charity. I can take care
of *my* wife."

"It's not charity. It's a present."

"Same difference. If you want a sewing machine, I'll buy you one."

"Fine." She bit the word off. "You can give my father two hundred dollars to pay for this one."

"Two hundred dollars? For that?" He pointed at the blue-and-white case that sat on the table.

"Two hundred dollars. You're so determined to buy it for me. Go ahead." She crossed her arms and glared at him.

He jammed his hands into his pockets, staring at the offending case. Pride roiled in his gut. He could take care of his own family. He *had* to take care of Beth and the baby. They had the money, and pride demanded that he march over to the big house and write her father a check. But practicality told him how impossible that was. They were going to need that money—that and every dime he could earn. Sometimes he allowed himself to wonder if it would be enough.

"Well, you're so all fired set on getting it for me. Go ahead."

He dug his hands deeper into his pockets. "No." The one word held a wealth of pain and brought Beth up short. His face was angled away from her as he looked at the sewing machine, but she could see the way the muscle ticked in his jaw, the hard set of his chin.

Her own anger and hurt faded as she realized that this was something that was important to him. He wasn't just asserting his rights as a husband.

"It's only a sewing machine. No big deal." Her voice softened unconsciously, pleading with him to understand, to see it the way she did. For a moment she thought he wasn't going to say anything.

"It isn't the damn sewing machine." His voice was raw with pride. "*I* should have thought of it. And *I* should be able to buy it for you. But I can't."

Beth struggled to understand, to comfort when she *didn't* fully understand. "It's not that big a deal. Daddy likes to buy me things. He always has. If it bothers you that much, I'll tell him I don't want it, after all."

The stiffness left Donovan's shoulders, and he reached out, pulling her close in a convulsive movement. "Oh God. What did I ever do to deserve you? I don't want you to give the stupid thing back to your father. I'm sorry I made such a fuss about it. It was a rough day. I guess I took it out on you. I'm sorry."

Beth wrapped her arms around his waist, holding him just as he was holding her. "It's okay. I understand." She didn't understand at all, but the important thing was that Donovan was holding her close. "I love you."

"I love you, too."

Beth didn't entirely comprehend Donovan's anger over the gift, but she did know that it galled him to accept help. After the sewing machine incident, she was very careful about accepting gifts from her father. If it was important to Donovan, she would try to do what would make him happy.

While Beth coped with the changes in her body and the pressures of having to grow up all at once, Donovan was trying to deal with a hundred different emotions, none of them comfortable, all of them demanding.

Guilt clutched at him every time he saw Beth. She was so young. The fact that he was only two years older didn't occur to him. He'd had to grow up quickly. Watching his parents' ruined lives made him realize at an early age that he was going to have to take care of himself. He'd accepted it the same way he accepted his parents' deaths, the same way he accepted the way people in Remembrance looked at him, expecting him to go bad.

But Beth . . . Beth was different. She was special. Her life should have overflowed with golden promises, all fulfilled. It was his fault that it hadn't been that way. Every morning he held her head while she was sick, and every morning his guilt was renewed, as was his determination.

Beth would have everything she deserved. He was going to make sure of that.

"Beth? Are you home?"

It had been three days since the argument over the sewing machine. Not another word had been said about it. Today was their three-week anniversary, and Donovan's hand tightened over the small bouquet of flowers he'd bought. Beth had been quiet, almost sad the past couple of days. If their fight was still bothering her, he hoped the flowers would ease the way to forgetting.

"Beth?"

"I'll be right out." The words sounded muffled, as if she were speaking through a pillow, and Donovan frowned, wondering if she was catching cold. Was it dangerous to catch a cold while you were pregnant? He heard the closet door shut and he followed the sound into the bedroom.

Beth was smoothing the already-smooth bedspread, her head bent forward so that her hair hid her face from him.

"Are you sick?"

She jumped at the sound of his voice, but she didn't look at him. "I'm fine. You're home early. I haven't done anything about dinner or anything yet."

Donovan frowned. "I told you not to worry about cooking. You should be resting and taking care of yourself."

"If I rest anymore I'm going to go into a coma." She laughed but the sound had little humor.

"I brought you some flowers. It's our third anniversary. They aren't much, but I thought they might brighten the place up some...." He trailed off and stared at the bouquet a moment, feeling silly. It was really such a small bouquet. It should have been a dozen red roses not a few simple flowers. "I wish I could give you more." He cleared his throat of huskiness and held the flowers toward her.

Beth took them from him, her hands shaking. "Oh, Donovan, they're beautiful. Thank you." Tears filled her voice as she smoothed the petals of a white daisy.

Donovan reached out, catching her chin when she would have turned away again. She kept her eyes lowered, but the blotchy redness around them spoke for itself. "You've been crying. What's wrong?"

She shook her head, forcing a smile that quivered around the edges. "It was nothing."

"It's not nothing when it makes you cry. Did someone say something to you?" Anger filtered through the words, boding ill for anyone who dared to upset her.

"Nobody said anything. I haven't seen anyone. I guess they're all afraid that pregnancy might be catching." There was a catch in her voice, but she swallowed hard. "I'd better go put these flowers in water." She edged by his taut figure and hurried out of the room.

Donovan could hear water running in the kitchen as she filled a vase. It hurt to think that Beth was unhappy, but there didn't seem to be much he could do. No one could have prepared her for the way her friends forgot her existence. He forced his clenched fists to unfurl. The only thing he could do was to make sure that Beth knew how much he cared. He turned to leave the room, but a flash of color caught his eye. Something was stuck in the closet door.

Opening the door, he started to tuck the scrap of fabric back inside, but his fingers froze on the peach-colored skirt. Moving slowly, he drew the garment out and hung it on the top of the closet door. It was the dress Beth had bought for the Homecoming Dance. He stared at it, remembering how excited she'd been. That was the day they'd made love in her bedroom.

It seemed so long ago. Years. Before they found out about the baby, before they got married, and when both of them still had all the normal dreams and ambitions. Their existence had been so different before reality crashed in on their heads. He fingered the soft fabric, seeing Beth's excited face when she'd shown the dress to him. She'd really been looking forward to that dance.

The puzzle pieces clicked slowly into place. She'd had the dress out, and she'd been crying. The dance was tomorrow night. Had she been thinking about how things might have been—how they *should* have been?

He turned when he heard Beth come into the room. Her eyes widened when she saw the dress.

"You were crying because of the dance, weren't you?"

"I told you, I was just being silly."

"You really want to go to this thing, don't you?"

She shook her head. "We can't so there's no sense in even thinking about it." But he saw the way her eyes shifted to the dress.

Rage swept through him. Beth hadn't done anything wrong. Her only mistake had been to fall in love with him. It was his fault. She'd done nothing wrong, but she was being treated as if she had the plague. It wasn't fair that she should lose her youth because of one mistake.

"We're going to the dance."

She stared at him, her mouth dropping slightly open when she read the determination in his eyes. "We can't."

"Like hell we can't."

"It wouldn't be right."

"Why not?" he asked coolly. "We haven't committed any major crimes. We didn't do anything to be ashamed of."

"What would people say?"

"Who gives a damn? They're already talking about us. Let's go to this dance and show them what we think of their opinions."

Beneath her uncertainty, Beth felt a glow of excitement. Donovan sounded so sure, so determined. What harm could it do? He was right, people *were* talking about them. It didn't matter whether they went to the dance or not, it wasn't going to change anyone's opinion.

"We can't." But the words had lost their conviction.

"Sure we can."

"You think so?" Maybe if they went, she could pretend for a little while that things hadn't changed. She could forget that nothing could ever be the same again. She'd had such high hopes for this dance. So many dreams had been wrapped up in that dress. She reached out and fingered the skirt, an abstract expression in her eyes. Maybe, just maybe...

The next evening she wasn't so sure there was any "maybe" about it. The whole idea was nuts. They couldn't go to the dance. It just wouldn't be right. She twisted her arms to reach the zipper on her dress, sucking in her breath as it hesitated at the waist and then slid the rest of the way up. Her hand was shaking as she smoothed it over her stomach. She was putting on weight. It wasn't obvious yet, but it wouldn't be long now. The realization added to her doubts. It was going to be a disaster.

She'd have told him so, but he wasn't there to tell. He'd made it a point that they dress separately, saying that he'd pick her up just as if it were a real date, which was why she was dressing in her old bedroom and Donovan was in the little apartment over the garage. She looked at the room through the mirror, wondering if it was the room that had changed or only the way she saw it. It felt strange, not quite right. Everything looked so young, so soft and frilly. She looked away, uneasy with the new perspective.

Downstairs, she heard the doorbell ring and her heart began to pound. That would be Donovan. She'd tell him that they couldn't go. It was crazy. She picked up her purse and took one last look in the mirror. The person who looked back at her was someone she wasn't quite comfortable with. She wasn't the girl who'd grown up in this room, but she wasn't quite a woman, either. She was somewhere betwixt and between.

She turned away from her reflection. Running her hand over her hair, she felt a sudden spurt of defiance. Donovan was right. They hadn't done anything wrong. Why shouldn't they go to this dance?

Donovan was waiting in the hall as she came downstairs. The look on his face banished the last of her doubts—or at least pushed them aside. He looked as if he'd never seen anything quite so beautiful in his life.

"Beth." He didn't say anything else, just her name was enough. With that one word, she knew how he felt. Her smile shook with nerves.

"Donovan." The intensity in his eyes was too much to bear for long, and she turned to her father, her smile hesitant. His own smile was wide, and there was a suspicious glitter in his eyes.

"I've never seen you look prettier, baby. You're going to knock all their socks off."

"Thank you, Daddy."

He hugged her, his arms tightening convulsively for a moment. "You keep your chin up, Beth."

"I will, Daddy." She turned to Donovan, her fingers clenched over her purse.

"I got this for you." Donovan stepped forward and held out a corsage of ivory rosebuds and baby's breath. "Shall I pin it on for you?"

"Please." Beth stood still as he slid his fingers inside the neck of her dress and pinned the corsage to her shoulder. Donovan could feel his hand trembling and hoped that Beth wouldn't notice. It was silly to be so nervous. This whole thing had been his idea.

The short drive passed in silence. There didn't seem to be anything to say. Donovan had borrowed her father's truck, since a motorcycle was hardly appropriate transportation. They were arriving late so they had to park almost a block away from the school.

Walking down the dark sidewalk, they could hear the music from the gym growing gradually louder. Beth's heartbeat speeded up. If she could have found her voice,

she would have told Donovan that she didn't want to go.
But she couldn't seem to do anything but cling to his
arm and keep walking.

Donovan pulled open the door and stepped into a
short, wide hall. Ahead of them they could see the big
doors opening into the gym. Music poured out on a
wave. There was a table set up near the door, and Donovan confidently walked up to it. Beth could only go
along, her heart in her throat. The two girls sitting at the
table had been staring rather forlornly at the dancers
inside. The dark-haired girl turned her head slowly, her
hand reaching out to take their tickets.

Under other circumstances, her expression might
have been funny. Her hand froze, half extended, her
jaw dropped slightly open and her eyes glazed over with
shock.

"Beth!" The name came out on a squeak, drawing
the attention of her companion, whose reaction was
much the same.

Beth hoped her smile didn't look as ghastly as it felt.
"Hello, Ann. Hi, Mary."

Donovan handed Ann the tickets and she took them
automatically, staring at the couple in front of her as if
they were ghosts.

"Nobody expected to see you," Ann choked out. "I
mean, what a surprise."

Donovan took the ticket stubs and drew Beth's hand
through his arm, pinning it firmly to his elbow as he
pulled her toward the door. Beth forgot about the two
girls at the table. Their reaction was nothing compared
to what she would face inside. She didn't want to go in
there. She tugged on her hand, her tongue glued to the
roof of her mouth, but Donovan ignored her.

They stepped through the doors just as the last notes of "Born to be Wild" faded away. The gym was brightly lighted. Streamers hung from the ceiling and balloons decorated the walls. To Beth's frightened eyes, it seemed as if the room was packed with people. The ripple started near the door as people saw them. She heard the shocked whispers and saw the eyes that couldn't believe what they were seeing. Information flowed across the room as everyone became aware that something was going on. In a matter of seconds, she and Donovan were the center of attention.

It was only Donovan's firm grip that kept Beth from collapsing in a terrified heap and crawling out the door. A space cleared around them as if by magic. For several slow heartbeats, the gym was dead silent. No one said a word. Donovan looked slowly around the room, his mouth set in an arrogant sneer, his eyes daring anyone to say a word.

The silence stretched until Beth was certain that the strain was going to kill her, and then there was a ripple of movement to one side as someone pushed forward. Beth held her breath as Carol ducked into the small circle that had grown between them and the rest of the school. She hadn't seen Carol since she left school. Her friend's parents had forbidden all contact. They'd talked once on the phone, but it had been a furtive, hurried call that left her wondering if she'd lost her best friend along with everything else that was lost.

Carol's eyes met hers, but it was impossible to tell what she was thinking. Was Carol going to snub her in front of the entire school? She felt Donovan's arm tense beneath her fingers and knew he was wondering the same thing.

Carol's thin face broke out in a wide grin. "Beth! It's great to see you." Her voice carried easily in the cavernous room and Beth felt her knees weaken as Carol hurried across the short distance between them. She had to blink back tears as she returned her friend's hug.

"It's nice to see you, too."

Carol linked her arm with Beth's so that she and Donovan flanked her. Carol's wide smile challenged the room, flicking over the other students, her look as much a dare as Donovan's was a warning. There was a mutter to the left of them, and Jane Masterson stepped forward, her face flushed.

"I'm glad you came, Beth. What a cool dress."

Someone put a record on, several people came forward to say hello. The tension was broken. Donovan's muscles eased, and Beth started to breathe again. It was going to be okay.

The dance was both nothing like she'd dreamed and more than she'd expected. Her dreams had been nebulous, unformed things in which she walked in with Donovan and everyone who saw them instantly recognized that they belonged together. Her father would then see how wrong he'd been and she and Donovan could be together without hiding their feelings.

Her life had shifted 180 degrees since then. The dream had become irrelevant, her expectations had become more realistic, her new hopes a little more hesitant.

Nice girls did not get pregnant and drop out of school to get married. But even Remembrance had to change with the times. Sluggishly, reluctantly, but it did change. There was room now for forgiveness, especially for a girl who did the right thing and got married, even if it was to Donovan Sinclair.

Her friends seemed genuinely glad to see her. No one mentioned the reason she'd left school, no one asked awkward questions. They all pretended nothing had happened. If there were whispers skating around the room, no one was rude enough to allow Beth to hear them—or perhaps no one wanted to chance the cool threat in Donovan's eyes.

It should have been wonderful, and in some ways, it was. But underneath the relief and pleasure, Beth was conscious of a vague sadness. She'd changed. She wasn't the same girl who'd started the new school year a few short weeks ago. She had a new life, new responsibilities. Gradually she realized that she could never go back and be that girl. The realization broke over her on a wave of melancholy.

The music changed before the sadness could get too firm a hold. The smooth sound of "In the Midnight Hour" poured out of the speakers, and she turned to Donovan. That song had been playing the night she'd met him, and it had been on the radio again the first time he kissed her.

Their eyes met and she saw the memory in his. Without speaking, he held out his hand and led her onto the dance floor. The lights had been dimmed for the slow tune, and couples filled the floor, swaying to the rhythm. As far as Beth and Donovan were concerned, they could have been alone. With Donovan's hands resting on the small of her back, his dark head bent close to hers, Beth felt as if she'd come home. He was holding her as though he'd never let her go. She leaned her forehead against his chest, linking her arms around his neck, letting the music flow over them.

"I love you, Beth." The words whispered against her hair, blending with the music.

"Oh, Donovan." There didn't seem to be any need to say more.

Driving home, Beth leaned her head against Donovan's shoulder. Her father's house was dark when they pulled into the driveway. Donovan's shoes crunched in the gravel as he stepped out, the sound strangely loud in the still night. Beth slid under the steering wheel, bracing her hands on his shoulders, letting him lift her out of the truck. The gravel felt rough beneath her stockinged feet, and she remembered that her shoes were still clutched in her hand.

"Thank you for taking me to the dance, Mr. Sinclair."

"The pleasure was mine, Mrs. Sinclair." The name sounded so right when he said it. Beth smiled at him, feeling truly happy for the first time since Dr. Morrison had told her she was pregnant.

Donovan wondered if she had any idea how beautiful she looked standing there in the moonlight. There was a full harvest moon in the sky and its soft light caught in her hair, turning it to pure silver. Her eyes were dark, mysterious pools and her mouth had never looked more kissable. Desire stirred.

They hadn't made love since they'd found out about the baby. The few short weeks had seemed like aeons. Lying next to her in bed at night, Donovan sometimes thought he'd go mad with wanting her, and then he'd be ashamed of himself. She was pregnant, her life had been torn apart. He'd give her all the time she wanted. All the time in the world, if that's what it took.

But she stood there in the cool light of an autumn moon looking so desirable. Almost too beautiful to touch—yet he had to touch her. His head dipped slowly, his eyes on hers. It was impossible to read her expression, but he could taste the softness of her mouth. The kiss deepened and her arms lifted to circle his shoulders, her shoes bumping against his back.

He angled his head to deepen the kiss, his arms tightening around her. Beth sighed, her lips opening, one hand slipping up to burrow into his hair, drawing him closer. With a groan Donovan bent and caught her up in his arms, catching her soft gasp in his mouth. Beth lay against him trustingly, her softness cradled in his arms as he carried her up the stairs and into the small apartment that was their home.

Chapter 4

"Donovan? Donovan, wake up. I think I'm in labor."
Beth's voice shook, its note of panic bringing Donovan
to attention even more than her words. He was offering reassurances almost before his eyes were open.

"I'm here, Beth. Don't be scared." He sat up, running his hand over his face and blinking the sleep away.
He snapped on the bedside lamp.

"How far apart are the pains?"

"I don't know. It hurts."

"I know, sweetheart. Just breathe and ride the pain.
We didn't drive all the way to Indianapolis for those
classes for nothing, did we?"

He was tucking pillows behind her as he spoke, easing her into a more comfortable position. He brushed
the hair back from her forehead, seeing the fright in her
eyes and hoping that he looked calm and reassuring.
Her hand came up to clutch his.

"I'm scared." Her voice broke and he had to force a smile.

"I'm right here and I'm not going to let anything happen to you. I promised to take care of you, didn't I?"

She nodded. "What if something goes wrong? What if..." Her fingers tightened over his as a contraction took hold.

Donovan laid his free hand over the taut mound of her belly, feeling the muscles ripple beneath his fingers. He swallowed his own panic. She was so young. What if something went wrong? How could he bear it if something happened to Beth—or to the baby who'd be his son or daughter? The contraction eased and he looked at the clock, automatically noting the time.

"Just relax and save your strength. Remember what the doctor said. It's probably going to be a while before it's even time to take you to the hospital."

"Don't leave me alone. I don't want to be alone."

"I'm not going anywhere. We've got plenty of time."

But the baby's idea of plenty of time was different than Donovan's. In less than three hours, Beth's contractions were coming five minutes apart. Donovan helped her down the stairs, afraid to carry her. Patrick was waiting to take them to the hospital, his face white and drawn in the dawn light.

Donovan held Beth during the short drive, brushing the hair back from her face, murmuring softly, promising her that everything was going to be all right, bottling up the terror that rose in his throat every time a contraction hit. Patrick pulled the truck up in front of the hospital entrance and Donovan lifted Beth down. A light spring rain was falling, and he eased her carefully up the concrete steps, supporting her swollen body as much as possible.

Once inside, the smell of antiseptic and the quiet bustle of the emergency room enfolded them. Donovan signed papers as they were thrust at him, holding those necessary for Beth to put her shaky signature on. Someone had found a wheelchair, and Beth sat in it, looking so small and fragile that Donovan felt fear engulf him.

When the last paper was signed, a nurse came to wheel Beth away, directing Donovan to the waiting room. Beth sobbed, her fingers closing around his wrist with bruising strength.

"Don't leave me. Please, please. You promised. You promised." Hysteria wrapped the words.

"Really, Mrs. Sinclair, having a baby is a perfectly natural thing. We don't need your husband—"

"I'm going with her." Donovan's calm statement cut through the woman's professional condescension.

"I'm afraid we don't allow that, Mr. Sinclair. Fathers have to wait in the waiting room. You'll have plenty of company."

"I'm going with my wife. We already discussed this with Dr. Grant."

The nurse sniffed, thus stating her opinion of Dr. Grant. "Then you'll just have to wait until she arrives. In the meantime, you can wait with the other fathers."

"You promised." Beth dug her fingers into his arm, her other hand pressed against her stomach as another contraction gripped her, her eyes hazy with pain. "You promised."

Donovan looked from her frightened face to that of the nurse, who was standing ramrod stiff beside the wheelchair, her expression filled with disapproval. "I'm staying with her."

"I can't allow that."

Donovan drew himself up to his full six-foot-two height, his frame muscular from hard work. "Do you want to stop me?"

The nurse stared at him, reading the determination in his eyes. He was less than half her age. By all rights, he should have been intimidated by her authority. *She* was the one in charge. But staring into those hazel eyes, she decided that this was one time she'd cut her losses. If she called security, it was going to cause a major scene. Looking at the boy's looming presence, she wasn't sure security would win anyway. He was damned determined. With a furious sniff, she capitulated.

"I'm going to discuss this with Dr. Grant the moment she arrives."

Donovan was no longer listening. He pried Beth's fingers loose from his arm so that he could take her hand, bending down to look into her pale face.

"It's all right, sweetheart."

"You're not going to leave me, are you? You promised you'd stay. You promised."

"You're not going anywhere without me. I'll stay right here."

He ignored the stunned disapproval of the nurses who prepared Beth for giving birth. He ignored the whispered consultations as to what to do with a father who planned on staying through delivery. He didn't care about anything but Beth. Each contraction seemed to drain more of her strength. He held her hand, whispering encouragement and wiping the sweat from her forehead.

When the doctor arrived, Donovan was vaguely aware of the hushed argument going on between her and the nurses. He assumed it was about his presence in the delivery room, but it didn't seem relevant. He was staying with Beth. That was the end of it as far as he was concerned.

"How are you doing, Beth?" Dr. Grant studied Beth's chart, her plain features reassuringly calm.

"I want to go home. It hurts."

"I know it does. Remember, the two of you decided that you wanted natural childbirth. This is part of bringing a beautiful child into the world. You're doing just fine."

"I'm not fine." Beth spit the words out on a wave of exhausted rage. What did this woman know about how she was? She was dying. Nothing else could hurt this much. They'd told her that having a baby was going to be a wonderful, glorious experience. There was nothing wonderful or glorious about this.

"I want to go home. Donovan, take me home." She struggled up on her elbows, her chin set.

"Beth, you can't go home now." Donovan pressed her back down, casting a panicked look at the doctor who looked as if this was all perfectly natural.

"I want to—" The words choked off as another contraction grabbed her. Her neck arched, her nails dug holes in his arm.

"Don't worry, Beth. You're doing fine." Beth wanted to scream at the doctor to stop lying. She wasn't fine. She was in agony. Her entire body felt as if it belonged to someone else, someone who was torturing her. She felt Donovan's arm beneath her hand and opened her eyes to focus on his face. As long as she focused on his face, she could get through this. He was the only thing linking her to the real world, the world she'd been a part of before this horrible creature took over.

"The head's coming now, Beth. Push. You can push now."

Stupid woman, Beth thought. I can't push. I don't have the strength. But somehow, she was pushing. Her breath came out in sobbing puffs, but she was pushing. There was a tremendous pressure and then a sudden emptiness.

"Good girl. You've got a beautiful little boy." The doctor's words came to her through a haze.

"A boy. Let me see." She'd never have believed it a few minutes ago, but she felt a tingle of excitement.

"Just a minute. Let the nurse clean him up a bit. And we're not quite through with you yet."

Beth's face tightened as she felt another contraction, but it was nothing like the earlier ones. She knew it must be the afterbirth. They'd been told about that at the classes. There was a quick tug and then the doctor was smiling up at her.

"You did a good job, Beth." Dr. Grant took a tiny bundle from the nurse. "I think you should introduce your wife and son, Donovan."

Donovan's hands were shaking as he took the baby from the doctor's arms and turned toward Beth. Beth pushed herself up on her elbows, oblivious to the quiet bustle going on around them or to the nurse who propped pillows behind her back.

Donovan carefully laid the baby in her outstretched arms, tugging back the soft blanket. Beth stared down at the wiggling red creature.

"He's beautiful," Beth said. She saw him through a haze of tears, but she knew he was perfect. From the thick, dark hair that covered his head to all ten of his tiny little toes, she'd never seen anything more perfect in her life.

Donovan reached out and nudged a flailing hand with his finger. Instantly the tiny fingers closed around his thumb. Beth's laugh ended on a half sob. She looked up at Donovan, and she wasn't surprised to see him wiping self-consciously at the dampness in his eyes.

"He's beautiful."

"Almost as beautiful as his mother." The husky words held a wealth of love, and Beth felt new tears fill her eyes.

"You need to let Beth get some rest now, Donovan." Dr. Grant bent to lift the baby from Beth's arms.

"I'm not tired." But even as she said the words, Beth felt exhaustion sweep over her. She barely felt the kiss Donovan brushed across her forehead.

Michael Patrick Sinclair arrived home on a spring day full of sunshine. The weather might have been celebrating his arrival. His grandfather carried him up the stairs to his first home while Donovan carried Beth. Beth protested that she was capable of walking on her own, but Donovan ignored her. She looked so fragile and felt so light in his arms.

"I think he smiled at me." Donovan set Beth on the sofa and glanced over his shoulder at his father-in-law. Patrick's face was bent over the small bundle that was his grandson. Donovan couldn't help but grin at the fatuous expression on Patrick's face. The fact that Beth had come through the pregnancy and birth as well as she had seemed to have eased the tension between the two men. In the long run, Donovan supposed that they had a strong common bond. They both loved Beth and now there was Michael.

"Are you sure you don't want to go to bed?" He smoothed the hair back from Beth's forehead, his eyes worried.

"Donovan, I've spent the past three days in bed. I'll let you know if I get to feeling too tired. I promise."

He smiled but the worry didn't leave his eyes. It wouldn't until she had the color back in her cheeks. Guilt washed over him again. It was his fault she'd gone through all this. Beth swore that it hadn't been so bad, at least not now that she had the baby, but Donovan's memories were too vivid, too frightening. Never again did he want to see Beth so frightened or in such pain. He'd promised to take care of her.

During the next few months, he kept that promise so well that Beth never suspected the tremendous toll it was taking on him. All her time and energy was taken up with the baby. She'd never realized how demanding an infant could be. There was more to motherhood than just an occasional feeding or diaper change. Michael needed to be held and talked to and played with. All the baby books she'd read said that it was important for a baby to live in an environment full of stimuli, and she worked hard to provide that.

During the summer months, Carol spent a lot of time amusing the baby, giving Beth a few much-needed hours to relax. Carol thought it was great fun to be Michael's "aunt"; Beth was just grateful to have a friend. The town had gradually accepted her marriage and child. She no longer felt as if she were wearing a scarlet "A" on her chest every time she took Michael to the store, but Carol was the only friend who'd managed to make the transition gracefully. Beth knew it hadn't been easy, but Carol had remained her friend without ever speaking a word of reproach.

The expenses that came with a baby were surprising, too. Donovan had to take on extra hours at the garage to make ends meet. Beth learned how to budget, sometimes shedding tears of frustration because the money never seemed to go as far as she hoped. But her eyes were always dried before Donovan got home. She knew instinctively that he would feel as if her tears were a symbol of some failure on his part.

Donovan took an active role as a father. During the first few months, he got up with Michael as often as Beth did. His hands, so much larger than Beth's, were just as competent when it came to warming a bottle or cuddling a fussy baby. Michael would stop crying for Donovan as easily as for Beth.

If Beth occasionally mentioned the lines of strain around her husband's mouth, he told her it was her imagination. She was too busy with Michael and the pressures of being a wife and mother before her eighteenth birthday to pursue the issue. Donovan was always there—she could always depend on him. Always.

Beth woke one night, about six months after Michael's birth. Next to her, the bed was empty and she leaned on one elbow, searching the room with sleepy eyes. She crawled out of bed, yawning as she reached for her robe. Michael's crib stood in the corner, but Michael wasn't in it. Maybe the baby had started to fuss and Donovan had been afraid he would wake her.

She wandered into the living room, tugging her hair from beneath the collar of her robe as she went. There was a light on in the kitchen, and it cast soft shadows in the living room. Donovan was sitting on the sofa, Michael asleep against his chest, his tiny body sprawled out across his father's much-larger frame. Beth stopped in the doorway, her face soft with love for both of them.

In the strange hours between midnight and dawn, she felt as if she was seeing Donovan for the first time in months. Caught up in the day-to-day pressures of living, it had been a long time since she'd really looked at him. He was wearing jeans and a heavy, flannel shirt that he hadn't bothered to button. His body was taut from hours of hard work. One broad hand lay across Michael's back, holding him secure, and Beth winced at the scrapes and bruises that marked his knuckles.

Donovan's twentieth birthday was just a few weeks away, but he looked much older—too much older. Somehow the dim light emphasized the lines of strain that framed his mouth. He looked drawn and worn, like a man who was reaching the end of his rope. Beth put her hand to her throat, trying to swallow the tightness there as she moved closer, her slippered feet silent on the worn, wooden floor.

Donovan was strong and tough. He'd always been there for her. From the moment he'd offered her that first ride home, through her pregnancy and the pressures of being a parent, Donovan had been strong. He'd offered her a shoulder to lean on, a hand to smooth the way across any rough patches. Now he looked vulnerable and tired. His lashes lay against his cheeks in dark crescents, emphasizing the pallor of his skin.

He wasn't aware of her presence until she sat next to him, the old sofa dipping beneath her weight. His eyes flew open, and he immediately turned his head away, running his hand over his face as if he had been asleep. But Beth had seen the dampness on his cheeks.

"Donovan? What's wrong?"

"Nothing. I guess Michael and I fell asleep." He didn't look at her, occupying himself with the baby.

"You were crying." Her voice shook.

"Don't be silly, Beth. You must be half asleep. Why don't you go back to bed, and I'll put Michael in the crib and join you." He still hadn't looked at her.

Beth put her hand on his arm, feeling the tautness of his muscles. "Donovan, don't lie to me. Please. If something is wrong, I want to know about it."

He didn't say anything. He stared down at Michael sleeping peacefully in his arms, confident that his small world was safe and secure. Beth saw Donovan draw a deep breath, his shoulders sagging slightly as if weighed down. For a moment, she thought he was going to refuse to talk about whatever was bothering him, and she felt the knot in her stomach tighten.

"Please, Donovan. I love you."

The whispered words seemed to break down some barrier held tight within him. His breath left him on a sound that was perilously close to a sob. He lifted his free hand to pinch the bridge of his nose, his eyes pressed shut.

"Sometimes I'm so tired, Beth. So damned tired. I'm afraid that one morning I'll just be too tired to get up." Exhaustion threaded through his every word.

"You've been working too hard. You shouldn't have taken on so many extra hours." Beth felt a wave of relief. This was something simple, something she could deal with.

"We need the money, Beth. But it doesn't really matter because I'll have to cut back my hours anyway. Things always slow down in the winter." He stood up abruptly, lifting Michael with him. "I'm going to put the baby to bed."

Beth didn't move. She watched him leave the room, trying to pin down the uneasiness nibbling at the back of her mind. There was something more here than just temporary exhaustion. She was ashamed that she hadn't noticed how tired he was, but she knew that wasn't the whole story.

When Donovan came back, he didn't sit down again. He moved around the dim room restlessly, and Beth could feel the tension building. Finally, she ended the silence herself.

"Are we broke?"

Donovan turned to look at her, his face shadowed. "We can get by. I suppose even if my hours are cut, we can survive. We've got this place rent-free, thanks to your father." His words were laced with suppressed anger.

Beth waited for him to go on, to explain what was bothering him, but he didn't say anything more. He stood next to the kitchen table, his fingers shifting restlessly over its edge. She moved over to him, taking his hand in hers, stilling the aimless movement.

"Donovan, what is it? What's bothering you? You said we could get by."

Donovan's gaze met hers. The light was at his back, his face all in shadow, but Beth could read the blaze of emotion, could feel it in the way his hand turned to grip hers.

"I don't want to 'get by.' I don't want that for you or Michael, and I don't want it for myself. You want to know what's bothering me, Beth? You really want to know?"

She nodded, half frightened by the intensity that shimmered around him.

"I'm scared. I'm scared half to death sometimes."

"Scared? Scared of what?" She swallowed the quiver in her voice. Her whole world was trembling. Donovan was her rock. He was always there, always strong.

"Sometimes, I look at our future and it scares me."

Beth drew a sharp breath as pain stabbed in her chest. She jerked her hand from his and stepped back, instinctively moving away from the light. He didn't love her anymore. All she wanted in the world was a future with Donovan, but he was saying that wasn't what he wanted.

He reached out and caught her hands. Ignoring her resistance, he pulled her toward him. Beth kept her face turned away. She couldn't bear to see the look in his eyes. She didn't want to see how he looked when he told her he was leaving.

"Beth, no. That's not what I meant. I love you." He took hold of her shoulders, shaking her gently, coaxing her to meet his eyes. "I'll always love you."

Beth lifted her eyes, seeing the truth in his face. With a muffled sob, she relaxed against his chest, letting him support her, her fingers clutching at the edges of his shirt.

"Then why did you say that a future with me looked frightening?" She sounded like just what she was. Very young, very frightened and in desperate need of reassurance.

Donovan stroked the back of her head, his long fingers offering wordless comfort. "I didn't mean that a future with you frightened me. I don't know what I'd do without you, Beth."

"What did you mean?"

"Do you ever look ahead, Beth? I mean really look ahead and wonder where we'll be a few years from now?"

"Michael will be in school, I suppose."

"I don't mean that kind of thing. I mean the future." The way he said it put the word in capital letters, and Beth drew back, staring at him.

"What do you mean?" There was a note in his voice that made her uneasy. It said her world wasn't safe yet and might not be safe again for a long time. "What kind of 'future'?"

"That's exactly what I'm talking about. Do you look ahead five or ten or fifteen years and see us still living here, taking charity from your father—me working in the garage and you keeping house?"

"I...I hadn't thought about it all that much. I guess I thought maybe we'd have another baby eventually, maybe even two or three. Aren't you happy?"

He stared at her, his expression unreadable. He seemed to be weighing something in his mind, and Beth held her breath, sensing that his answer might hurt.

"No. No, I'm not happy." He caught her hands before she could pull away. "I'm happy with you. You know that. I love you. I love Michael. Maybe that should be enough, but it isn't. Beth, I don't want to work in a garage for the rest of my life. I don't want you to be a housewife unless that's what you want to do. I want us to have some choices."

"We do have choices."

"What? Whether we should have hamburger or splurge on a chicken for dinner? Whether to buy you a winter coat or buy Michael new shoes? Whether we're going to have to ask your father for another loan to pay our bills?"

"Daddy doesn't mind—"

"*I* mind! Dammit, Beth, I don't want to live like this. I don't want it for me, I don't want it for you, and I sure as hell don't want it for our son. I want him to have choices, too. I want him to be able to go to college. *I* want to go to college. I'm twenty years old. You're barely eighteen. I don't want to give up all our dreams."

"If I hadn't gotten pregnant, we could have done a lot of things. But I did get pregnant." Her voice was thick with tears, and Donovan softened his tone, trying to get her to see what he was saying without making her feel as though she was being accused of something.

"Beth, you're talking like we have to be punished for what we did. We made a mistake. *I* made a mistake. But I love Michael, I wouldn't wish him away if I could. We didn't do anything wrong, and I don't see why we should have to give up all our dreams because of it."

She stared at him, her eyes bright with unshed tears. "I love you. I just want to be with you."

"God, Beth, I want that, too." He drew her close, feeling the dampness of her tears against his chest, feeling her pain as if it were his own. "I want that more than anything in the world. But I want to be able to give you all the things you should have. A nice house, a car. I want those things for you. I want to be able to buy Michael a bicycle when he's old enough, and I don't want to have to scrimp and save for months to do it."

They were silent for a long time. Around them, the little apartment was quiet. Michael slept securely in the next room. Beth had no such security. She felt as if she were standing on a patch of ice that was threatening to throw her off balance.

It had taken her a long time to adjust to all the changes in her life, but she'd adjusted and she'd worked hard at it. If she sometimes had twinges of discontent or wondered if this was all there was to life, then she suppressed them. One thing her father had taught her was that when you made your bed, you had to lie in it.

Now, Donovan was throwing all her careful thinking out of whack. Everyone knew that children took priority. Parents didn't have dreams except for their children's futures. She'd been living day to day, not really looking at anything but the present. His words made it impossible to go on that way.

She stepped back, wiping her eyes with her hands. "I could get a job. We could get someone to baby-sit Michael, and I could go to work. If we saved carefully, we could get a house and—"

Donovan laughed. "Beth, that's not going to do it. It would take years to save enough money for a house. And you going to work isn't going to do any good because anything you earned would have to go right in to paying whoever was taking care of Michael."

"Well, then I don't see what we can do. We can't turn the clock back."

"I don't want to turn it back, but I'm not willing to give up our dreams, Beth. Remember the way we always talked about our future together? I want those dreams. Dammit! We're going to have those dreams."

"What are you going to do?"

Donovan stared at her, his eyes old far beyond his years, deep lines tightening his mouth. "I'm going to join the marines, Beth."

Beth forgot how to breathe. Her gaze clung to his, pleading with him to say that this was all a bad dream. She read the pain in his eyes, but there was iron determination in the set of his jaw.

"No. There must be some other way."

"There is no other way. I can spend a couple of years in the marines, and when I get out, I can go to school on the GI bill. Money will still be tight, but once I've got a degree, I'll be able to start earning a good salary.''

"If you come back." The words were out before she could stop them, and she pressed her hands to her mouth, staring at him as if she'd never seen him before. If he loved her he wouldn't even consider doing this to her.

The war in Vietnam had been nothing more than a frightening but distant news story. Parts of the nation might be protesting and boiling with discontent, but Remembrance went peacefully about its business. She knew a few girls at school who had older brothers in Vietnam, but none of them were her close friends. It was something that had no relevance to her own life. With one sentence, Donovan changed all that. Suddenly the fighting was very real. Those men she'd seen on the television all had Donovan's face.

A sob escaped her and she pressed her hands tighter against her mouth. But she couldn't do anything about the tears that welled up in her eyes and spilled onto her cheeks.

"Oh, Beth, don't cry." Donovan took her in his arms, holding her close.

"What if you get killed? Please don't do this." The pleas came out between ragged sobs, her face pressed tightly to his chest.

"I have to, sweetheart. If I don't volunteer, I might be drafted. At least this way I have some choice about it. Nothing is going to happen to me. Didn't I promise I'd take care of you? I can't do that if I let myself get shot. Come on, sweetheart, don't cry like that. You'll make yourself sick."

Beneath the loving concern lay determination, and Beth knew she'd lost the war before the first battle was ever fought. Donovan was going to do what he felt was right, and there was nothing she could do but learn to live with it.

Two days after Michael's first Christmas, Donovan caught a bus to Indianapolis. From there he would take a plane to South Carolina and start boot camp. Beth didn't cry when he left. She'd already shed all her tears, and she swore she would send him off without them. But she stood in the bus station long after his bus was gone, unable to break the last link and move from the spot where he'd kissed her goodbye.

He had to come home safely. He'd promised. And Donovan never broke his promises.

Never.

Chapter 5

Dear Donovan,

I hope this letter finds you well and drier than you were when you last wrote. The weather here has been unusually warm. We're having a hot summer—not much rain.

Michael is starting to walk. He's really starting to fall down, I suppose. He does pretty well if he's got something to hold on to, and I know he'll get the hang of it soon. He's talking now, enough to get across what he wants.

I've started the night school I told you about in my last letter. Carol or Daddy take care of Michael the nights I'm in school. Carol will be starting college this fall. I feel a little stupid trying to get my high school diploma, but I guess it's a good idea. Anyway, it fills some time.

I'm enclosing pictures of Michael. He's grown so much since you left. I wish you were here to see him, but I've taken a lot of pictures so that you'll be able to see those when you get home.

When will you be home? I promised myself I wouldn't ask, but I can't help it. I miss you so much. Michael tries but he can't fill the gap his daddy left. Our home feels empty without you. I feel empty without you.

We hear so many frightening things on the news. I dread turning on the TV for fear I'll see your face, maybe lying in the road somewhere hurt or dying. I probably shouldn't tell you how frightened I am. I don't want you to worry about me. I want you to think about yourself.

Remember you promised to come home to me.

I love you.

                                                             Beth

Donovan folded the letter and carefully slipped it back into the envelope before picking up the pictures. His fingers were trembling as he sorted through the half-dozen photos. They were all of Michael, and he felt an ache in his chest as he realized how much his son had grown. He looked happy and healthy, his smile proudly showing off his first few teeth.

Beth was holding him in one picture, and Donovan stared at that one the longest. It had been taken outside and the sunlight poured over her, turning her hair to pure gold. She was smiling at the camera, her arms wrapped around Michael's sturdy little body.

"Letter from your wife?"

He dragged his eyes away from the photo. "Yeah. She sent pictures."

"Pictures, huh? Of her and the kid?"

"Mostly Michael, but one of her."

Smitty sat up, swinging his feet off the cot. "Let me see. I want to see if she's as pretty as you said she was."

Donovan grinned and handed the photos across the short space that separated them. Lowell Smith—Smitty, if you didn't want to carry your teeth in your hand—fancied himself a connoisseur of women. In the months Donovan had known him, he'd discovered that Smitty had opinions about everything, from the proper way to chew tobacco to the proper way to hold a rifle. He didn't really expect anyone to follow his suggestions, but he made damn sure everyone knew what he thought.

Smitty shuffled through the pictures until he found the photo of Beth. Donovan leaned back on his cot, already knowing what the Southerner's comment was going to be.

"Ooooeee! That's one powerful pretty woman. I bet her mother was from the South. The prettiest women—"

"Grow in the South." Donovan finished the comment for him. "Beth's mother was born and raised in Indiana."

Smitty shrugged, not in the least disturbed. "Might'a been her grandma, then. But I can tell she's got southern blood in her."

Donovan shook his head, reaching out to take the photos back. Smitty handed them over, his thin face wistful. "That's a nice little boy you got there, too. You're a lucky man, Dono. A lucky, lucky man."

"You hear from your girl?"

"No. But I reckon Sue Ann is pretty busy with college and all. She's going to be a doctor. That takes a lot of work."

"Yeah, I guess it does." Donovan slipped the photos back inside the letter and put both under his pillow. In the months they'd trained together and then shipped out, Smitty had received two letters from Sue Ann.

Outside, the rain poured down without showing any signs of stopping. Donovan lay back on his cot, hearing the soft crackle of Beth's letter beneath his head. It made him feel closer to her. If he closed his eyes, he could almost imagine that the endless sound of the rain was the dusty rustle of a cornfield, the silks no brighter than Beth's hair.

"We're heading farther in tomorrow."

"So I heard."

"Don't you ever lose your cool, Dono?"

"I might if you don't stop calling me Dono." Donovan's voice was lazy. It was an old argument, one they'd had since boot camp.

"I mean it. You always look like you expect to go home in one piece. Don't you ever worry, ever think that some of us ain't gonna make it?"

Donovan opened his eyes, turning his head to look at his friend. "I don't think about it. I'm going home. I've got a wife and kid to take care of."

"You think the VC care? A lot of guys got wives and kids. They ain't all going home."

"I promised Beth."

"Dammit! Don't it ever occur to you, you might not keep that promise?"

Smitty's voice held a ragged edge, and Donovan sat up, clasping his hands between his knees. He stared at the canvas floor.

"Don't you ever get scared?" Smitty's question was quiet, blending with the rain.

"Yeah, I get scared. We're all scared. This is supposed to be a war. I'd be nuts if I wasn't scared. But it doesn't do any good to think about it. I try to think about Beth and Michael and how much they need me."

"Must be nice to have someone need you that much."

Donovan looked at Smitty and then looked away. There was too much vulnerability there, too much pain. No man wanted another to see him like that.

"Sue Ann needs you." Whatever his personal thoughts on Smitty's girlfriend, he knew how much it meant to know that someone was waiting for you, that someone cared about you coming back.

"Hell, she don't care none. That last letter I got a month ago? It didn't say how much she missed me, like I told y'all. It said that she thinks we got no business being over here, and it wouldn't be moral of her to keep writing to me. She said I should refuse to fight, even if they send me to jail for it."

Donovan stared at his hands. He didn't need to see the naked pain on Smitty's face, it was in his voice. Somewhere in the distance, they could hear a staccato burst of gunfire, too far away to be a threat, too close to ignore. Someone was dying out there. Someone would never go home. In both their minds was the thought that tomorrow it might be one of them.

The firing died away and Smitty spoke again. "I wrote her a letter. I tried to explain what it was like over here. The jungle and the rice paddies and how you never know when a sniper is going to pick you off. You just don't refuse to fight because of some moral issue. How else am I going to stay alive? I guess I don't think much about the politics of it. I just want to keep me and my buddies in one piece."

"That's about all any of us do. We're just trying to stay alive. There's nothing wrong with that."

Smitty rubbed his hand over his face, his angular features twisting in a smile that held so much pain, Donovan felt an ache in his gut. "I suppose. I never sent the letter. I reckon she ain't going to change her opinion none."

"She probably doesn't really mean it. I bet in a few weeks you'll get a letter saying how sorry she is. She's young, Smitty."

"I used to think I was pretty young. I guess maybe I won't never be young again. None of us will."

Donovan stared at him, the words echoing in his mind. He opened his mouth and then closed it again. There didn't seem to be anything to say.

"Incoming! Incoming! Hit the dirt! Hit the dirt!"

Donovan dove for the floor, hearing the whine of the rockets endless seconds before they hit. Time was suspended between life and death as he and Smitty braced for the impact, wondering where the ammo would land, wondering if these were their last seconds alive.

The explosion rocked the ground. The gunfire must have hit one of the few solid buildings in the camp. Boards smashed against the tent, ripping the walls apart. Debris scattered over them. The light went out. Donovan put his hands over his head, his cheek pressed to the thin, canvas floor, feeling the hard dirt underneath. The second rocket hit nearby, the sound shattering around them. The tent collapsed like a badly stacked deck of cards, smothering them in damp canvas.

"Come on, we've got to get out of here." He groped for Smitty, finding his arm in the darkness and tugging. There was no response, and Donovan edged to his knees, fighting the layer of canvas, finding Smitty's

shoulders and dragging him toward where the entrance
had been. Two more rockets slammed into the ground,
and he heard the sound of answering fire, knew that
their gunners were trying to get a fix on the enemy's lo-
cation. He didn't think about any of that. All he
thought about was getting the two of them out. Smitty
was a deadweight, knocked unconscious in the blast.

Donovan edged backward, groping for the opening,
finding it at last and backing out into the rain, dragging Smitty with him. The rain fell steadily, not the
gentle rain that fell on Indiana cornfields but a heavy
curtain that seemed smotheringly thick. Donovan wiped
his hand over his eyes, casting a quick look around the
camp, seeing the scurry of activity, then hearing the
heavy boom of a rocket launcher. All of that was secondary to his concern for Smitty. He wiped the rain out
of his eyes again and reached for his buddy. The medic
was across the camp. He was halfway to his knees,
Smitty cradled against him, when he realized that there
was no rush.

There wasn't anything a medic could do for him.

It must have been the first rocket that did it. From the
looks of it, a board must have caught him, breaking his
neck and killing him instantly. Donovan laid him down
gently. He reached out to close his friend's eyes, vaguely
disturbed by that blank stare. He knelt there for a long
time . . . until someone came along and took him by the
shoulders, lifting him to his feet and pulling him away
from the body. He didn't say anything while the med-
ics dabbed antiseptic on his numerous cuts, cuts he
hadn't even been aware of. They released him, going
back to the more seriously wounded.

Donovan walked back to the remains of the tent.
Smitty's body was gone, but there had been no time to

do anything about the collapsed tent. There were more important priorities. But not to Donovan. He shifted through the debris to find Beth's letter. It was wet but it would be all right once it dried out. He tucked it in his pocket and then went through Smitty's belongings methodically, packing them up to be shipped home to his folks.

He found the letter Smitty had written to his girlfriend. Without thinking about it, he tucked it in his pocket. The next day, it was on its way back to the States, exactly as Smitty had written it but with a simple postscript written by Donovan.

''He's dead.''

Dear Beth,
I wish I could be there for Thanksgiving dinner. I know you'll be having turkey and all the trimmings. Eat some for me, would you?

I know I said I might be able to make it home for Christmas but, as it turns out, that won't be possible. If everyone who wanted Christmas leave got it, there wouldn't be a war during the month of December because no one would be here to fight it. I'll be home in January, though. Save some Christmas ham for me.

I can't wait to see you, Beth. I miss you so much. It's like an ache in my gut every minute. I don't know what I'd do if I didn't have you to think about. You and Michael are what keeps me going.

I didn't tell you before because I didn't want to worry you, but Smitty was killed a few weeks ago. I guess I mentioned him in some of my letters. He was a great guy. I don't want you to worry about me, though. I've been really lucky. Nothing but a few cuts and scrapes.

There doesn't seem to be any real sense to anything that happens over here. Who lives and who dies seems to be a matter of luck sometimes. Or being in the wrong place at the wrong time. I'm doing my best to be in the right places at the right times.

I miss you and I love you. I'll send you all the dates for January just as soon as everything is cleared. Kiss Michael for me. I wish I was there to do it myself.

                                        Love, Donovan

"Do I look okay? Do you think this dress is too wild? Or too uptight? What about my hair? Maybe I should have cut it."

"Beth, you look just fine. Donovan is going to be dazzled. Besides, it's a little late to start worrying about that now. Your plane takes off in twenty minutes. Did you tell him you were going to meet him in San Francisco?"

"No, I wanted to surprise him." She stared at the open gate. Passengers were filing onto the plane, but she couldn't seem to move. "What if he doesn't recognize me, Daddy? What if he's changed and he doesn't love me anymore?"

"Don't be silly, muffin. That boy loves you enough to find you in the dark."

"What about Michael? Are you sure you can take care of him?" She fussed with the fringes on her suede purse, her eyes anxious.

"Stop stalling. I didn't buy you a ticket just to wait here at the airport while you missed the flight. I raised *you* okay. I think I can take care of my grandson for two days.'' He picked up her small case and handed it to her, edging her toward the gate. At the last minute, Beth turned and threw her arms around him, giving him a fierce hug.

''Thank you, Daddy.''

''Just have a good time, muffin.''

The flight to San Francisco was endless. Beth felt as if she could have walked to California in less time than it was taking the plane to get there. Her flight was supposed to get into San Francisco two hours before Donovan's arrived from Honolulu.

Despite the way time crawled, she was soon standing in the terminal, watching Donovan's plane taxi up to the building. She smoothed her hair again, hoping the upswept style made her look older and more mature. She wanted Donovan to see how she'd grown up in his absence. She'd coped without him, dealt with being a single parent, and she wanted him to be able to see it all.

Her heart started to pound with slow, heavy thumps as the first passengers exited. She watched anxiously, her thoughts scattered in a million different directions. There were several men in uniform, but she knew Donovan the minute he stepped off the plane even though his head was bent, and his cap shielded his face.

She opened her mouth to call his name, but nothing came out. Her voice was caught somewhere in her throat, and she could only stand and stare at him, her eyes filling with foolish tears. He seemed to feel her gaze, because he suddenly looked up and looked directly at her.

She wanted to run forward, but her feet were frozen. Time was frozen as they stared at each other. She'd never seen anything more wonderful in her life.

She wasn't sure which of them moved first. But all
that mattered was that she was in his arms, feeling them
tight and warm around her. He was holding her so close
that she couldn't breathe, but that didn't matter, either.

"Oh God, Beth. Are you really here? I'm not
dreaming you?"

"Donovan, Donovan." She couldn't seem to get out
more than his name. His hand cupped the back of her
head, destroying her carefully pinned hair as he tilted
her face back until he could look at her. She knocked
his cap off, oblivious to everything around them as his
mouth found hers. It was only a kiss, but it held a solid
year of loneliness—twelve months of being apart and a
lifetime of worry.

She had no idea how long they stood in the middle of
the terminal kissing. People bumped into them, but she
didn't care. She didn't care about anything but the feel
of Donovan's mouth on hers.

"Sir? I think you dropped this."

It took a bit for the voice to penetrate. Donovan lifted
his head, his eyes locked on Beth's.

"Sir?" the voice prodded again.

Donovan dragged his gaze away, lowering Beth to her
feet. His arms slid away as he took his cap from the
stewardess dusting it off on his sleeve and setting it back
on his head. He bent to pick up his case, throwing his
other arm around his wife.

"We'd better hurry if we're going to catch our flight.
You're flying with me?"

"I canceled your reservations. We've got reservations at a hotel, and we've got two days together before
we go home. It was a Christmas present from Daddy.
He's taking care of Michael. Please don't get mad. I
didn't let him get me anything else. I didn't even let him

buy me a birthday present, so this isn't like taking charity from him or anything.''

"I don't care what it is. All I care about is that you're here. I guess even my pride has its limits. Do you have a bag?''

The ride to the hotel was short and full of news. Donovan wanted to hear everything Beth had done and everything Michael had learned in the past year. It seemed as if there was so much to tell him, and he was hungry for every little detail.

A light drizzle was falling when they got to the hotel. San Francisco was damp and gray, and a shadowy fog blanketed the bay. The tall, narrow buildings and famous hills might have been flat desert and wooden shacks for all Donovan and Beth cared.

It wasn't until the door to their room was shut and they were completely alone that Beth felt a wave of uncertainty. In the warm lamplight, Donovan looked different. He looked harder, older. She was suddenly out of things to say. She glanced at him and then looked away, moving to the window to stare out at the rain.

It had been a year. They'd both changed.

She felt him come up behind her, but she didn't turn. What if he didn't love her anymore? He laid his hands on her shoulders, and Beth felt a shiver run up her spine. It had been so long. She responded to the gentle pressure he applied and leaned back against him, letting the broad strength of his chest support her.

"I missed you so much, Beth.''

"I missed you, too.''

He slid his arms around her waist and rested his cheek on the top of her head, staring out the window with her.

"Nervous?'' His breath whispered against her hair.

She nodded, vividly aware of his arms around her.

"So am I. All I could think about was getting back to you. It's what kept me going, kept me alive. Now that I've got you, I'm afraid you're going to disappear. I'm afraid I'll wake up and find out that you're not here at all."

Beth felt some of the tension slip away. He was as nervous as she was. His arms loosened as she turned. She laid her hands on his chest and looked up at him, her eyes searching his face. Yes, there were changes there, but his eyes were the same—green gold and warm with love.

"I love you, Donovan."

"Oh, Beth. I love you so much." The last word was a caress against her mouth. Beth closed her eyes, her hands sliding upward as he pulled her closer. The kiss was full of love, full of healing.

Gradually, the texture of the moment changed. Desire slowly edged in. Donovan's mouth firmed over hers, his tongue tracing the edge of her lips. With a sigh Beth opened her mouth to him and his tongue slid within, tracing the ridge of her teeth before moving on to softer territory. He relearned the velvety softness of her mouth, their tongues tangling, twining.

He broke the kiss slowly, easing away. Beth's eyelids felt weighted as she forced them to lift. His gaze was on hers, heating to gold, half asking, half demanding. She let her eyes drift shut again, her hands sliding upward into the thickness of his hair, giving him an answer without words.

He kissed her again, this time more a demand—less a question. A year of hunger lay dammed up in both of them. A year of nights alone, days of worry. Passion lay simmering near the surface. It took only a kiss to set it free.

Donovan's fingers fumbled with the zipper at the back of her dress, finding the tab and sliding it downward. Goose bumps came up on Beth's back as the zipper opened, but it wasn't because the room was cool. Her bones seemed to melt with every inch.

Donovan flattened his palm against the small of her back, pressing her closer, letting her feel the heat of his arousal. Beth moaned, a soft plea muffled by the pressure of his mouth, and suddenly desire was an urgent presence in the room.

She tugged at his uniform, anxious to feel his skin against hers. Donovan gave a choked laugh as he dragged his mouth from hers and stepped back. Beth would have protested, but she saw his hands on the buttons of his jacket, his fingers shaking with urgency, his eyes never leaving her face. She shrugged out of her dress, letting it drop to the floor.

The afternoon sunlight filtered through the sheer drapes, filling the room with soft, gray light. The last of Donovan's clothes hit the floor, and he was reaching for her. Beth went into his arms, knowing it was the only place in the world she wanted to be.

Her breath left her in a sob as he lifted her, cradling her to his chest as he crossed the few feet to the bed. He tossed the covers back impatiently and set her on the cool, linen sheets. Beth reached up to pull him down to her but he held back, catching her hands and pressing them against the pillow, holding her a gentle captive.

"Let me look at you. Do you know how many nights I dreamed that you were lying next to me? I can't quite believe you're here, really here."

She tugged her hands free, reaching up to cup his face in her palms. "I was always there. Always. There wasn't a moment when I wasn't thinking of you, praying for you. A part of me will always be with you."

"You are so beautiful."

Beth's smile was shaky. "Kiss me. Love me."

"Always, Beth. Always." The promise was whispered against her lips.

She moaned as he lowered his weight onto the bed. He lay half over her, half beside her, his chest gently crushing her breasts, one thigh resting across her hips. She was captured, a willing prisoner. Her hands slid over his shoulders, testing new muscles, feeling the feverish heat of him.

His mouth slid down her neck, his tongue tasting the frantic pulse that beat at the base of her throat. Her short nails dug into his shoulders as his mouth sought softer territory, his tongue swirling across one pink nipple before taking it inside and suckling deeply.

A year's separation had only made the fire burn hotter between them. Beth arched against the pressure of his leg across her thighs and Donovan shifted, allowing her to draw one knee up so that she cradled his hard thigh between her own. The pressure was tantalizing, but not enough. She could feel his arousal burning against her, the pressure urgent, but no less urgent than the pressure building inside her.

He switched his attentions to her other breast, painting it with quick strokes of his tongue, building the fire higher and higher until Beth was sure that she would be consumed in the blaze of need.

"Please, please." She wasn't even aware of the breathless repetition, but Donovan heard it. He lifted his head from her breast, capturing her mouth in a hard kiss, his body shifting.

Beth drew her knees up, cradling his body. She could feel him against her, hot and hard. She arched, her body quivering, but he drew back. She whimpered as he caught her head in his hands.

"Look at me, Beth. Open your eyes, baby." Her lashes lifted slowly, weighted down with passion. His eyes were pure gold, reflecting her hunger, burning with her need. "I've spent a year dreaming about this. Show me, Beth. Show me."

Their eyes never shifted as she reached between them, her slim fingers closing over him. His breath caught, his lashes flickering at the feel of her cool hand on his heated flesh. She drew him to her, leading him home, her fingers sliding away to rest against his hip.

He thrust forward slowly, ever so slowly, giving her body time to adjust. At last he was sheathed in the velvet warmth of her. He rested against her for a moment, their eyes still locked, each savoring the feel of his warmth within her. He shifted and her lashes dropped, her body arching hungrily.

"Beth." Her name was a mere breath as he lowered his weight, his chest gently crushing her breasts. Beth swallowed a moan as he began to move, a slow, undulating movement that quickened, gaining power, hurtling them both along the path to fulfillment. Pressure built, wonderful, delicious pressure, demanding release, promising pleasure.

"Donovan." His name broke from her on a whimper as the pressure exploded into satisfaction. Her nails dug into his shoulders, her body arching beneath his. Donovan groaned, feeling the delicate contractions tighten around him, holding him, caressing him. With a sound that was almost a sob, he released the tight control he'd held. Beth held him, her hands clutching his shoulders as the shock waves raced through them, tossing them both high and leaving them to float down to earth on a cloud of contentment.

It was a long time before Donovan moved. He shifted to one side, ignoring her whispered protest.

"I'll mash you."

"I wouldn't mind."

He chuckled, his breath stirring the fine hair at her temples as he pulled her close. "I would. I like you too much the way you are."

She snuggled up to his side, her fingers sifting through the light dusting of hair on his chest. "I missed you."

"All I thought about was you."

"I don't want you to go again. I don't think I can stand saying goodbye again."

"Shh." He lifted her until she lay along his body, feeling the strength of the muscles supporting her. He reached up to tuck her hair back, his eyes tender. "Don't think about it now, Beth. I'm home now. Don't think about anything else. I'll always come home to you."

"Promise?" Her voice broke on a sob, and she buried her face in his shoulder, ashamed of her tears. His hand stroked the back of her head.

"I promise. Hey, don't I always keep my promises?" She nodded against his shoulder.

"Sometimes I get so scared."

"I know, baby. But it's going to be all right. I'm not going to let anything happen to me. I've got too much to come home to. Now, stop crying and kiss me. Tell me you love me. I've got a year to make up for."

She lifted her head and his hands cupped her face, his thumbs stroking away the tears, his smile coaxing her.

She smiled. It was shaky around the edges, but it was still a smile.

"I love you, I love you, I love you, I—" His mouth stopped the rest of her words. He rolled, pinning her beneath him, making her forget all her fears. Making her forget everything but Donovan. For now, he was home. That would have to be enough.

Chapter 6

When Beth had time to think, she was amazed by how quickly time passed in some respects and how slowly it seemed to go in others. Now Donovan was home for good, but when they'd been apart time had seemed to be deliberately holding back. Every endless day he was away was time to wonder if he'd been wounded, if he was cold or wet or hungry.

Then she'd look at Michael and time was running on winged feet. He'd changed so quickly, moving from infant to toddler to little boy. One minute he was learning to walk, the next he was riding a trike.

And her own life seemed to be spinning by so quickly. When Donovan was gone, Beth had grown up in a hurry. After night school the next logical step was to get a job.

When a new shopping mall had opened on the outskirts of Remembrance, she'd gathered up all her courage and applied for a job in a department store. When they'd asked if she had any special skills, she stretched the truth so thin she was afraid they would be able to see the holes in it. She'd told them she had some experience in decorating, which wasn't exactly a lie. She *had* done the decorating in the tiny apartment over the garage, and everyone agreed it was exceptionally nice.

She'd gotten a job in the furniture department. Her age was a mark against her, but she learned to style her hair so she'd look older and introduced herself as Elizabeth Sinclair, since that sounded more mature than Beth.

While the girls she'd gone to school with were going to college—some marching in protests, some looking for a man to take care of them—Beth was raising her son, working a job and praying for Donovan's return.

Now Donovan was home—older, harder, toughened by things she couldn't imagine, things he wouldn't discuss. She'd always thought that if he just came back safe and sound everything else would fall into place. She was still young enough to believe in happily ever after. What she discovered was that happily ever after didn't come without a lot of work.

The afternoon was still and quiet. Beth set down the small shirt she was attempting to mend and leaned her head against the sofa back. Summer had barely arrived, but summer's heat was here early. Rain had been threatening for two days, but so far all that had arrived were low clouds that held the heat next to the earth, promising relief but never delivering.

Outside, Donovan sat on the tiny landing, a book in his lap, a notebook set next to him. When she'd thought of having him home, she'd never gone beyond having his arms around her again, keeping her safe, loving her.

She hadn't thought about things like having him go back to school and get a job.

She picked up the shirt. She shouldn't complain. At least he'd made it home, and he was only working so hard because he wanted a better life for her and Michael.

"Dammit, Michael! I told you no!" The words were punctuated by a terrifying crash as something bumped down the wooden stairs. Beth was halfway across the apartment when Michael began to scream, heartrending sobs of anguish that brought her mothering instincts to full alert. She nearly crashed into Donovan as he stalked into the living room, Michael's arm clutched firmly in his hand.

"Mommy!" Michael's face crumpled in anguish as only a four-year-old's could. Tears streamed down his flushed cheeks. He reached toward her, and Beth's arms opened automatically, only to drop to her side at Donovan's stern voice.

"No. Michael, go to your room. You're not hurt so you can stop the crying."

Beth's hands clenched. Every instinct was screaming for her to go to her son and comfort him. But it would not be a good idea to contradict Donovan's order. With his father's gentle push giving him a start, Michael dragged toward the tiny storage room that had been converted into his bedroom. Heartbreaking sobs trailed behind him, telling of permanent psychological damage being done.

Beth barely contained herself until the door shut behind him. "How could you be so cruel? Can't you see how upset he is?"

A muscle ticked in his jaw, but Donovan kept his voice level. "There's nothing wrong with him except that he got a good swat on the butt. He's more startled than hurt.''

"You *hit* him?" She couldn't have sounded more appalled if he'd just confessed to beating the child. "I've never hit him. No wonder he's so upset."

"No wonder he's so damned spoiled," Donovan shot back.

"Spoiled? He's not spoiled. He's a normal four-year-old who's been treated with love and kindness, not brutality."

"Brutality? For crying out loud, I didn't tear him limb from limb. Most children survive an occasional swat without permanent damage."

"I've never found it necessary."

His eyes glittered with anger. "It hasn't even occurred to you to ask why I felt it necessary."

Beth glared at him. "He was probably trying to get some of your attention. God knows that's in short supply these days. The least you could do was have a little patience with him. He hardly knows you. You can't expect to come home and step right into being his father again."

The words spilled out without plan. She hadn't even been aware of thinking most of them until she heard herself. Donovan paled.

"I don't think that's fair, Beth. I spend as much time with him as I can. Part of being a father is disciplining when it's necessary. I'm not going to apologize for that."

"So, what horrible crime did he commit?"

"He wanted to ride his trike down the stairs and, when I refused to let him do that, he pushed it down the stairs. Next time, he might have been on it."

Beth looked away. "I'm sorry. I should have asked before I jumped all over you."

The silence stretched, and she thought he was going to ignore her apology. "I suppose it's difficult for you to get used to having someone else help you with Michael."

"It is. It was just the two of us for quite a while. I'm sorry."

"Don't worry. This weather has everybody on edge."

He ran his hand around the back of his neck, offering her a smile that said that everything was back to normal. Beth smiled back but she didn't feel very happy. Everything wasn't back to normal. She was beginning to wonder if this funny tension that lay beneath every moment they were together was going to become part of their lives.

"So, how's the happiest couple in Remembrance?" Carol's voice turned heads, and Beth found herself wishing there was something to hide behind besides Donovan's bulk.

"Fine." She hugged her friend as Carol edged through the crowd of graduates and families. "Congratulations. You look great."

"Sure. Black is my best color, and don't you love the cool tassle?" She grinned, her mild sarcasm a shield for her obvious excitement. "Well, Donovan, I'm glad to see you made it back in one piece. I told Beth you were too stubborn to get killed."

Donovan smiled, the first relaxed smile Beth had seen in weeks. She swallowed a twinge of jealousy when he hugged Carol. "Congratulations."

"Thanks. I can't wait to see you in one of these horrible robes."

Donovan looked at the stage that had recently held the graduates, and Beth had no trouble reading the hunger in his eyes. "It'll be a while, but I'll get there."

"So, what did you do with the curtain climber?"

"Michael is staying with my dad for the night. We thought we might make an evening of it. Dinner, maybe a movie."

"A cheap motel in the anonymous big city?" Carol waggled her eyebrows suggestively.

Beth laughed and then wondered if it sounded as strained to her companions as it did to her. They talked with Carol for a few minutes. But Beth didn't feel like laughing and smiling. She felt like standing in a corner somewhere and screaming over and over again. She wanted to scream and scream and beat her fists against something nice and solid—like Donovan. That thought slipped in unwanted, and she shoved it aside, not wanting to face it.

She had no reason to be angry at Donovan. She loved him. He hadn't done anything to deserve her anger. He'd come home just as he'd promised. He was working very hard between his job and school. She was proud of him.

"Beth? We're home." She looked up, startled. She hadn't realized how long she'd been silent, thinking. Her father had left the porch light on for them. In the thin illumination, Donovan's face was questioning. She looked away, not wanting to see the questions, knowing she didn't have the answers.

"I really enjoyed dinner. It was nice to get out of the house. I hope Daddy didn't have any trouble with Michael. Carol looked so nice. Her parents are really proud of her for getting her degree, though I don't know what she's going to do with a degree in botany. I don't think she does, either."

She was aware of Donovan following her up the stairs. For some reason she felt she should keep talking, as if a moment's silence might be fatal. Donovan reached around her to unlock the door. She flipped on the light as they walked in.

"Feels funny without Michael here, doesn't it? I hope Daddy didn't have any problems with him."

"You said that already." Donovan's voice was level, and Beth felt a spurt of rage, quick and uncontrollable.

"Excuse me for repeating myself." She shrugged out of her jacket and dropped it on the sofa.

"Beth, what's wrong?"

"Nothing's wrong." She snapped the answer out without looking at him.

"Something's bothering you. You've been uptight for weeks."

"I'm not uptight."

"I've been walking on eggs around you and so has Michael."

"Michael? What do you know about how he feels? Has he told you?" She turned to look at him, her eyes full of anger. Donovan struggled with his irritation, his expression carefully calm.

"I can see the way he watches you. I'm not criticizing you. I just want to know what's wrong."

"You're not criticizing me? Well, isn't that nice of you. You'd damn well better not criticize me! Who the hell do you think you are? Telling me what my son thinks."

"He's my son, too." Anger threaded through his quiet words, but Beth was too angry to care.

"Your son? *Your* son? I wonder if he knows that. You've been gone most of his life. You're home a few weeks and you're already beating him."

"Beating him! I swatted him once, more than a week ago. I don't think that qualifies as a beating."

"If you don't like the way I raised him, maybe you should have stayed home to help me."

"Do you think I wanted to leave you? Do you think I *chose* to spend that time away from both of you?"

"Didn't you? You volunteered. You decided it was the best thing for both of us."

"It was the only way out for us. Don't tell me you want to live in this place for the rest of our lives."

"There were other ways. My father would have helped us."

Donovan gestured sharply, his hands cutting through her words. "Your father has already helped us enough. I wouldn't have gone to him to ask for more."

"No, of course not. You'd rather go off and get shot at. You went off to your stupid war and left me with all the pieces. *I* had to take care of our son. *I* had to cope with faucets that leaked and cars that wouldn't start. *I* had to wonder every minute of every day if you were still alive or if someone had put a bullet through your head."

Tears blurred her vision and her voice shook but she didn't slow down. She was only just now realizing the rage that had been building inside for years, dammed up by conventions that taught her that a woman endured without resentment.

"*I* was the one who stayed up with Michael when he had the measles. *I* was the one who watched the news, wondering if I was going to see your body lying in a ditch somewhere. Every time someone knocked on the

door, I had to wonder if it was going to be a telegram
telling me you were dead.''

"Beth, I—"

But she didn't give him time to say anything. "Do
you know what I felt today, watching Carol get her diploma? I thought, that could have been me. I could
have been up there. My father could have been sitting
with the other parents, proud of me.''

"Your father is proud of you." If she hadn't been so
upset, Beth might have heard the unaccustomed tightness in Donovan's voice, the way his eyes glittered with
emotion.

"Oh sure, he's really proud of me. For what? I
haven't done anything to be proud of. You want to
know what I was upset about today? I'll tell you. I gave
up everything to marry you. Everything. I had to grow
up in a matter of months. And then you went off to play
soldier and left me with the pieces. I—"

The crash of Donovan's fist going through the wall
stopped her words in midsentence. Beth gasped, her
eyes widening as he spun to face her. For just an instant, she wondered if he was going to hit her, but he
didn't move from where he stood. She was too shocked
for tears, too frightened for words. This wasn't the
Donovan she knew. This was someone else, a man capable of violence.

His eyes glittered with a rage that dwarfed hers, his
hands were clenched into fists. Blood oozed from the
hand he'd put through the wall, but he didn't seem to
notice. Beth couldn't drag her gaze from his face.

"*You* gave up everything? What about what I gave
up? You watched the news and wondered if I was alive
or dead? Well, I woke up every day and wondered if I'd
be alive long enough to go to sleep again. I watched my

buddies get killed and wondered why it wasn't me, why I was the one surviving. I learned to carry a machine gun and I learned to kill people. I learned to kill because it was them or me and I had to stay alive. I had to stay alive because I had you and Michael to come home to, because you needed me.

"Ha! You needed me. I get home to find that you've done just fine without me, thank you, and you don't much want interference. I feel like a visitor here, I feel like a visitor in my son's life. And I feel like a visitor in our bed.

"Why don't we compare notes and see just who the hell gave up the most? And you know what the most ridiculous thing is?" He crossed the distance between them so quickly that Beth didn't have time to move. Not that she was sure she could have moved. Her feet seemed rooted to the floor.

"Do you know what the stupidest part of this whole damn mess is?"

She shook her head, mesmerized by the glitter of his eyes.

"The stupid part is—I still love you." There was so much pain and anger in the words that it took a minute for Beth to realize what he'd said.

They stared at each other, tension humming between them. Years of pain and anger both separated and drew them together. She wasn't sure just when Donovan had taken hold of her shoulders, anymore than she knew just how her hands had come to rest on his chest.

"I love you, too." His mouth caught the sob that ended the vow. Beth's hands slid up, her arms circling his neck, her fingers sliding into the thick, dark hair at his nape.

"Beth, Beth." His mouth slid down her throat, her name a prayer.

The tension that had lain between them since he returned home now lay exposed, its power shifted from anger to passion in the blink of an eye. In the aftermath of harsh words and harsher feelings, each needed reassurance that they still loved each other.

Donovan's hands were rough on her dress. She heard the fabric tear, but she didn't protest. Nothing mattered except that his hands were on her bare skin. She struggled with the buttons on his shirt, popping two of them off, but then her palms were flattened against hard muscle and crisp hair and nothing else was important.

Donovan's laugh held an undercurrent of pain as she fought with his belt. He stripped the ruined dress from her, and seconds later she was naked but for a pair of panties. His belt gave way before her determined assault, and he kicked his jeans aside before crushing her against his body.

Beth gasped, feeling the feverish heat of him warming every inch of her body. Her nails bit into his shoulders as he lifted her, holding her easily, her toes off the ground as his mouth found her breast, suckling and licking until she thought she'd surely go mad with need.

He set her down, his mouth devouring hers. Never before had passion been so quick to fire, nor had the fire ever burned quite this hot, consuming all the pain and anger, leaving nothing but need behind.

He lifted her again, his mouth locked on hers as he cradled her against his chest and carried her into the bedroom. It was dim and cool, illuminated only by the light that spilled in from the living room. But they didn't need light. Donovan's image was burned into her soul, a part of her, never to be forgotten, never to be left behind.

He set her on the bed, stripping the last of their clothing, leaving nothing between them. Beth lay back, opening herself to him, body and soul, heart and mind. With a groan Donovan lay over her, his weight braced on his arms.

"I don't think I can wait, Beth. I want you so much."

"Now. Please now." Beth's whisper echoed in the small room. Her body arched, her nails biting into his shoulders as he thrust home, his heat finding the deep core of her, making them one.

Their passion burned too hot, too fiery for it to last long. Each rocking movement, each whispered word seemed to meld them closer together until Beth and Donovan ceased to exist as individuals and became one being, their love the glue that bound them to each other.

The climax, when it came, was stunning, as explosive as the passion that built up to it. Beth's whimper was drowned in Donovan's guttural moan. He collapsed against her. She took his weight willingly, her arms circling his back, holding him even closer, feeling complete for the first time since he'd come home.

The silence lasted a long time. After a while, Donovan lifted himself from her with a mutter of apology. He rolled to the side, pulling her with him. Beth tucked her head on his shoulder, curling into his warmth, needing the feel of him against her.

"I love you, Beth."

"I love you, too. I'm sorry I threw a fit."

"I'm not." His breath stirred her hair and his arm tightened around her. "I think we've been building up to this for a long time. I'm sorry I yelled at you."

"It's okay." She rubbed her fingers through the hair on his chest. "Did I really make you feel like I didn't need you?"

"A little. I guess maybe a part of me wanted to believe that you couldn't live without me. When I got back, you'd done so well without me, it kind of hurt. You had a job, you'd gotten your diploma. You took care of Michael."

"But I did it because I knew I had to hold things together for you. I wanted you to be proud of me."

"I am proud of you. I was always proud of you. I know you gave up a lot because we had to get married."

She put her fingers over his mouth, stopping the difficult words, tilting her head back to look into his eyes.

"We both gave up quite a bit, but I think maybe we got even more in the bargain. I love you, Donovan. Being with you is the most important thing in the world to me."

"I don't know what I'd do without you, Beth. You're everything to me. You always will be."

"We'll always be together. No matter what, we'll always have each other."

"Always." Donovan's kiss sealed the promise.

Chapter 7

Michael Sinclair tightened his grip on his backpack and pushed open the front door. Stepping into the wide entry, he dropped the pack and stretched.

"Mom, I'm home." Dead silence greeted his call. He shrugged. She was probably at some committee meeting or something. He straightened and then almost dropped the pack. His father was standing in the door to the study, his face tight, his body rigid.

"Dad! What are you doing home? Where's Mom? Is something wrong?"

"Not unless you count sheer insanity as something wrong." The words were snapped off, each one distinct.

"What?"

"Your mother is upstairs packing."

"Packing? Where's she going?"

"She's going to 'find herself.'" Donovan turned and stalked into the study, leaving his son staring after him.

"Find herself? What do you mean?"

Donovan picked up a glass of Scotch, his fingers grasping the heavy crystal. Michael's eyes widened. He'd *never* seen his father drink in the middle of the day. It wasn't something that he talked about, but Michael was aware that Donovan's father drank himself to death. He'd always assumed that was why Donovan didn't drink. To see him with a drink in his hand and the sun shining outside was enough to punch home just how serious the situation must be.

"What's wrong with Mom?"

Donovan took a swallow of the Scotch, grimacing in distaste before he set the glass down. "Damn stuff tastes like battery acid," he muttered. His gaze slid to his son and then away. He stared at the pine-paneled wall opposite, his college degree neatly framed in the middle of it. When he spoke, it was clear that he was trying to be calm for Michael's sake.

"Your mother is moving out."

"Moving out? You mean *moving out*?" Michael couldn't quite grasp the concept. "What for?"

"To find herself. She needs an identity apart from me. I'm not offering her enough support."

"I didn't say anything of the kind, Donovan." Michael turned with relief. His mother could explain this mess.

"Mom. I don't understand what's going on."

"That makes two of us," Donovan muttered.

Elizabeth ignored her husband's comment and moved into the room, hugging her son. "How was Colorado?"

"The trip was fine. I want to know what's been going on here while I've been gone. Jeez, I leave the two of you alone for a week and you get all messed up." The attempt at humor fell flat, and Michael swallowed hard. Whatever was going on here was major.

Elizabeth linked her hands together, her gaze skittering over Donovan's looming figure to focus on her son.

"I'm moving out. I'm putting the last of my stuff into the station wagon right now. It has nothing to do with you. I don't want you to think for even a minute that it does."

"Why? What happened?" Michael suddenly felt very young and confused.

"Ha! If you can get her to explain that one, you're doing better than I did."

Elizabeth glanced at her husband and then looked back at Michael. "It's nothing specific, Michael. It's just that your father and I don't have much in common anymore."

"Just eighteen years of marriage."

"And we don't talk much."

"Only every morning and every evening."

"It's just time to end it now, while we still care about each other."

"A great way to show how much you care." Donovan didn't look at her. His eyes were focused on the Scotch glass, watching the patterns of light in the amber liquid.

Michael thrust his fingers through his hair, feeling his world crack and then resettle. He searched for some surprise and didn't find it. On some level, he'd been aware that this was coming for a long time. It wasn't something he'd ever dwelled on, but now that it was here, he didn't feel as shocked as he should have.

"So, how come you're the one moving out?"

"Because it's what I want." She twisted her fingers together, her eyes pleading with him to understand.

"I've been a wife and mother for so long that I'm not sure who else I am. I want to find out if I am something more."

"Of course you're more than a wife and mother. Don't be an idiot."

Elizabeth looked at Donovan, her eyes full of pain. "What else am I, Donovan? You tell me."

He frowned. "You're Elizabeth. Beth. Yourself. What more do you need to be?"

"Don't you understand? I've got to find out who that is. I don't know anymore."

They stared at each other across an abyss of pain, Elizabeth's eyes pleading with him to understand. Donovan looked at her for a moment and then snorted in contempt.

"Sounds like a lot of pop psychology. You are who you are and tearing your life apart doesn't change that."

He slammed the glass down on the desk, splashing the liquid up over the side. He stalked from the room without another word, but not before Michael saw the loss in his eyes.

There was silence until the front door slammed and they could both hear the sound of an engine starting up. Donovan's car roared down the street and Elizabeth sighed, looking up at her son.

"I'm sorry, Michael. I know it's not a very good homecoming this time."

"It's okay, Mom. I think I understand what's going on."

"God, I wish I did." She moved to the desk, picking up the abused glass and using her shirttail to mop up the alcohol before it could damage the finish. "I'm not asking you to choose between your father and me, but it would mean a lot if you could accept what I'm doing and wish me luck.'' She set the glass on a coaster and turned to look at him.

Michael stared at her, for the first time seeing the vulnerability she'd been working so hard to conceal. ''I do, Mom. Really I do. I just wish it didn't have to be so hard on Dad.''

''I wish it didn't, either. I didn't think it would be.'' She stared at the door Donovan had stalked through. ''I didn't want to hurt him.''

''I know, Mom.''

She forced a smile and moved away from the desk, giving her son a tight hug. ''I love you, Michael Patrick Sinclair. And your father loves you. Don't you forget it.''

Michael's arms circled her awkwardly. ''I love you, too, Mom. I...hope you find what you need. And I know Dad wants to see you happy, too.''

Elizabeth blinked back tears, the first she'd shed in the three days since she'd asked Donovan for a divorce. She had to have done something right to have a son like Michael.

Donovan scraped the remains of his supper into the garbage disposal. Michael joined him, and two charred pork chops joined overcooked peas and undercooked potatoes.

''We could send out for a pizza.'' Donovan glanced over his shoulder, his mouth twisting in a smile.

''Go ahead. At this rate, we're both going to either starve to death or die of cholesterol overdose from all the pizza we've been eating.''

''I'd rather risk the cholesterol. I'm starved.'' Donovan rinsed the dishes and set them in the dishwasher, vaguely aware of Michael's voice in the background

ordering an extra-large pizza with the works. He shut
the dishwasher and stared at the panel of buttons.
Sooner or later he was going to have to dig up the instructions on the damn thing and figure out how to run
it. Eventually, either they were going to run out of
dishes or the dishwasher was going to burst.

Funny, it wasn't until somebody left that you realized all the little things they'd done in your life. The
kitchen was immaculate, if you didn't count the rapidly filling dishwasher. Some people might have
expected him to let the place fall to pieces now that he
and Michael were living alone, but he wasn't going to
fall into that stupid trap.

"Danny's says they'll have the pizza here in thirty
minutes, tops."

"That means it will be at least forty-five. I don't
think they've delivered a pizza on time in the last twenty
years."

"You and Mom used to go there, didn't you?"

Donovan could feel his muscles tighten at the memories the simple question evoked. "That was a long time
ago." He opened the refrigerator door and made a production out of looking inside. "You want a soda or
something?"

"Sure." Michael took the can his father handed him
and popped the tab. Aside from the hushed fizz of the
soda, the kitchen was silent. Donovan sprawled in one
of the kitchen chairs, his long legs out in front of him.

Outside, the autumn night was chill with the promise
of winter's cold. Remembrance was already settling
down and bracing for snow. Donovan stared out the
window at the darkness. Funny. They'd lived in this
house for almost twelve years. He could remember how
excited Beth had been to move in.

Michael had been just six, and he'd been beside himself with the idea of a room of his own. He'd boasted about how he was going to sleep all by himself and that no one was to come into his room without knocking first. They'd promised to respect his privacy, which was a big thing to Michael at age six.

Half an hour after the lights were out and Donovan and Elizabeth were snuggled in their new bed, Michael had come scooting into their room, his eyes wide in the dim light. He'd skidded to a halt at the side of the bed, panting from the sprint between the rooms. Elizabeth had asked him what was wrong, and he'd gathered all his six years of dignity about him and announced that he thought they might like some company.

Donovan's mouth softened, his eyes distant as he remembered lifting that sturdy little body into bed and tucking him under the covers. His eyes had met Elizabeth's and . . . He frowned, cutting the memory off and reaching for his cola. That was all a very long time ago.

Michael looked at his father. It wasn't hard to see the pain he was going through. It was almost a week since his mother moved out, but not once had Donovan mentioned Elizabeth's name. He seemed to be trying to pretend that nothing had happened, as if she were on a vacation or something.

"I saw Mom today."

Donovan's eyes jerked toward his son and then away. "Oh?" The question was flat, as if he weren't really interested.

"She moved the last of her stuff into her new apartment. It's pretty nice. It's in that new development over on Bush."

"Cracker boxes. The guy who designed those places ought to apologize for calling himself an architect."

"Well, it's certainly not a Sinclair design, but the apartments are pretty nice inside."

Donovan grunted and took another swallow. Michael decided that it was encouraging that he hadn't tried to change the subject.

"She's got a nice, little one-bedroom place on the second floor. Aunt Carol was over all afternoon. She's going to fill the place up with plants."

"At the rate Carol gives plants away, it's a wonder that nursery of hers didn't go belly-up a long time ago."

"I thought you gave her a lot of the work on your projects."

"I didn't say she wasn't good with plants. She's just not much of a businesswoman."

"She seems happy enough."

"Meaning I don't? I suppose you agree with your mother and think I haven't spent enough time at home."

Michael said nothing, disconcerted by this sudden flare of temper. The silence was full, pulsing with tension. Donovan stared at the table for a minute and then looked at his son, his mouth twisting in a half smile of apology.

"I'm sorry, Michael. I shouldn't have snapped. It's not your fault."

"That's okay." Michael shrugged awkwardly and took a swallow of cola. "It's not Mom's fault, either, you know."

"Well, it's sure as hell not mine. I'm not the one who came home one day and announced that I had to go 'find myself.' Hell, I didn't even know you could lose yourself. I don't understand her at all."

"Maybe that's part of the problem." Michael didn't look at his father as he spoke. His finger traced the distinctive pattern on the soda can.

Donovan stared at the table, his expression brooding. "If she was unhappy, why didn't she come to me? I would have done something. Anything."

Michael looked at him and then looked away. "You know, Dad, you aren't really home all that much. And a lot of times you bring blueprints or schedules or whatever with you. Maybe she felt you didn't have time for her."

"I've always had time for her." Donovan winced at the defensiveness he heard in his own voice. "Maybe I have been pretty busy lately, but a business doesn't run itself. Somebody's got to take care of it."

"I guess maybe you could say the same thing about a marriage." Michael's words were punctuated by the mellow chimes of the doorbell. "Great! Food at last." He loped out of the kitchen, leaving his father to stare after him, his eyes stunned.

"You realize, of course, that I think you're completely bananas. Only a mental case would give up a man like Donovan Sinclair." Carol raised her voice to be heard over the roar of the vacuum. "And I don't know why you're vacuuming when you don't have everything unpacked. You're just going to have to do it again."

Elizabeth shut off the vacuum, trying not to wince at the sudden silence. She'd hoped that the noise would keep Carol from harassing her, but she might have known her ploy wouldn't work. A little thing like a vacuum cleaner wouldn't have made Carol hesitate to state her opinion when they were young, and nothing had changed with age. Elizabeth looped the cord around the handle, aware of her friend watching her, her blue eyes bright with curiosity.

"Well?"

"Well what?" Playing dumb wasn't going to do much good, but it was a stalling tactic.

"Why did you do it?"

"Vaccum before the packing was through? I don't know. It seemed like the thing to do."

"Don't be an idiot. You and I both know that I'm not going to leave you alone until you tell me what on earth drove you to leave a gorgeous man like Donovan."

Elizabeth shrugged. "I don't know." The answer sounded weak to her own ears, and she knew it would never be enough to satisfy Carol. She was right.

"You don't know? You just up and dump him and you don't know why? Beth, my dear, you've gone over the edge. It's mid-thirties delirium."

"Beth. That's part of it."

Carol cocked her head to one side. "You are sick. My name is Carol, remember? How many fingers am I holding up?"

"No, that's not what I meant. He calls me Elizabeth."

"*Everyone* calls you Elizabeth."

"You don't."

"That's because you can't teach an old dog new tricks. In my case, you couldn't teach me tricks even before I was an old dog." Carol reached for a doughnut, part of her housewarming present to Elizabeth. She took a bite, leaving a line of chocolate frosting on her upper lip. "Let me get this straight. You left Donovan because he called you Elizabeth, just like everybody else does. I thought you *wanted* to be called Elizabeth.

You've been Elizabeth to most of the town for years. Seems to me like it would have been easier to ask him to call you something else.''

Elizabeth reached for a doughnut. She didn't want one. She didn't even particularly like them. But she needed something to do with her hands.

''I didn't leave him because of that. It's just part of everything else that was wrong. He hasn't called me Beth in years. Beth was someone young and pretty that he was in love with. Elizabeth was an adult, mature and responsible and not very interesting. I know I'm the one who wanted to be Elizabeth because I wanted to seem older than I was, but couldn't I have still been Beth sometimes, too?''

Carol stared at her. ''I don't know. I get the feeling I'm talking to several different people here. You wanted to be Elizabeth but you wanted to be Beth, too, only Elizabeth and Beth are the same person but different.''

Elizabeth took a bite of her doughnut, scattering powdered sugar over the front of her sweatshirt. ''I suppose it does sound kind of ridiculous.''

''No. I think it casts serious doubts on my sanity, but I understand what you're saying.''

''He didn't even seem to miss Beth. It was like she never existed. Somehow I got all caught up in being Elizabeth, wife of a successful architect, mother of a terrific son, member of every charitable committee in Indiana. Only where was Beth in all that? I had dreams, too, you know.''

''I know you did.'' Carol licked the chocolate from her fingers. ''You've got to take some responsibility for that yourself, you know. I don't think Donovan expected you to give up your dreams for his or for Michael's.''

"Maybe he didn't expect it. But he let me do it."

"What did you expect him to do? Sit you down and insist that you take time out for what you wanted to do? Maybe he thought you were already doing what you wanted to do."

"I think it's been years since he's even wondered what I wanted to do. He just accepted that I was there."

"He does have some workaholic tendencies."

"I know you think Donovan is perfect, but he's got his flaws, too." She sounded like a four-year-old and she knew it. The problem was that she felt like a four-year-old at the moment.

"I've never thought he was perfect." Carol reached for another doughnut and bit into it thoughtfully. "I just think he's about the best thing I've seen in men. And I think what you two have together is pretty special, and it's not going to be easy to replace."

"What we *had*. *Had* is the operative word. Somewhere along the line we lost it. He got all caught up in being the world's greatest architect and I got all caught up in playing suburban wife and we drifted apart. You know, we'd always planned to have more kids. But we always put it off until 'things' were more settled. We haven't even talked about it in years. We haven't talked about *anything* in years."

"Maybe that's all the two of you need. Just a chance to talk."

Elizabeth shook her head. "No. It's too late for that. After a while, love dies if it isn't fed."

"Has your father called since you moved out?"

Two years ago Patrick had remarried, and he and his new wife had decided to travel around the country. He called once a week from whatever state they happened to be in.

Elizabeth's voice softened. "Donovan gave him my new number when he called the house. Dad was pretty confused, but he said that I had to do what I thought was best. All he wants is for me to be happy. He also said I shouldn't throw away anything I might want back. Only there's not much to throw away anymore."

Carol swallowed the last of her doughnut, her eyes thoughtful. "I just can't believe that a love like the two of you had can die that easily."

"It wasn't easy. It was a long, slow process, but it's dead."

"Maybe."

Carol's stubborn determination to believe what she wanted drew a short laugh from Elizabeth. "You're a closet romantic, that's all. Life doesn't offer a lot of happily ever afters, Carol. Donovan and I had some good years together, and we've got a wonderful son. That's more than a lot of people ever have."

"I think you're fooling yourself, but it's certainly none of my business." Her features took on a saintly cast, and Elizabeth laughed again.

"The day when you can keep your nose out of someone else's business will be the day they bury you."

"I'm the soul of discretion."

"I didn't say you weren't discreet. I said you were nosy." Elizabeth looked at the clock that was stuck haphazardly on top of a crate. "You'd better get going. It's late and you've got a business to run. And tomorrow, I start job hunting."

Carol stood up, reaching for a third doughnut. "I'll need something to keep me awake on the drive home."

"Most people consider driving reason enough to keep their eyes open."

"In Remembrance? You've got to be kidding. The streets are as dull as the rest of the place. Food is the only thing that keeps me breathing."

"If I ate like you do, I'd look like a blimp."

"Yes, but you'd be a much prettier blimp than I would be." Carol hesitated in the doorway, her blue eyes unusually serious. "Are you going to be all right? You know, you'd be welcome to stay at my place as long as you wanted. It's kind of nice to have someone to talk to besides the plants."

Elizabeth hugged her friend, her eyes stinging. "I'll be fine. I've got a brand-new apartment to play in, and tomorrow I'm going to find a terrific job."

Carol looked doubtful, but she didn't argue any further. If Beth wanted to pretend that she was happy as a clam, Carol wouldn't be the one to burst her bubble.

Elizabeth shut the door behind Carol and let her smile fade. She stared around her new apartment, still full of boxes, the furniture stuck wherever was convenient. It didn't look like a home yet, but it would soon.

She clasped her hands over her upper arms and rubbed. The chill she felt had little to do with the temperature. She was alone, really alone, for the first time in her life. Nobody was going to come in the door unless she invited them.

She hadn't realized how much it was going to hurt to break the ties with Donovan. She'd moved out a week ago, and she hadn't seen him in all that time. Surprising how much you could miss somebody. She told herself that it wasn't love causing this ache in her gut, but Donovan had been a part of her life for a long time. His absence left a big gap.

But she was going to fill that gap with new experiences and growth. She had this big, roomy place all to herself. She could do anything at all she wanted with it. She didn't have to consult anybody's taste but her own.

She had a sudden image of the cramped, little rooms over her father's garage where she and Donovan had started their married life. They'd worked so hard to make them seem like home. It had been the beginning for them.

She blinked, clearing the image away. This was a beginning for her. And she was just as happy as she had been then. She could do anything she wanted, anything at all. And that was exciting and wonderful.

Which explained why she was sitting on a packing crate full of dishes in the middle of her wonderful, new apartment crying her eyes out.

Chapter 8

SIX MONTHS LATER

What did you buy for a young man about to turn nineteen? Elizabeth stared at a display of action figures without seeing them. She'd wandered into the toy store more out of nostalgia than anything else. It had been a few years since she'd been able to shop for Michael in one. He'd outgrown such presents a long time ago.

Sometimes it seemed like just yesterday when he'd been clamoring for the latest toys touted by his cartoon friends. And sometimes it seemed as if centuries had gone by.

Moving down the aisle, she paused in front of a shelf full of Legos. The bright, primary colors brought a surge of memories. The hours she'd spent putting those things together. She must have built enough houses to create a small town. And anything she hadn't built, Donovan had. He'd been good at the more-exotic things like cars and rocket ships. During the months after he got back from 'Nam, Legos had been one of his strongest links to Michael.

He had made up for his absence. He'd been a good father. Loving, but not afraid to be firm.

"Daddy, look!" The shrill voice shook her out of her memories and Elizabeth moved aside just in time to avoid being run over by a little girl in pink overalls. The child skidded to a halt in front of a display of bright puzzles.

"Please, Daddy. Please could we get a puzzle?" The words held a wealth of longing.

"You've got lots of puzzles, Bethany." Bethany's father stopped next to his daughter and stared at the boxes. "I don't know which ones you've got."

"*I* know."

Elizabeth bit her lip to control a smile. The scorn in the little girl's voice would have done justice to a duchess ten times her age.

Her father glanced at Elizabeth, sharing her amusement. He looked as though he was about thirty-two or thirty-three, not that much younger than Elizabeth. Somehow, watching him, she felt centuries older. Michael had been a teenager by the time she was this man's age.

She moved away, leaving father and daughter to hash out the question of how many puzzles they should buy. He was standing firm on two, but Bethany was bargaining for a jillion. Elizabeth wouldn't have laid bets on who would win.

She wandered down the aisle and turned a corner. Dolls. She stopped next to a display of baby dolls, her face softening. The toys she'd played with as a little girl had mostly disappeared, relegated to the ranks of collectibles. But baby dolls never changed. She reached out to touch the smooth, vinyl skin on a plump infant that promised to do nothing but be soft in a little girl's arms.

Elizabeth didn't have to close her eyes to picture a little girl cuddling the doll. She had Donovan's hair, inky black and as soft as silk, and maybe his eyes, too. Her father would teach her to ride a bicycle, but he'd also be willing to play dolls with her or baseball. She'd definitely be Daddy's girl, but she would be close to her mother, too.

She blinked and the picture vanished. She pulled her hand away from the doll. It was foolish to hope for something that would never happen.

After six months she still envisioned Donovan as a father. She shrugged uneasily. There was nothing significant in that. They'd been married a long time. There had never been another man in her life. The little fantasy had nothing to do with the hollow feeling she sometimes had when she thought about Donovan.

She turned away from the dolls, shoving her hands into her jeans' pockets. It was only natural that she was feeling a bit nostalgic. Shopping for Michael's gifts was something she and Donovan had always done together. Even in the past few years, when they did so little as a couple, that was one tradition that had survived. This was the first time since Donovan returned from the war that she'd had to shop for Michael's gift alone.

Nostalgia was all this empty feeling was. It had nothing to do with regrets, because she didn't regret leaving Donovan. She'd done the right thing. It was just that, sometimes, she felt a little hollow. She was free to do as she pleased, but there was no one to care that she did.

Donovan ducked out of sight behind a display of

stuffed dinosaurs, feeling like a fool. He had to be nuts, hiding from his own wife behind a purple stegosaurus, but he wasn't ready for her to see him yet. He wasn't sure he'd ever be ready.

It felt like centuries since he'd seen her. He'd almost managed to forget the softness of her skin and the way her hair caught the light. In slim-fitting jeans and a bright blue sweatshirt, she looked young and vibrant and stunningly beautiful.

He'd been watching her ever since she entered the store, dogging her down the aisles, ducking out of sight to avoid being seen. He'd gotten some funny looks from a couple of kids but, so far, no one had called the cops. More likely, they'd call the men in white coats. He was acting like a demented teenager, not like a mature man of thirty-eight.

He edged farther behind the stegosaurus as Elizabeth wandered toward the front of the store. When had he stopped noticing how beautiful she was? How long had it been since he'd really looked at her?

She stopped next to a rack of children's books. The harsh, fluorescent lighting gilded her hair. She looked so young—not that much different than when they'd first met. God, that seemed like so long ago. She glanced up and Donovan squatted down, turning his face away as if vitally interested in the toys displayed on the lower shelf.

"Are you playing hide-and-seek?" The voice was solemn and unusually deep considering its owner was under three feet tall.

Donovan's startled eyes met those of the little boy who must have been standing right behind him. Serious brown eyes studied him. Donovan felt a flush slowly creep up from his neck. He cleared his throat, searching for the authority that was supposed to go with being an adult. Only he didn't feel much like an adult at the moment.

"I...ah...I'm trying to find a present for someone."

"For who?" The child looked prepared to wait as long as it took to get his answer.

Donovan glanced over his shoulder. Elizabeth was still scanning the books. He turned back to his inquisitor. "For my son."

Brown eyes studied him, considering that answer. "How old is he?"

"He's going to be nineteen."

"I like these."

"I...ah...Michael probably does, too."

"I don't have the leader yet, but Mom says I might get it for my birthday."

"I don't think Michael has it, either. Maybe I'll get him that."

"They're at the front."

Donovan glanced over his shoulder to see Elizabeth leaving the store. "At the front. Thanks."

"You're welcome."

Donovan was just in time to see Elizabeth wander down the mall. He waited a few seconds and then followed her, feeling like a second-rate James Bond. Did spies feel this stupid following someone?

She stopped to look in the window of a clothing store and he turned, staring intently at a display of copper cookware. This was ridiculous. He'd been married to the woman for eighteen years. They were *still* married if it came right down to it. He had no reason to be lurking behind her—no reason except the knot in his gut that threatened to climb into his throat and choke him.

Elizabeth felt him behind her an instant before his hand touched her shoulder. She forced herself to turn slowly, keeping her expression utterly calm.

"Hello, Elizabeth."

"Hello, Donovan." She'd almost managed to forget his height and the width of his shoulders. He was wearing a blue plaid, flannel shirt tucked into a pair of brown corduroys. He looked fit and trim and amazingly handsome. His hair was still inky black, with just a touch of gray at the temples. His eyes were still that wonderful green-gold shade, impossible to read, impossible to ignore.

"How have you been?" It was a simple question. Why was it that she couldn't find a simple answer? Did she tell him how hard it had been to make the break; how she'd cried herself to sleep more than once? Or did she tell him about her job and how much she loved it? Did she mention the sense of pride she felt when she came home to an apartment that she paid for herself?

"I'm fine. You?"

"Fine. You look . . . well." What had he been going to say? Had he been going to tell her that she looked pretty? Did he still think she was pretty? She tugged at the bottom of her sweatshirt, unaware of the way it molded the fabric to her breasts.

"So do you."

Silence stretched between them. Each of them avoided looking at the other, but neither of them could think about anything else. Around them the mall bustled with people. They could have been all alone for all the awareness they had of anyone else.

"I—"

"Well—"

Each started to speak and then stopped abruptly. Their eyes met.

"You go ahead," he offered.

"I was just going to ask if you were shopping for Michael's birthday present."

"What else would drag me to a mall?"

Elizabeth smiled, a quick expression gone immediately. "You designed this place. I don't see how you can hate it so much."

"Too many people in too small an area."

"I suppose. I was shopping for Michael, too."

"I know. I've been following you."

Her eyes jerked back to his face in time to see him flush. "You've been following me?"

He shrugged. "Sounds dumb, I know. But I saw you in the toy store and I couldn't quite get up the nerve to say anything, so I sort of followed you."

"You were watching me?"

"Well, not exactly watching. Just sort of... following..." He trailed off and shrugged again. "I said it was dumb. You should have seen the funny looks some of the kids in there gave me. One little guy even gave me advice on what to get Michael."

Elizabeth's mouth twitched, picturing Donovan lurking around the toy store. She supposed she should be angry. At another time, maybe she would have been. But, somehow, at this moment, she just couldn't find the anger.

"Why didn't you just come up and say hello?"

"Well, it's been quite a while. And we didn't exactly part on the best of terms."

"I suppose." Her smile faded, reminded of just how they'd parted. She stared past him at the people who hurried back and forth in the mall. The silence stretched.

Donovan cleared his throat. "You know, since we're both here and we're both shopping for Michael, maybe we should talk about what we're going to get him. That way we could avoid duplicating anything. We could have a cup of coffee."

There wasn't any real need to discuss what they were going to buy for Michael. She'd say no, of course. This encounter had been awkward enough already, and who knew how much worse it might get if they spent more time together. Donovan was part of her past, and she was quite content to keep him that way. There wasn't any reason to renew any old ties.

"It *would* be awkward if we both ended up getting him the same thing."

Five minutes later they were seated across a table from each other. Coffee steamed in front of them. The bustle of the mall was muted in the restaurant. It was too late for the lunch crowd and too early for the dinner crowd.

Elizabeth stared at her coffee and listened to the silence stretch. She'd been an idiot to agree to this. Donovan was undoubtedly regretting the impulse that had made him suggest it. The whole point of her leaving him was that they hadn't any more to say to each other. So why was she sitting here, pretending there was something to talk about now?

"Michael tells me you've got a nice place."

Elizabeth shrugged. "It's small but it's comfortable. I don't really want a lot of room."

"I know what you mean. With Michael in school most of the time, I rattle around in that house. I've been half thinking of selling it."

"You *can't*." Donovan's head jerked up at her vehement denial, and she tried to soften the words. "I mean, isn't the real estate market soft or hard or something? It probably wouldn't be a good time to sell." She stared at the table.

"I wouldn't do anything drastic without talking to you. It's your house, too."

It had been their dream house—one of the first projects Donovan designed. Once they'd had the money to buy the lot, they'd still had to put a lot of their own labor into the place in order to afford to build the house itself. A lot of sweat and a few tears were built into that house. Funny how she didn't want to live there, but it still hurt to think of it being sold.

"I wish you'd let me give you at least some of the value of it. I feel guilty about living in the place."

"That's okay. I don't need the money right now. If you... if you sell it, then we can talk about it."

Silence hung over the table again, a third party to the conversation. Again, it was Donovan who broke it.

"So, Michael tells me that you really like your job."

"I do. I'm working at Mason's. They needed an interior decorator, and they didn't insist that I have a certificate or a degree. It's a great place to work."

Donovan looked away. It hurt to hear her sound so happy. It hurt to realize how long it had been since he'd seen her face light up. How long had she been unhappy, and why hadn't he seen it?

"You always did have a flair for decorating. It's great that you found something you liked."

"I was pleased." If the conversation got any more stilted, it was going to require medical attention just to revive it. She took a swallow of coffee and searched for something to say. Funny how they were both being so careful not to talk about what was really on their minds. They'd talked around her leaving, but neither of them had said anything definite. They avoided words like *separation* and *divorce*.

She looked out the window that opened into the mall in time to see a young couple walk by, arm in arm and obviously very much in love.

"That guy looks just like Brad Mossman."

Elizabeth glanced across the table to see Donovan's eyes following the same couple. "He doesn't look anything like Brad."

"Sure he does. Same I'm-adorable chin, same you're-lucky-to-be-with-me-baby walk."

She laughed, the naturalness of it surprising. "You never did like Brad. Looking back on it, I think you did your best to intimidate the poor guy every chance you got."

"Hell, yes. That guy had a personality that would make the Pope want to punch him in the lip."

"Careful. You're talking about my first real boyfriend. I wore his ring for two whole weeks."

"Until you got in a fight with him and I gave you a ride home."

"On the back of that scruffy motorcycle. All the girls thought you looked really sexy riding that thing, and they all wanted to know if you'd tried anything."

"On the back of a moving motorcycle? I think that would have discouraged even Casanova. I wanted to, though. You looked so sexy in those tight, little hip-huggers and that green shirt. I didn't dare get off the bike when I got to your house."

Elizabeth flushed at the memory. She could remember that short ride as if it were yesterday. The wind streaming by them, Donovan's hard body in front of her. She'd felt so safe.

"So what did you tell all your girlfriends when they wanted to know if I'd made a pass?"

"I told them you'd been a perfect gentleman, of course."

"Liar."

Her head jerked up. He took a swallow of his coffee, his eyes on hers over the rim of the cup. Mischief danced in his gaze.

"What do you mean? I'm not a liar."

"Yes, you are. Carol told me the truth years ago. You told all the girls that I kissed you thoroughly when I took you home. As I recall you went into fairly vivid detail. I think I put my hand—"

"All right. All right." Elizabeth waved her hand in surrender. Her face felt as if it were on fire. "Remind me to murder Carol next time I see her. Every girl in town had the hots for you, whether they'd admit it or not. You could hardly expect me to go back to school after leaving Danny's with the infamous Donovan Sinclair and tell them you really had been a gentleman."

"Every girl in town?" He laughed. "I think you're exaggerating my appeal."

"Every girl. You looked so dangerous, so adult. And of course, any parent would have had apoplexy if their daughter went out with you. That was icing on the cake."

"I had no idea I was so popular. No one ever spoke to me."

"Of course no one spoke to you. You were too sexy to talk to. Besides, you had such an aura of mystery and danger, we were all too scared."

"*You* weren't too scared. I couldn't believe you'd actually come to the garage to see me."

"I wanted to thank you for giving me a ride home."

"Four times in one week?"

"I wanted to be sure you knew how much I appreciated the ride."

"Sure you did. You were so beautiful. You know, the first time I kissed you, I expected you to dissolve because I knew it had to be a dream. You couldn't really be there in my arms."

Elizabeth couldn't pull her gaze away from his. She felt flushed all over, remembering the feel of him against her, remembering the way his slightest touch had made her skin heat.

They stared at each other, a wealth of memories between them, the present almost forgotten. They'd shared so much. Their surroundings faded away. For a moment there was only the two of them, all alone.

"Beth, I—"

She jerked her eyes away and made a point of looking at her watch. "Good heavens, look at the time. I'd better get going."

Donovan stared at her and, for a moment, she was afraid he was going to insist on finishing whatever he'd started to say. She didn't want him to finish. She didn't want to hear it. She'd made her decisions and she didn't regret them. She didn't.

She fumbled with her purse, aware of him watching every move she made. After a long moment, he slid out of his seat and stood next to the table, waiting for her.

She stood up, conscious of his size, aware of the way her body wanted to lean into his. Her skin tingled with his nearness. All those memories had served to remind her of so many things she wanted to forget—was afraid to remember.

"I'll walk you to your car."

"That's really not necessary. I'm not parked all that far away."

"I'd feel better if I saw you to your car."

She glanced at the stubborn set of his jaw and shrugged. It wasn't worth arguing over. In a few minutes, she'd be gone. Neither of them spoke as they left the mall and stepped into the softly lit parking lot. A light rain was falling, not enough to require an umbrella. The rain somehow created a feeling of intimacy, as if it were just the two of them.

She unlocked her car and turned to him. Silhouetted in the lamplight, he looked bigger than ever—safe and warm and secure. But the uneven rhythm of her pulse had nothing to do with safety.

"It was nice to see you." God, she talked as if he were a casual acquaintance. How did you say goodbye to someone who'd once been your entire life?

"Maybe we could have dinner some night. There's a new steak house on the north end of Main."

Elizabeth wanted to say yes. She wanted to say it so badly it hurt. The very intensity of the feeling frightened her. She stared up at him, blinking against the sudden burning in her eyes.

"I . . . don't think that would be such a good idea." Could he hear how hard it was to say the words?

The light was behind him, making it impossible to read his expression. His shoulders seemed a little stiff, as if held too tight. The silence stretched, building until Elizabeth could stand no more. It hurt too much.

"Goodbye, Donovan." She slid into the car, shutting the door on the rain, shutting him outside. There were tears on her face. It was only the rain. That's all it was.

Donovan watched as she backed out of the parking place and drove down the aisle, tires hissing on the wet pavement. He didn't move until her taillights turned out of the parking lot and disappeared in the traffic.

Rain soaked his hair, seeping through his shirt. He shoved his hands into his pockets, hunching his shoulders against the dampness as he turned toward his own car.

Was it always going to hurt this much to say goodbye?

Chapter 9

You can't hibernate forever, Beth. You're hardly old enough to take up celibacy as a hobby." Carol waved a Danish for emphasis.

"I'm not planning on hibernating forever. It hasn't been that long. It's only been a few months, and I'm just not ready to start dating. And I'm definitely not ready to sleep with anyone."

"I didn't say you had to go to bed with a guy on the first date. That may be the rule in some parts of the country but here in Remembrance, we expect our womenfolk to have more discretion than that.

"All I'm saying is that if you don't want to spend the rest of your life alone, you'd better start looking around now. There aren't that many great guys lying around waiting to be found. Look at me, I haven't found one yet."

"That's because you're so finicky."

"I know. I always insist on a man who can walk and chew gum at the same time. And in this town that's a rarity. Donovan is one of the few good ones, and you're crazy to have turned him loose. If I managed to get hold of a man like that..." A sigh completed the thought, and Elizabeth forced herself to smile.

Carol pulled herself away from her daydream. "Anyway, you'd better start looking around. We ain't getting any younger, you know."

"I know. It's just that it's only been a few months, and Donovan and I were together for so long." She pushed a crumb across the table with the tip of her finger.

In the bright warmth of her kitchen, it was almost possible to forget that meeting with Donovan a week ago. Until then, she'd been proud of the way she was putting her life together. She was proving that she could make it on her own, and she was happy. Somehow seeing him again had made it all seem so hollow, as if it was just a facade and he'd shown her the emptiness underneath.

"Beth, I know it's not going to be easy for you to see other men. But unless you want to spend your life alone, you ought to start looking around. Take my word for it, living by yourself isn't all it's cracked up to be. Right now it seems okay, but wait until you've done it a few more years. Sure, there's nobody to tell you what time to get home, but there's nobody to care if you don't make it home at all. It can get damned lonely. It's okay for me. I'm used to it, and I've gotten pretty set in my ways over the years, but you aren't used to it, and I don't think you'll like it."

Elizabeth reached out to squeeze Carol's hand, knowing that anything more concrete by way of sympathy would be dismissed with a laugh and a joke. The picture Carol drew was not inviting. She loved her job, but it wasn't enough to fill her life.

"Even if I wanted to date—and I'm not saying I do—I don't know how to go about meeting men. If there's a singles' bar in town, I don't know where it is."

"Not to worry." Carol set down her Danish and leaned across the table to pat her friend's hand. "Just let Matchmaker Carol take care of everything. I have a guy in mind."

"Wait a minute. What kind of a guy?"

Carol grinned. "A male kind of a guy. Two legs, two arms, two eyes, one—"

"I can fill in the rest. I mean what does he do for a living? Do I have anything in common with him? What makes you think he'd even want to go out with me?"

"Beth, Beth. Don't be an idiot. Have you looked in a mirror lately? You're gorgeous."

"I thought I wasn't getting any younger."

"You're not but some things age well. Believe me, George will be more than happy to pay for dinner just for the chance to drool at you from across the table." She waved a hand, cutting off Elizabeth's next objection. "Trust me. Would I lie to you?"

Three days later Elizabeth was still debating the answer to that question. It wasn't that she thought Carol would actually lie. But she'd been known to poke the truth into a shape that fit her wishes.

She smoothed her hands over her hips, turning to check the fit of the pale aqua silk dress. She felt a little reassured by the reflection in the mirror. She wasn't sixteen anymore, but she didn't look half-bad. Maybe Carol was right, perhaps she had improved with age. The dress was new and very flattering if she did say so herself. She'd bought it just the day before, and the fitted top and flared skirt suited her.

Would Donovan like it? He'd always liked her in anything blue. She traced her fingers over the scooped neckline. He'd definitely approve of the fit. She stared in the mirror. With her eyes half closed, she could almost imagine him coming into the room, could see his reflection in the mirror. He'd pause when he saw her, his eyes flaring for an instant. Then he'd come up behind her, and his hands would slide around her waist, pulling her back to rest against his chest. He'd hold her, and then maybe he'd reach up to pull the pins out of her hair because he always preferred it down. Her hair would spill over his fingers, and he'd brush it aside to kiss her ear. She'd turn and—

Her eyes snapped open, and Elizabeth stared in the mirror, horrified by the direction her thoughts were taking. She hadn't put this dress on for Donovan. She didn't dress for him anymore. She had to get it through her head that he wasn't the center of her life. Not now, not ever again. It was her choice and it was the right choice.

She tucked a strand of hair into place and reached for her earrings. Donovan Sinclair had no business intruding into her daydreams. He was part of her past, and she wanted him to stay that way. The immediate future belonged to George Bonner.

Her hands were shaking as she slipped her shoes on and took one last look in the mirror before going into the living room to await the arrival of her date. *Her date.* The words sounded funny even in her head. She hadn't had a date in almost twenty years. What was she supposed to say to him? What did a man expect on a date these days? Would he expect her to be full of witty conversation?

As it turned out, she didn't have to worry much about what to say to George Bonner. George didn't need outside help with the conversation—he carried it quite efficiently by himself.

Seated across the table from him at the Haufbrau, Remembrance's one genuinely fancy restaurant, Elizabeth was able to carry her end of the conversation with little more than an occasional yes or a mumbled sound of agreement. He didn't seem to need anything more than a periodic indication that she was still conscious.

He ordered for her, a gesture that Donovan would have made seem courtly. George made it seem officious. She smiled and said nothing. This was her first date in twenty years; she was going to enjoy it if it killed her.

Staring at him, she couldn't help but make a few comparisons. George was about the same age as Donovan, give or take a year, but he had none of Donovan's hard strength. He was shorter, wider, softer, paler and duller.

She reached for her wineglass and took a sip of the California Chenin Blanc he'd ordered. He hadn't consulted her, but he had informed her that it was a very modest little wine with no pretensions to greatness. Too bad the same couldn't be said of George. The wine tasted rather thin to her, but she smiled and made polite noises about it. Donovan had always allowed her to order the wine, admitting quite bluntly that it all tasted alike to him. Too bad George didn't know he had a cork for a palate.

"Carol tells me you're an interior decorator." Elizabeth looked at him, hardly able to believe her ears.

Good heavens, was the man going to let her talk? Was he actually expressing an interest in something she might have done?

"Yes, I am."

"You wouldn't believe how important some people think interior decorating is. It can make or break a house sale. I've had clients refuse to buy a house because they didn't like the decoration. Slap on a little paint, I tell them, but they don't listen. Just last week I had a place that was done in lime green, and I told the owners, I said—"

Elizabeth tuned him out. She could imagine what George had told the owners. It was amazing but, after only an hour or so in his company, she had the feeling that she could imagine what George would say in just about any situation.

Suddenly, she realized that hadn't been the case with Donovan. She'd known him as well as it was possible to know another human being, and yet he'd always managed to surprise her. She took another sip of her wine. What was Donovan doing tonight? Was he at home? Was he thinking about her at all?

Actually, at that moment, Donovan was about twenty feet away, sitting at a table just around the corner from Elizabeth. He smiled at his dinner companion and hoped that the glazed feeling in his brain didn't extend to a glaze in his eyes.

This date had been a major mistake. He should have known better. It was too soon to start dating. In fact, it might never be the right time if tonight was any indication.

"You know, they've done studies that prove that a woman in my age group has a better chance of being struck by lightning than she does of getting married."

Donovan resisted the urge to look hopefully upward. There hadn't been a cloud in the sky when they drove here. Lightning was unlikely.

"I'm sure that's not true."

"It was in the paper." She stared at him, the expression in her eyes solemn. Clearly, if it was in the paper, there was no arguing with it. He thought of pointing out that it was possible to skew statistics to prove just about anything, and then he decided against it.

"Well, I'm sure any woman who truly wants to get married can find a like-minded man."

He took a sip of his wine, wondering if it tasted as much like lamp fuel to her as it did to him.

She shook her head, her mouth pursed. "It's not that simple. You see, statistically speaking, there aren't as many men as there are women, and then you have to figure in the necessity of finding someone with like interests. Oh, and someone who wants children. Not all men want children, you know."

He could have said the same about a lot of women, but he didn't. He'd already learned that it was simpler to say nothing at all. He took another sip of his wine and then reached for the water glass. It was going to be a long evening.

Seeing Elizabeth last week had made him realize that he'd only been marking time since she left. He'd been living in limbo, not thinking about the future, trying not to think about the past. It couldn't go on forever.

Jane Bartholomew was a sales rep for a firm he'd dealt with for several years. They'd talked at the office, and she'd always seemed to be intelligent and interesting. When she walked into the office on Monday, he'd found himself asking her if she'd like to have dinner with him on Friday. He hadn't thought long and hard, hadn't analyzed the decision to ask her out. He'd just decided that it was time he started giving up the past and this was as good a way as any to start.

Unfortunately, Jane didn't see it quite that simply. Donovan leaned back as the waiter brought their food. He smiled across the table at Jane and wondered why he'd never noticed the hungry gleam in her eyes that had nothing to do with the trout almondine the waiter set in front of her.

It wasn't that he didn't sympathize with her. She was thirty-seven and clearly feeling the pinch of the biological time clock. She wanted a husband and a baby and she wanted them now. The minute he asked her out, she'd refiled him in her mind from unavailable to available, and the change in her attitude toward him was nothing short of stunning.

Donovan cut into his steak, trying not to notice the way she watched him. He now knew how a stallion must feel when it was being considered for stud. Any minute now he expected her to lunge across the table and pry open his mouth to study his teeth.

It wasn't that he didn't like Jane. He did, despite her not-too-subtle hints about marriage and children and time running out. She was a nice woman, and he wished her the best of luck. But he wasn't interested.

He speared a mushroom and stared at it glumly. The problem was he wasn't interested in any woman except Elizabeth, and he'd been stupid enough to lose her. Asking Jane out had been a foolish attempt to pretend that he was going to get over Beth. It hadn't worked. She was deep in his soul. It was only now that she was gone that he realized just how much he needed her.

The past six months had been gray and barren, an empty wasteland without her. She was probably perfectly happy without him. After all, she hadn't lost that much. She'd been right, he *had* let their marriage drift away while he pursued his work. He'd thought somehow that it would simply maintain itself, without any effort on his part. He knew now that it was too late.

He took another bite of steak, forcing himself to smile. It was too bad he wasn't a drinking man. Right now the idea of being stinking, filthy drunk had a definite appeal—if only to help him forget what he'd lost.

The date wasn't a raging success, but it wasn't a total disaster. Eventually Jane did allow him to turn the conversation away from marriage. When the small band began to play in the bar, he forced himself to do the gentlemanly thing and ask Jane if she'd like to dance.

She was light on her feet and, if their steps didn't match quite like his and Elizabeth's had, Donovan didn't allow himself to think about it. The music was slow and mellow, and they moved around the dance floor in reasonable harmony. At least she didn't feel as if she had to carry on a conversation while dancing.

He casually gazed over her head, looking at the other couples. He nodded to one or two acquaintances. In a town the size of Remembrance, it was impossible to go out without running into someone you knew. There was Jase Bower, who owned the local feed store, out with his wife, who was pregnant again, and Levar Davis who was the closest thing to a celebrity Remembrance could boast. He'd been on *Jeopardy* three times and had actually won some money. Levar was with his wife. George Bonner, the local real estate agent, was dancing with—

Donovan mumbled an apology as his foot came down on Jane's toe. *Elizabeth*. He wasn't imagining things. She was actually here dancing with George Bonner, that annoying pip-squeak. She looked up and her gaze fell on him. George seemed to stumble, as if confused by the sudden rigidity of his partner. Then Elizabeth dragged her gaze away from Donovan's and stared fixedly downward, her feet moving automatically to the music.

Donovan turned Jane so that his back was to the other couple. He hadn't expected to feel the absolute, blinding rage that gripped him. If he'd thought about it, he would have expected Elizabeth to be dating. After all, she was the one who'd left him, so it made sense that she would be ready to see other men. How long had she been dating George, and what did she see in the little twerp?

Had George kissed her? Were they sleeping together? Jane squeaked in protest as his hand tightened on hers.

"Sorry." But the muttered apology was automatic. Even though his back was to her, Donovan was aware of Elizabeth with every fiber. She had no right to be going out with other men. She was his: his wife, his woman. She had been since the moment they met.

He turned Jane again. Now Elizabeth's back was to him, and Donovan scowled at the way George was holding her. His hand was too low on her hips. He was too close. They were making a spectacle of themselves.

The music came to a halt, but Donovan wasn't aware of it until he realized that no one else was moving. George started to lead Elizabeth off the dance floor. Without thinking, Donovan moved forward, pulling Jane with him.

"Elizabeth, George. How nice to see you." Elizabeth stiffened before turning slowly toward him. George turned, and Donovan was maliciously pleased to see a twinge of uneasiness in the smaller man's eyes.

"Sinclair. Nice to see you."

"Have you met Jane? Jane, this is George Bonner, our local real estate whiz kid, and this is Elizabeth Sinclair—my wife."

"That's not quite accurate." Elizabeth kept the smile on her face, but Donovan could see her annoyance.

Jane murmured hello, clearly uncomfortable. Donovan barely noticed. The band had started playing again, and his smile became even more sharklike. "George, would you mind if I danced with Elizabeth. This used to be our song, didn't it, Beth? Why don't you and Jane dance? I bet the two of you have a lot in common."

It was rude. It was ruthless. But he didn't care. He pushed Jane's hand toward George and reached around her to take Elizabeth's arm. Without creating a scene, there was nothing anyone could do but go along with the arrangements he'd so cavalierly made.

Elizabeth was stiff as he led her onto the floor and pulled her into his arms. Her steps matched his automatically even as she tried to avoid letting him draw her close.

"I hope you're proud of yourself. That was quite a performance."

"I don't know what you're talking about. I just wanted to dance with my wife."

"I'm not your wife," she spat out, but the words lacked impact. It felt remarkably nice to be in Donovan's arms. "And this isn't our song. I don't even know what song this is."

"Neither do I. Who cares?"

"You were very rude."

"I know."

"George probably thinks you're nuts and so does Janet."

"Jane."

Beth's perfume was just as evocative as ever. Soft and floral, it always made him think of wildflowers and bedrooms. He drew her a little closer, liking the way her breasts pressed against his chest.

"I wish you wouldn't hold me so close."

"You didn't object when George held you like this."

"He wasn't holding me this tight. Besides, George is my date."

"Do you let all your dates hold you like this?"

"No. Yes. It's none of your business. Besides, this is the first date I've been on." She could have bitten her tongue out the minute the words were said. She could actually feel the pleasure they gave him.

"So, is George showing you a rollicking good time? I bet you could qualify for a real estate license by now."

Elizabeth bit her lip against a smile. Obviously Donovan had spent a little time with George. His hand tightened on her back, shifting her still closer. Not even a whisper could have worked its way between them. It was foolish. She'd regret it. But, for just a moment, she allowed herself to savor the hard length of his body against hers.

"I suppose Janine is a barrel of laughs."

"Jane. Actually, Jane is looking for a stud."

"What?"

Donovan ignored the pressure of her hands on his chest and kept her close. "She's looking for a husband and a baby, and she wants them immediately."

"And she thinks you're a good candidate?" A confusing mixture of emotions churned inside, angering her.

"She seems to think I qualify." He sounded so smug it made her want to hit him. Hard.

"Tell her to talk to me first. She doesn't realize what she'd be getting into. A man who's married to his career first and his wife second, a man who's never home. And when he does come home, he brings the office with him." She was aware that her words were taking on an hysterical edge, but she couldn't seem to stop them. "And as far as having a baby is concerned, she'd have a hard time getting pregnant. A rabbit couldn't have gotten pregnant with our sex life the past few years. The music has stopped. Would you please let me go?"

She didn't look at him as he let his arms drop. Without a word, she turned and left the dance floor, searching blindly for her date. She found him on the edge of the floor, holding an animated conversation with Janine or Janet or whatever her name was.

"I'm sorry, George, I've got an awful headache. Would you mind if we went home now?" She directed a vague smile toward the other woman, wondering quite viciously what bottle she'd found her hair color in. She was acutely aware of Donovan standing just behind her, but she didn't look at him. She couldn't.

George might have wondered that she'd developed a headache immediately after dancing with her semi-ex-husband, but he was gentleman enough not to question. He took her arm, murmuring solicitously as he led her away. Elizabeth could feel Donovan's eyes on her until she and George turned a corner.

George had the good sense to remain relatively quiet on the way home. Elizabeth struggled to find answers to his polite comments regarding how pleasant he'd found the evening. He left her at her door without trying to kiss her good-night, which raised him a couple of notches in her estimation. He might be a bore, but he wasn't totally insensitive.

She shut the door and leaned against it, staring at her apartment. She had gone to so much trouble to turn it into a home. It *was* her home. Why was it that a chance meeting with Donovan should suddenly make the place feel empty? She closed her eyes against burning tears. He'd been part of her life for so long, she'd been a fool to think that it wouldn't hurt to cut him out of it.

A tear escaped to slide down her cheek. He'd put his career ahead of their marriage for so long. She'd waited and waited, and was devastated when she finally realized that nothing was going to change because he wasn't unhappy with the way things were. She didn't love him anymore. *She didn't.* It shouldn't hurt so much to see him again.

Outside, the street was dark. Most of the small town slept. Donovan hunched his shoulders inside his leather jacket, staring up at the angular building. He knew she was in there crying as surely as if he were standing next to her. It hurt to know that she was in pain and that he was the cause of it. He hadn't meant to hurt her, but he couldn't help but feel a small flicker of satisfaction. If she didn't care, she wouldn't be hurt.

Elizabeth might not be ready to acknowledge it, but she did still care about him. She couldn't cut him out of her life so easily.

He pulled his collar up and shoved his hands into his pockets. The spring air was cold late at night. He should go home. He was acting like a lovesick teenager. He'd never told her about the nights he'd spent standing outside her bedroom twenty years ago. Sometimes, he'd walk to her house late at night and just stand outside her window, imagining her asleep in her ruffled bed.

He'd always felt so unworthy and he'd never been able to believe that she really loved him. She could have had anyone, and she'd chosen him. Maybe that was part of what went wrong. He'd spent too much time trying to prove he was good enough for her, and in doing so he let his ambitions take precedence over their marriage.

A chill breeze wove its way down the street and he shivered, staring at the building another long minute before turning to get in his car. He'd lost so much.

Michael's birthday party was only two weeks away. Maybe that was long enough for tonight's wounds to fade and for him to remember how to court his wife again. She hadn't filed for divorce, hadn't even asked for a formal separation. That had to mean something.

Chapter 10

The party to celebrate Michael's nineteenth birthday was a small gathering for family and friends. In a stilted phone conversation, Elizabeth had offered to come over and help with the preparations. Donovan had been very casual about refusing her offer, telling her that he had everything under control. The caterers dropped everything off the afternoon of the party along with written instructions spelling out oven temperatures and serving times.

Donovan spent the day cleaning the house. Michael, who had a few days off from college, watched his father whirl around the house like a maniac. He didn't ask why. He might be only nineteen but he understood exactly what his father was doing. Donovan didn't want any evidence that the house wasn't running as smoothly as it had when Elizabeth was in charge. The fact that several of the closets could have been registered as lethal weapons and that he finally had to spray oven

cleaner on the bathtubs to get them clean were things
that no one needed to know.

So Michael offered an occasional hand and was tactful enough to swallow his amusement. As the day wore
on, Donovan's expression became more harried, his
hair stood on end and his jeans looked like the place
where dirt came to die. He'd never realized how much
work went into cleaning a house.

When the first guests arrived at seven, the place was,
if not immaculate, at least presentable. Donovan's hair
was still damp from his shower, and he had the nag-
ging feeling that he'd forgotten a hundred things, but
none of that showed in his face. He was the very picture of masculine calm.

It might have consoled him to know that Elizabeth
was at least as nervous as he was. She was bringing the
cake, and no one but her and the ficus in her kitchen
would know that the cake she brought was her third attempt. The other two resided in the trash can.

It felt very strange to be parking her car on the street
and walking up the familiar brick walkway. She reached
for the doorknob and then stopped herself. She had to
remember that she was a guest here now. This wasn't
her home anymore, and she didn't regret that choice,
she reminded herself fiercely.

Ringing the bell, she stared at the closed door and
swallowed nervously. She hadn't seen Donovan since
that disastrous evening two weeks ago. She should never
have let him see that he was capable of upsetting her.
She should have remained cool and calm. Tonight
would be different. She was going to make it clear that
she didn't regret her decisions.

Her heart bumped when the door swung open, and she felt almost weak-kneed with relief when she saw that it was Michael.

"Hi, Mom. I hope that's chocolate." The casual normalcy of his greeting put her at ease. He reached out to take the plate from her.

"Is there any other flavor?" She stepped into the hallway and hugged her son, feeling a rush of foolish tears. He was so tall, as tall as his father and already broadening out. He wasn't a little boy anymore.

He returned her hug with one arm, balancing the cake on his other hand. "This smells great."

She drew back, smiling, hoping he wouldn't notice that her eyes were a little too bright. "Don't sound so surprised. My cakes always smell great."

"They taste great, too." She stiffened at Donovan's quiet voice, frozen for an instant before she forced herself to turn, hoping she looked more casual than she felt.

"Hello, Elizabeth." He was standing at the bottom of the stairs wearing a pair of crisp jeans and a green cashmere sweater. He looked relaxed, at home and so intensely masculine that, for a moment, it was a little hard to breathe.

"Hello, Donovan." She was acutely aware of the way his eyes went over her, taking in the soft, cotton dress with the full skirt that swirled just above her ankles. His eyes told her that he liked what he saw—not that she cared whether he liked her clothes or not.

Michael looked from one parent to the other, sensing the tension between them, wondering at its cause. "I'll put this in the kitchen. You should see the great spread the caterers left, Mom. Shrimp and mushroom and all kinds of great stuff."

Elizabeth dragged her gaze from Donovan. "I'll go with you, just to make sure you don't sample the frosting."

"Would I do that?" His face was the very picture of innocence.

She laughed. "I'll just make sure temptation doesn't get the best of you."

Donovan shoved his hands into his pockets, watching the two of them disappear into the kitchen. He hadn't realized how hungry he'd been for the sight of her until she was on his doorstep, or how possessive he'd feel once she was back in this house. This was her home, it was where she belonged.

The party was apparently a success, though neither Donovan nor Elizabeth could have said exactly what happened during the evening. Though they spoke directly to each other only a few times, there wasn't a moment when they weren't intensely aware of each other.

Everyone had a wonderful time, Michael was thrilled with his gifts, the party was pronounced great fun. All Elizabeth knew was that she felt breathless, almost hunted. Donovan didn't say anything to her. He didn't watch her every move, but she was intensely aware of him. Even when her back was to him, she knew where he was.

It felt so natural to be back in this house, playing hostess to their friends, celebrating their son's birthday. When everyone began to leave, it felt natural to start cleaning up. Michael yawned and reached for a plate, and she took it from him, shooing him off to bed. As the birthday boy he wasn't expected to help with the dishes.

He trailed off upstairs, and Elizabeth felt the sting of tears. It seemed as if he'd grown up in such a short time.

"Hard to believe he's nineteen. Seems like just a couple of years ago we were worrying about him riding his bike to school." Elizabeth's words were quiet, fitting with the slight melancholy of the late hour.

"I was just thinking the same thing. I guess children always grow up too fast to suit their parents." She moved back into the living room and lifted a stack of plates. They worked in companionable silence for a few minutes.

Without speaking, Donovan filled the sink with water and began to wash the crystal. Elizabeth hesitated, loath to give up the quiet intimacy that had settled between them, knowing she should go home. She moved forward and picked up a towel.

"I think everyone had a good time."

"They seemed to." His arm brushed hers as he rinsed a fragile glass and set it in the drainer. She picked it up and dried it automatically. He was so close, she could smell the woodsy scent of his after-shave. The scent brought back so many memories.

"How is the job going?"

"Really well. I'm redoing some of the store displays. Next week I'm supposed to go out and see Mrs. Buckman about redecorating her house."

"Mrs. Buckman? She hasn't changed a thing in that place in the past thirty years."

"I know but her sister is coming to visit and I think she wants an updated image."

"She must have been impressed with you."

"Well, she hasn't let me do anything yet. We're just at the talking stage."

"You'll get the job."

His confidence in her lit a small glow. She'd almost forgotten that Donovan had always believed in her, no matter what she wanted to do. It had been so long since they'd talked about dreams and hopes for the future.

He seemed to be taking a long time washing the last goblet. With the sleeves of his sweater shoved up above his elbows and his forearms disappearing into mounds of fluffy suds, he looked distractingly attractive. She should have gone home as soon as Michael went to bed.

"I'm thinking about buying another motorcycle."

"What for?"

He shrugged. "I don't know. Maybe to recapture my lost youth. I seem to have gotten a bit stuck in the mud lately."

"They're dangerous." The protest was automatic. She could sense that the idea excited him.

"You didn't seem to mind that when we met."

"I was sixteen. Sixteen-year-old girls don't really think about things like motorcycle wrecks. All I knew was that you looked sexy in a black leather jacket and it was exciting to feel the wind in my hair."

"Did you think I looked sexy in a black leather jacket?" The look he slanted 'her was dangerous. Its effect wasn't lessened by the suds that coated his forearms. She took the last goblet from him.

"Of course I thought you looked sexy. Every girl in school thought you looked sexy."

She was grateful when he didn't pursue the question. She set the sparkling crystal on the counter and folded the towel, her movements precise, matching the corners perfectly, smoothing the damp cotton into perfect folds. She was disturbingly conscious of Donovan draining and rinsing out the sink.

"You know, there's going to be a reunion concert of some of the sixties groups in the city this weekend."

"Oh, really?" She put another fold in the towel, not looking at Donovan.

"I . . . I've got a couple of tickets." His tone was elaborately casual, his attention all for the sink. It was apparently important that every trace of suds be rinsed away.

"You do?"

"Yeah. It's supposed to be a great concert." He named some of the popular groups from that decade.

"Sounds interesting." She folded the towel again, making sure the corners met precisely.

"Do you . . . Would you be interested in going?"

"It sounds like fun." She was cautious, not sure if he was asking her to go with him or suggesting that he could let her have the tickets.

"I could pick you up Saturday afternoon. We could go into Indianapolis and get something to eat before the concert starts. Make a day of it."

"I'd like that." She didn't look at him, staring at the towel in her hands.

"Would one o'clock be too early?"

"No, that would be fine."

"Great. It should be fun."

"Yes." Elizabeth set the towel on the counter. She'd folded it to a size only slightly larger than a postage stamp. What on earth was she thinking? She'd just agreed to go on a date with Donovan. They were practically divorced and she was going to a concert with him. It was crazy.

"Michael, have you seen that dark green shirt of mine?"

"Have you checked the closet?" Michael leaned in the doorway of the bedroom his parents had shared.

Donovan straightened from looking under the bed. "No. I know I wore it three days ago, and I didn't hang it up."

"The laundry delivered everything yesterday afternoon while you were at work. I hung a bunch of stuff in your closet, and I think I saw that shirt." He took a bite out of the apple he held, his eyes curious.

Donovan hurried to the closet, stumbling over a pair of shoes. They were only one of several pairs stacked haphazardly at the foot of the bed. The bed itself held half a dozen pairs of jeans and a handful of shirts.

"You cleaning out your closet? 'Cause if you are, can I have that gold shirt? My girlfriend likes the way I look in gold."

"Take it." Donovan's muffled voice came out of the depths of the walk-in closet. Michael took another bite of apple.

"How about the gray slacks? They'd look great with some of my shirts."

"Sure."

"You know, I've always liked this bedspread. It would be terrific on the wall of the dorm."

"Okay."

Michael crunched some more apple. "Dad? I need a loan. Could you spare ten thousand or so? I was thinking of taking a trip to Europe instead of finishing out this quarter. Maybe joining a gang in Paris or Rome or something. I thought I might break into the Louvre and steal the *Mona Lisa*. And then I could smuggle it back to the States and we could hang it in the bathroom. Of course, we'd have to change the towels. I don't think that color would go."

"Fine. Have you seen my black boots?"

"They're out here on the floor." Michael finished his apple and measured the core between thumb and forefinger, eyeing the wastebasket across the room. The core hit it with satisfying precision just as Donovan came out of the closet, the green shirt dangling from one arm, his expression distracted. He sorted through the tangle of shoes to find his boots. With them in hand, he looked at his son, apparently truly aware of him for the first time.

"Don't you have a date tonight?"

"Not tonight. Sara went home to her parents for the weekend. Are you nervous about having a date with Mom?"

"It's not a date."

"I thought you two were going to get something to eat and then go to a concert with a bunch of old guys." He dodged the shoe Donovan threw at him, his grin full of mischief. "Seems to me that qualifies as a date."

"Your mother and I are just getting together for a casual meal and a concert."

"What's the difference between that and a date?"

Donovan ignored the question, pulling on the short, black boots. "When you and Sara go out, what do you do?"

"We get together and we go somewhere. Pizza. A movie. Sometimes a concert."

Donovan stood up, stomping his feet to settle the boots into place. "No. I mean, do you buy flowers or candy or anything like that?" His tone was elaborately casual. Too casual. His son's eyes narrowed.

"Are you asking me for pointers on how to date?"

"Of course not. I was just curious." Donovan shrugged into his shirt, his head bent to conceal the flush in his cheekbones.

Michael reached into his back pocket and pulled out a banana, peeling it with careful movements. Donovan waited a few moments and then prompted him.

"Well?"

"Well what?" Michael glanced up, his expression all innocence. His father clamped his teeth together and thought longingly of the time when his son had been too young to speak.

"Do you buy her flowers or something?"

Michael took a bite of the banana and chewed slowly. "Sara is allergic to flowers and she hates candy."

"Oh."

"Now, if you were asking me if I thought you should get Mom some flowers for this nondate, that would be a different story."

"It would?"

"Sure. Mom loves flowers. Of course, since this isn't really a date, then flowers would probably be kind of silly." He peeled the banana another careful inch.

"I should have beaten you more often when you were little. It's your mother's fault that you've turned out this way."

Michael grinned and didn't shift his comfortable position slouched in the doorway. Donovan buttoned his shirt, aware of the way he had to concentrate to get the buttons through the proper holes. He hadn't been this nervous in years.

"Are you trying to get Mom back?"

His hands stilled and he angled a glance at his son. Damn, when had he grown up?

"Do you think I should?"

"Do you still love her?"

This was no conversation to be having with his son. He was sure any psychology book would tell him that.

"I . . . yes, I do."

Michael nodded, folding the banana peel neatly and tucking it back in his pocket. "I thought so."

"You did, huh?"

"Sure. Mom's terrific. How could you not love her?"

The simplistic answer was impossible to argue with, especially since Donovan felt much the same. He finished buttoning his shirt and unsnapped his jeans to tuck the tails in.

"It's not going to be easy to get her back, you know. You better not take it for granted that she's just going to fall back into your arms."

"I'm not."

"She's dating again, I think."

Donovan's jaw set, remembering the one date he'd been witness to. If he had his way, there wouldn't be any more. Elizabeth belonged with him. All he had to do was convince her of that.

"Well, here I am to help you prepare for the big night." Carol's cheery greeting drew a distracted smile. Elizabeth shut the door behind her friend.

"It's not that big a deal. Donovan just happened to have tickets for this concert and he thought I might enjoy it. That's all."

"Is that why you look like you're facing a firing squad at dusk?" Carol's sharp eyes skimmed over Elizabeth, taking in the pale features, the half-done makeup, the rumpled bathrobe clutched in a white-knuckled grip at the throat.

"I'm just a little nervous, that's all."

"So was Marie Antoinette just before they chopped off her head, and I bet she didn't look as nervous as you do. What are you planning on wearing?"

"I don't know." The question appeared to cause Elizabeth some distress.

"Show me what your choices are."

"Well, I've tried on a few things, and everything makes me look too fat or too old. I should have gone out and bought something new, but it's too late now." She led the way into her bedroom as she spoke. "I just couldn't find anything that looked right." She ran her fingers through her hair and gave Carol a helpless look.

Carol stared at the bedroom solemnly. Clothes were draped over every possible surface except the vanity table, which was covered with opened bottles and eyeshadow cases. Shoes were piled here and there in forlorn little heaps.

"I can see your problem. Have you tried all this stuff on?"

"Most of it. I just can't find anything that looks right. What do you wear to a concert these days?"

"Well, I'm no authority, but it seems to me that something in between the blue terry-cloth rompers and the black silk sheath would probably hit about the right note."

Elizabeth stared at her friend blankly and then looked around the room, seeing the mess for the first time, really looking at all the things she'd tried on.

"Oh, Lord."

"I don't think divine intervention is called for. Why don't you finish your makeup while I sort out a few things that seem reasonable. Maybe if you don't have so many choices, it'll be easier to make a decision."

A few minutes of Carol's sensible company and Elizabeth could feel her nervousness subsiding to a manageable level. She forced herself to concentrate on her makeup, trying not to jam a mascara wand in her eye. Behind her, Carol sorted through her clothes, finally setting aside a few things and then sitting on the edge of the bed to watch her.

"You love him, don't you?"

Elizabeth muttered a curse as her lipstick pencil swerved and, instead of outlining her mouth, she created a new and impossible lip line. Her hand was shaking as she reached for a tissue to repair the damage.

"I don't know what you're talking about. I'm just a little worried about this, that's all."

"You weren't this worked up about going out with George."

"George wasn't this important." The words were out before she thought about them. Her hand stilled on her face. Her eyes met Carol's in the mirror, and then she pulled her gaze away.

"There's nothing wrong with loving Donovan, you know. I've always thought he was a pretty terrific guy."

"He is. I never said he wasn't." She stirred a finger through some spilled powder. "I don't know how I feel anymore. I always thought I'd love him forever, that nothing could ever make me change my feelings for him. And then, these past few years, we just didn't have anything to say to each other anymore. I began to feel lost, like I didn't have any identity of my own. I just stopped loving him."

"Did you really?"

Elizabeth shrugged without looking at her friend. "I don't know. I thought I did. Then I moved out and a whole new world opened up to me. Only there was this hole where Donovan had always been. We've shared so much of our lives, Carol. I've been with him since I was sixteen. We raised a son together. You can't break those ties.''

"Do you really think that's all that holds you two together? Look at yourself. If it was just old ties that bind, you wouldn't be so upset by a simple date. It really would be 'no big deal.' ''

"I don't know. No one else has ever made me feel like Donovan does. I just don't know if we can recapture what we had. I don't even know if I want to recapture it—or if he does. But I'm not settling for anything less. I'd rather live alone than go back to what it was the past few years.''

"I think the two of you were meant for each other, and I think you're going to get back together, stronger than ever.''

"Maybe.'' Elizabeth stood up. "Okay, show me what you think I should wear.''

Half an hour later she was suitably attired in a pair of snug, black jeans with white pinstriping and a bright blue blouse that made her eyes seem bluer than ever. Her hair reached her shoulders in a soft fall of golden blond. She felt like she was sixteen again, waiting for Donovan's knock, wildly excited and scared.

"You look terrific. You're going to knock his socks off. I'll clean up the mess here after you've gone and let myself out.''

"You don't have to do that. I can clean it up tonight or in the morning.''

"It's the least I can do to aid the cause. You don't want to come home to a place that looks like a tornado went through it.''

"Thanks." Elizabeth hugged her friend, blinking back tears. "I don't know what I'd do without you."

"A lot worse." But Carol's hug was equally fierce.

Elizabeth took one last look in the mirror, jumping when the doorbell rang. Her eyes met Carol's, panic flickering in their depths.

"I think I'm going to throw up."

"No, you're not. You're a grown woman, and you're going to handle this date with the sophistication that comes only with maturity. Donovan will be stunned by your beauty, impressed by your wit, and left speechless by your suavity."

"Suavity? I'm not even sure that's a word, let alone something to impress someone with."

Carol shrugged, pushing Elizabeth toward the door. "Who cares? You get the idea. You look dynamite. Go knock 'em dead."

Elizabeth wiped her hands down the sides of her jeans and took a deep breath, trying to still the foolish pounding of her heart. Carol was right. This was just a simple evening out, nothing to panic about. It was only Donovan waiting on the other side of the door. It was only the one man she'd ever loved, the one man who could still reduce her to a puddle of quivering mush with just a look. No big deal at all.

She reached for the doorknob and took a deep breath, feeling as if fate waited on the other side.

And perhaps it did.

Chapter 11

It's nothing fancy, but steak and lobster didn't seem like a good prelude to a rock concert.''

"This is perfect." Elizabeth picked up a barbecued rib and bit into it with delicate greed. She'd been too nervous to eat all day, and the hot and spicy ribs tasted wonderful.

The small restaurant was crowded. Families, couples and groups of friends filled every table, and a line waited outside. Best Ribs in Indianapolis announced the sign outside. Elizabeth wouldn't have sworn to that, but they were certainly superb. And it was impossible to remain nervous with a snowy-white napkin tucked into the top of your blouse like a bib and your fingers covered in barbecue sauce.

Besides, there'd been nothing to be nervous about in the first place. True, Donovan did look devastatingly attractive, and he had presented her with flowers, but he'd also been comfortably casual about the whole thing.

A family with a little girl was seated at the table next to them, and Elizabeth glanced over, holding back the urge to laugh out loud. Her parents watched in helpless wonderment as the child managed to dress herself completely in barbecue sauce, all in the course of eating one rib. Elizabeth glanced at Donovan, her eyes alight with laughter.

He'd been watching her. In the instant before his gaze shifted away, she read a hunger that had nothing to do with the food in front of them. Her laughter faded and she stared at the table, feeling a nervous jump in her stomach that wasn't caused by the spicy food.

"I looked at motorcycles yesterday. I think I'm definitely going to buy one. Probably in the next week or so." He picked up another rib and bit into it, and she wondered if she'd imagined what she'd seen a moment ago. He didn't look as if he had anything more on his mind than food and motorcycles.

"What are you going to do with it? Ride it to the office?"

"Maybe. I could strap my briefcase onto the back, or I might get one of those enormous bikes with the saddle bags."

"I still think they're too dangerous."

"If you're careful, they're not that bad. Besides, you only live once."

"That doesn't mean you have to try and get yourself killed."

"I'm not going to get myself killed. I'm just going to have a little fun. Come on, admit it. Don't you think I'd look great sitting on a Harley in a black leather jacket? I could do my hair in a DA and get a pair of really cool shades and wait outside Mason's for you to get off work.''

''There's only one problem with that scenario. I wear skirts to work, and I'm not climbing on a motorcycle in a skirt. Besides, my boss would probably call the police as soon as she saw you lurking outside the store.''

''Lurking? I wouldn't be lurking. I'd be sitting there looking tough and cool.''

She reached for a French fry. ''I don't think Mrs. Tancredi would recognize 'tough and cool' as a good thing. She might decide that you were casing the joint. She watches a lot of television, and she's got a vivid imagination.''

''You're taking all the fun out of it.'' He sounded so disgruntled that Elizabeth grinned. Seeing that, Donovan leaned across the table, his expression coaxing. ''Come on, wouldn't it be exciting to go whizzing down the highway on the back of my bike?''

She set her mouth very primly, her eyes dancing. ''I think you're trying to capture a piece of your lost youth.''

Donovan stared at her, and that hungry look was back in his eyes. ''Would that be so bad? It seems to me that our lost youth was pretty good.''

She looked at him, the noisy restaurant fading away, a thousand memories tangling with the present. He was right, but a past together didn't make up to a future.

Donovan leaned back, deliberately breaking the tension that had crept between them. ''The problem with you, Beth, is that you're too practical. You wait till I get my bike. You're gonna love it. You done?''

She nodded, dipping her hands in the battered stainless steel bowl of water in the middle of the table and drying them on her napkin. He kept throwing her off balance. One minute they might have been casual friends and the next he was reminding her of all they'd shared in the past.

Donovan dug into his pocket and threw some bills on the table. "Let's get out of here. I bet the arena is going to be packed."

The arena *was* packed, but no one seemed to mind. The crowd swayed back and forth and clapped their hands and lost themselves in the cheerful rhythms of twenty years ago. Memories seemed to float on the air. Every song brought new cheers, and it was impossible not to have a good time.

Donovan's arm around her shoulders seemed perfectly natural, and Elizabeth leaned into him, letting him shield her from occasional jostles, enjoying the feel of his muscular body against hers.

For just a little while, it was almost possible to pretend that it really *was* twenty years ago. She felt young and excited, the whole world opening up in front of her. With Donovan's arm around her, she could do anything.

The concert ended at last with a rollicking chorus in which the entire crowd joined. There was a lot of good-natured jostling and laughter as people began to make their way out of the stadium. Elizabeth allowed the fantasy to stretch as they walked across the parking lot. There was no need for Donovan to keep his arm around her, but it felt so right there.

"We could go out for a late supper, if you'd like."

Somewhere, a small voice cautioned her that she was letting things drift along and she might regret it later, but she ignored the warning. There was magic in the air, and she was going to savor every minute of it.

"I'd like that."

He took her to a small restaurant, full of dimly lit tables and quiet conversations. Looking at the menu, she was surprised to find that she was hungry. It didn't seem possible after all the ribs she'd consumed.

"I think music must burn up a lot of calories." Donovan's comment fit her own thinking so exactly that he might have read her mind. It was a pleasant thought.

"Why don't we split the seafood platter?" she suggested. Her mouth watered at the thought and he laughed at her eager nod.

Once the order was given to the waiter, Donovan leaned back and looked at her, his fingers toying with his silverware. "Did you enjoy yourself?"

"Couldn't you tell? I must have sung fifty-four choruses of every song. Thank you for inviting me. I wouldn't have missed it for the world."

"The pleaure was all mine." The quiet sincerity in his voice brought a flush to her cheeks, and she looked away, feeling very young and deliciously vulnerable. "It brought back a lot of memories."

"I think it did that for just about everyone there."

"A lot of good memories."

Elizabeth looked across the table, her eyes soft. "A lot of good memories."

Their eyes held for a long moment, all the good times they'd had together lying between them like a thick, warm quilt. The waiter was a welcome interruption, at least as far as Elizabeth was concerned. Too much seemed to lay unspoken, things she wasn't sure she wanted to hear.

The meal passed in uncomplicated pleasure. The seafood platter was beautifully prepared and definitely enough for two. She and Donovan squabbled amicably over who ate more than their share. Donovan graciously allowed her to have the last shrimp, she returned the favor by insisting he take the last oyster.

On the road home, Elizabeth felt wonderfully relaxed. It had been so long since the two of them had simply gone out and had fun together. Whenever they went out, there was an underlying purpose to it—something at Michael's school or dining with a client Donovan was designing a building for.

She'd almost forgotten how much fun they'd always had together. She leaned her head back against the smooth leather of the car seat. Outside the fields rushed by in a blur of open spaces. A full moon hung overhead, ghosting the land with pale light. It was nearly summer, but the late-night air was cold. Donovan had turned the heater on low, just enough to make Elizabeth feel pleasantly cosseted. The radio was set to a station playing classical music, and smooth cellos and horns added to the feeling.

She closed her eyes, letting herself imagine—just for a moment—that everything was still perfect between them. They'd never grown apart, love hadn't faded. They were going home to the house they'd built together, full of memories and dreams.

The fantasy was so pleasant that, when Donovan stopped the car, she was surprised to find herself in front of her apartment building.

"You looked very content. What were you thinking?" Donovan's voice was quiet.

Elizabeth hoped that the light from the streetlamp wasn't enough to reveal the flush in her cheeks. "Nothing in particular. I was just thinking how much fun I had this evening. Thank you."

"Maybe we could do it again."

"Maybe." She reached for her purse. "Well, good night."

"I'll walk you to your door."

"That's really not necessary." But the words went unheard. Donovan was already out of the car and walking around to the passenger side. He opened the door and she slid out, murmuring another thank-you.

"You really don't have to do this. It's a very quiet neighborhood."

"It's no problem."

The street was silent. In the late-night hours, everyone was in bed, the lights out. Even the dogs were quiet. Elizabeth walked across the street beside Donovan, his presence looming next to her. Where had all those relaxed feelings gone? Tension crept over her with each step.

They walked upstairs to her apartment and she pulled the keys out of her purse. Donovan took them from her, turning the lock but not opening the door. Elizabeth didn't move. She stared at the door, feeling the tension stretched taut as a wire between them.

Slowly, feeling as if she was fighting herself, she looked at him, her gaze traveling across the broad width of his chest, pausing on the stubborn strength of his chin and the masculine molding of his mouth. When her eyes at last met his, her heart was bumping against her chest and she felt breathless.

His eyes were a warm, liquid gold that looked deep into her soul, pulling out needs she didn't want to know existed. When his hand curled around the back of her neck, she closed her eyes, her palms coming up to rest on his chest but not to push him away. Some dim, half-heard voice said that she was taking too many chances, but the warning was smothered by the feel of Donovan's mouth on hers.

At the first touch of his lips, she felt her knees weaken. It had been so long since she'd felt this way. She leaned into Donovan, opening her mouth to the hard pressure of his. His hand tightened on the back of her neck, tilting her head to his, his other arm circling her waist, lifting her onto her toes, her breasts crushed against his chest.

His mouth was warm and hard, demanding and receiving total surrender. His tongue traced the ridge of her teeth before sliding past to explore the softness of her mouth. Elizabeth moaned, her body melding to his, her arms circling his neck, her fingers burrowing into the silky blackness of his hair.

His tongue fenced with hers—touching, withdrawing, only to touch again. It was an ancient duel without winner or loser. His tongue stabbed deep into her mouth and then withdrew, only to return. The suggestive rhythm pulsed through her body, like waves breaking in the pit of her stomach.

She was breathless, half fainting when his mouth left hers. The day-old beard that stubbled his chin rasped gently over her face as he kissed his way to her ear. His tongue traced its contours, making every nerve in her body quiver.

"Beth. Let me stay with you."

The words shivered across her skin, tempting her. Her body screamed at her to say yes. She didn't want him to leave. She didn't want to go in to her empty apartment and her lonely bed. She wanted to feel his hands on her, his hardness against her softness. She ached with the wanting. His tongue swirled against the pulse that beat so heavily at the base of her throat. Another minute, another second and she'd be lost.

"Donovan. No." The word was not particularly loud. She could barely force it out past the need to say yes, the need to let him stay.

His mouth stilled against her. For a moment, neither of them moved. She wasn't sure of her answer, and they both knew it. If he ignored her words, held her closer, let his mouth coax her, she'd say yes. He wouldn't be leaving, she wouldn't be sleeping alone tonight. His arms tightened around her and Elizabeth held her breath, half hoping he'd take the decision out of her hands.

"All right." His hands slid reluctantly away, lowering her to stand on her own two feet. Elizabeth's fingers left the softness of his hair reluctantly. She leaned back against the door, uncertain about her knees' ability to hold her. Donovan's eyes simmered gold, stealing what little breath she had left.

"Thank you."

He shrugged, his mouth twisting. "Think nothing of it. I'm insane, of course, but think nothing of it."

"It's too soon. I'm not ready for... for this."

His hand came up to cup her chin, his thumb stroking her soft cheek. "Cold showers are good for my circulation."

Elizabeth turned her face into his hand, leaning against that strength for an instant.

"I'm sorry. I—"

His thumb pressed across her lips, silencing her apology. "Hush. You've got nothing to apologize for. I shouldn't have pushed it. I swore I wouldn't, but you looked so delicious and you tasted even better." He grinned. "The devil made me do it."

Her smile was shaky, but the tension was reduced to a bearable level. Nobody but Donovan had ever been able to spark her emotions so quickly with so little effort. He could take her from passion to laughter in a matter of seconds, leaving her breathless from the ride.

"When can I see you again? Can you make dinner Wednesday night?" It was phrased as a request, but his eyes spoke a demand. Elizabeth ignored the small voice that warned her things were moving too quickly.

"I'd like that." His relief told her he hadn't been as sure of her answer as he'd seemed.

He reached behind her to open the door, easing her inside. "I'll pick you up at seven." He dropped a quick, hard kiss on her mouth that left her tingling, and then pulled the door shut, closing her inside.

Elizabeth leaned against the door, listening to the sound of his footsteps disappearing in the quiet night. She lifted her hand to her mouth, aware of the way her fingers trembled.

She hadn't felt so alive, so wonderfully, marvelously alive in months, years maybe. It was frightening, it was fabulous. She felt like a teenager, with everything life had to offer all spread out in front of her. And all the frightening, wonderful feelings that boiled inside were because Donovan was back in her life.

She closed her eyes, pushing aside the thought. She wasn't going to think about it now. For now, it was enough that she was happy, that life was exciting. She would think about the whys and wherefores another time. Right now, all she wanted to do was go to bed and dream about the day just past.

Wednesday night seemed aeons away.

Wednesday night eventually came, as did Friday

night and Saturday and Sunday and the next Tuesday. And every one of those days, Donovan filled her life with picnics and dinners and movies. On the days she didn't see him, Elizabeth thought about him and looked forward to the next time they'd be together.

He courted her with beautiful flowers and wonderful late-spring days. Even without Carol's blunt summation of the situation—"The man obviously wants you back, dummy"—Elizabeth could hardly doubt his intentions.

He cared for her, she knew that and she cared for him. In her weak moments she might even admit that she might be falling in love with him again. But only in a weak moment and only to herself.

Nearly two weeks after their first date, Elizabeth was putting her notes together for a redecorating project. It was near the end of the day and she was looking forward to getting home. Her tiny office was stuffy and the warm sun had been trying to coax her outside all day.

Donovan had said he might come by this evening. He'd been very mysterious, promising that he'd have something to show her. Her mouth softened and her pencil slowed. Donovan. In a couple of weeks, he'd somehow become central to her life again, and she wasn't even sure what she wanted out of a relationship with him. After all, he was practically her *ex*-husband.

"Elizabeth." Mrs. Tancredi's voice interrupted Elizabeth's thinking. She looked up to find her manager's short, stout figure standing in the doorway, her plump features set in an expression of stern disapproval.

"There's a man here who says you're expecting him."

"A man?"

Mrs. Tancredi sniffed. "I nearly called security but, on the off chance that you do know him, I decided to wait."

Elizabeth stood up and edged her way around the desk. Donovan? He hadn't said anything about picking her up at work. Besides, if it was Donovan, why on earth would Mrs. Tancredi consider calling security? He was a respected businessman. He looked respectable if you didn't notice the wild streak that sometimes sparkled in his eyes. He was—

She came to a screeching halt between a sofa covered in green-and-blue plaid and a chair covered in brown tufted tweed. He was standing a few feet away staring at an abstract print. From the way his head was tilted, he seemed to be considering the possibility that it was upside-down. It was Donovan all right, but not a Donovan she'd ever seen before.

Her astonished eyes started at his feet and worked their way up. Size twelve feet were encased in black boots decorated with gold chains. Worn blue jeans disappeared into their tops. The jeans fit as if they'd been molded to him, outlining the muscles in his long thighs. A black leather belt cinched his waist, and a black T-shirt disappeared into the waistband. His shoulders looked enormous in a leather jacket. The jacket could only be described as "bad boy black." If the clothes weren't enough, he'd combed his thick hair back off his forehead. Not only combed it back—he'd greased it so that every heavy wave caught the light.

He turned, meeting her stunned eyes. Elizabeth was aware of Mrs. Tancredi standing behind her. She wondered vaguely if the other woman was depending on her for protection.

"Hi, Babe."

Babe? "Donovan?"

His eyes held a wicked spark that caused a convulsive bump in her chest. He should have looked ridiculous. He *did* look ridiculous. Why did he have to look so sexy, too?

"You ready to blow this joint? I've got my new wheels." He pulled out a pair of wraparound sunglasses and slid them on his nose.

"New—wheels?" she said weakly.

"Yeah? You ready? This place is like a tomb." He looked around him, his mouth set contemptuously. Elizabeth bit her lip to hold back a giggle.

"Have you gone nuts?"

"If you don't know this man, Elizabeth, I really think it would be best to call security." Mrs. Tancredi's hurried whisper brought another choked giggle out of Elizabeth.

"I know him, Mrs. Tancredi. Or at least, I think I know him. I don't think it will be necessary to call security."

"Hey, Babe. I don't want to hang around this place too long. It's not good for my image, ya know what I mean?" He hunched his shoulders inside the jacket, giving the impression that he might be allergic to the conservative tastes that surrounded him.

"I know what you mean. Let me get my purse."

She ignored her manager's muttered protest and hurried back to her office. Her notes were only half finished, but she didn't give them a glance. She grabbed her purse and hurried out.

Neither Donovan nor Mrs. Tancredi had moved during the few minutes she'd been gone. Donovan still wore the sunglasses, his mouth was still molded into an expression of insolent contempt. Mrs. Tancredi was still watching him as if expecting him to whip out a switch-blade at any moment and start slashing the stock. It was all Elizabeth could do to keep from laughing.

"I'm ready."

Donovan hunched his shoulders again. "Let's make tracks."

He slung an arm over her shoulders and pulled her close. "All this respectability is makin' me itch."

Elizabeth waved to Mrs. Tancredi, pretending not to see her completely scandalized expression. As soon as they'd turned a corner and were out of sight, Donovan reached up to take off the sunglasses.

"Couldn't see a thing," he muttered.

Elizabeth collapsed against him, giggling. "You idiot. What is all this in aid of?"

He looked hurt. "Don't you think I look tough?" He guided her wavering footsteps toward the exit. "I was hoping to impress you with my macho image."

"Well, you certainly impressed my boss."

"Was that your boss?"

"*Was* may be the operative word. After this, she may decide I'm too wild to risk having me in the store."

"You can always tell her that you only went with me to protect the store's image. She looks like the type to love a little noble sacrifice."

"Maybe. What are you doing here? I thought you were going to come by my house later tonight."

"I couldn't wait to show you."

"Show me what?" But she had a sinking sensation that she knew what.

Donovan's grin was appealingly boyish, his eyes excited as he ushered her through the door. Parked illegally at the curb was a shiny, new motorcycle. Bright red with black trim, it looked enormous, fast and danger-ous.

"Isn't it great? I just picked it up."

"It's very—red." She hoped she sounded enthused enough.

"I thought I could follow you home and wait while you changed, and then maybe we could go for a ride. I bought you a helmet." His expression was coaxing. He was well aware of her doubts about two-wheeled trans-portation.

She looked at him and then looked at the bike. It *did* look reassuringly large. Besides, Donovan was an adult. He wasn't going to be doing crazy things on the high-way. And, though she was reluctant to admit it, there was something exciting about whizzing along with the wind in your face.

An hour later she climbed gingerly onto the back of the motorcycle. The helmet that covered her head made her feel like an extra in a science fiction movie, and once on the bike, it seemed an amazingly long way to the ground. Donovan had clearly bought the machine with his measurements in mind, not hers.

On the road, she was grateful for the solidity of the machine between her legs and even more grateful for the hard strength of Donovan's body in front of her. The countryside flashed by, the wind roaring in her ears. She'd expected to be nervous. She hadn't been on a motorcycle since Donovan had sold his right after they got married. She'd underestimated her confidence in the man who controlled the machine.

"Like it?" He had to shout to be heard, and she caught just the edge of his grin as he turned his head.

It had been years since she'd seen him so excited about something that didn't have to do with his profession. That alone made this expensive toy acceptable.

"It's great."

Late spring turned to early summer, and the weather remained bright and perfect. Elizabeth couldn't remember the last time she'd felt so happy and alive. She tried not to analyze what was happening or ask herself what the future might hold. For now, it was enough that Donovan was in her life, a large, warm presence that somehow completed something vital to her happiness.

Michael watched his parents without comment. Carol was not so tactful, and expressed her opinion anytime the subject came up. Clearly, Elizabeth and Donovan were destined to be together, and Elizabeth was a fool if she didn't just face the fact and accept her fate. Elizabeth wasn't quite ready to admit any such thing, but she couldn't deny that she was happier than she'd been in a long time.

Chapter 12

Would you like some coffee?" The moment the invitation was spoken, Elizabeth wondered why she'd made it.

"Thanks."

She smiled, hoping her nervousness didn't show, and opened the door wide. Donovan stepped into the living room, bringing all the tension in with him.

"I'll just go put it on. It won't take a minute." She escaped to the kitchen, wishing there was a door to shut between them. Her hands shook as she opened cupboards and got out cups.

She'd been nuts to invite him in on tonight of all nights. In the six weeks they'd been dating, she'd avoided having him in her apartment, and she'd flatly refused his invitations to have dinner at their old home. There were too many memories there and there was too much intimacy here. She wasn't sure where their relationship was going, but she wasn't going to rush.

Whatever happened, this time around she was going to give it a lot of thought. She would be thirty-seven on her next birthday. A mature woman by anybody's standards.

She put water on to heat and leaned against the counter, taking deep breaths. She couldn't see Donovan from here, but she could feel him. He was only a few feet away, and the tension that had been building between them reached out to catch her in its web.

It was that stupid movie. She'd been crazy to suggest that they go see a film billed as a passionate love story. The love scenes had been enough to make the screen threaten to melt. She'd sat through them, her arms held against her side, avoiding any contact with Donovan's muscular shoulder.

It wasn't as if there hadn't been sexual tension between them right along. She knew Donovan wanted her, and physically, she wanted him. But she wasn't jumping into anything, and he'd respected that wish. When he kissed her good-night, she could feel his tension and she knew it would take only a word from her to change everything.

Tonight, she wanted to say that word. But she wasn't going to give in to temporary desire sparked by a sensuous movie. She was going to remain rational and calm. If and when she slept with Donovan it was going to be after they'd discussed their relationship and clarified just what each of them wanted from it. That was the adult, sensible way to handle things.

She was so absorbed in her thoughts that she wasn't aware she was no longer alone until Donovan's mouth settled on the nape of her neck, which had been left bare by her chignon. A shiver ran through her, leaving her knees weak. Her logical thoughts scattered in a thousand directions as his lips moved against her tender skin, finding every nerve ending and bringing it to life.

"Donovan." She'd intended his name to be a protest, but it came out as more of a whimper.

"Hmm?" His teeth nibbled gently at the curve where her neck and shoulder met, one hand tugging aside the neckline of her blouse to give him more room.

"Donovan. I want you—" She forgot what she was saying when his mouth found her ear. His tongue traced every curve, his teeth nipped at her earlobe. If it hadn't been for the counter in front of her and the length of his body behind her, Elizabeth would have melted to the floor.

"I want you, too." His kisses moved down the side of her neck. One of his hands found its way to her waist, sliding upward to cup the weight of her breast, his thumb brushing across the tip, bringing it singing to life. The thin cotton of her blouse was no protection.

"I mean I—" What did she mean? She couldn't think.

He slid his other hand downward, boldly cupping the warmth between her legs, drawing her backward until she was pressed against him. She drew in a quick, hard breath. His arousal pressed against her was a potent call for her to abandon logic and caution. How could she think when his hands held her so close, reminding her of how long it had been since he'd touched her like this.

She didn't protest as he turned her into his arms, his hands sliding across her back. Her head tilted back, her eyes closed. Her hands came up to press against his chest, somehow losing their impetus and sliding up to his shoulders.

"Beth."

No, don't say anything. Kiss me. Make me stop thinking.

"Beth, look at me." His voice was husky and she could feel his tension.

He wanted her. She could feel the proof of that like a hot brand against her stomach.

"Beth, open your eyes."

Her lashes fluttered and then slowly lifted. She wanted him to kiss her, to make her forget all her logic and caution. His eyes blazed down at her, hunger and need mixing in a potent combination.

"Is this what you want?"

Why was he making her decide? Didn't he know that all he had to do was kiss her and she'd melt? She didn't want to think about what she was doing.

"Beth, I ache with wanting you. But, if this isn't what you want, I'll walk out of here right now."

Her hands tightened on his shoulders. He wasn't going to let her pretend that she didn't know what was happening. He was going to make her face her choice head-on. If she said she wanted him to stay, he would make love to her. Their relationship would change, and there would be no going back to the quasi-safety of the past weeks.

"Are you going to stand there all night, or are you going to kiss me?" She could hardly get the words past the nervous lump in her throat. The golden flare of his eyes made her pulse jump, and the reckless grin that slashed his face stole her breath.

He bent, sweeping her off her feet to cradle her against his chest, his mouth capturing hers. With her last remnant of sanity, Beth reached out to shut the stove off. Somehow, she didn't think they'd be wanting any coffee.

He carried her through the apartment, his long strides covering the short distance to her dark, cool bedroom. He set her down. His hands cupped her face, and he kissed her over and over again until she was breathless.

The desire that had been building between them during the past weeks bubbled up, full and rich, a driving force that would not be denied. She fumbled with the buttons of his shirt, sighing with pleasure when her palms were at last able to press against his skin. Crisp, black curls covered hard muscles.

Donovan tugged at the shirt impatiently, his attention on Elizabeth's blouse. She reluctantly let him pull the blouse over her head. Her bra was quickly removed, tossed into some corner of the room.

A sob caught in the back of her throat as he drew her toward him again. The crisp, curling hair brushed against her swollen nipples, teasing, building the fire higher. She would have melted onto his chest but he held her away, tantalizing, moving her so that her nipples were barely touching him.

"Damn you." The words left her on a moan, and she heard him laugh just before he gave her what she wanted. She sobbed as he pushed her back onto the bed, lying over her, his chest crushing her breasts with delicious weight.

His mouth found hers, his tongue stabbing inside, tasting her, making her his. His fingers fumbled with the side fastening on her skirt, stripping the garment away. He slid his hand beneath her bottom, cupping her through the fragile silk of her panties, arching her upward as his jean-clad thigh slid between her legs.

It was too much and it wasn't nearly enough. Elizabeth was filled with need. Only Donovan had touched her like this. Surely no other man would ever know just the way to set her on fire. His head bent and his mouth captured the swollen peak of one breast, his teeth nibbling at the tender flesh. His thigh pressed upward, giving her a tantalizing glimpse of what she really wanted.

Her fingers clenched around his shoulders, her breath leaving her on soft moans. He held her helpless, leaving her no choice but to feel everything he was doing, every demand he was making. She pushed at his shoulders, her movements weak. She didn't want him to stop the delicious assault, but she wanted more—needed more—had to have it.

Donovan dragged his mouth from her breast, his breathing as ragged as hers. Elizabeth's fingers found the waist of his jeans. The snap gave easily, and her hand slid inside. Donovan shuddered as her fingers closed around him, cool against the fiery heat of his arousal.

The jeans hit the floor with a soft thud. Elizabeth's panties followed, a whisper of light without sound. His legs slid between hers, his skin fiery hot. But no hotter than the passion he'd created inside her. She felt him against her, hot and hard, and she forgot how to breathe.

"Look at me, Beth." His voice seemed to rasp in his throat.

Elizabeth dragged her eyes open to stare into the green-gold depths of his. The passion she read there only stoked the flames higher. No one had ever wanted her the way Donovan did. Body and soul, every inch of her belonging to him. No one would ever want her like that again.

"Donovan." The name was a whisper, a breath. It said everything and told him nothing.

His eyes holding hers, he slid forward, possessing and being possessed. Elizabeth arched, her breath leaving her on a sob as he filled the aching emptiness within. It had been so long. She'd almost convinced herself that it hadn't been this wonderful, this right. After the first, heavy thrust, he rested against her a moment, giving her body time to adjust, drawing on all his control.

He started to move, bracing his weight on his hands, his eyes never leaving her face. She could feel herself spinning out of control. Her hands slid up and down his back, seeking something to cling to, something to slow the spinning madness that beckoned her. There was nothing but Donovan's sweat-dampened skin, the muscles rippling beneath her fingers.

She wanted it to last forever. It had to end soon or she'd fly into a million pieces, never to be put back together again. Her head turned back and forth, scattering golden-blond hair across the pale blue bedspread. She couldn't breathe, couldn't think. All she could do was feel. Tension coiled low in her belly, each thrusting motion tightening the coil until she was begging him to end it.

"Please, please, please."

And he gave her what she sought.

He thrust deeply, seeming to reach to the very core of her, and the coil sprang apart, shattering the tension that held her together. Donovan's mouth caught her cry, swallowing it, absorbing it into himself, just as he seemed to have absorbed her into himself. Elizabeth's nails dug into his shoulders, her body tightening around him, demanding that he follow her into the spinning maelstrom that threatened to swallow her and drown her in pleasure. She tasted his groan of surrender, felt his shudder of completion and was filled with a purely feminine pleasure. In the taking, he had been taken. In the giving, he had received.

For a long time, there was no sound in the room beyond the ragged rhythm of their breathing. She murmured a protest when he shifted, lifting his weight from her. If he moved, she might have to acknowledge that the rest of the world existed. Right now, she didn't want to think of anything beyond this room, beyond this night.

"I'll squash you." He kissed her softly and lifted himself away.

"What a nice way to go." The words came out on a yawn, and she sensed more than saw his grin. She didn't open her eyes as the bed shook with his movements. He pulled down the covers and then bent to scoop her up and lay her against the sheets, her head on the pillow. She frowned but, before she could voice her protest, Donovan slid beneath the covers, his long body a warm contrast to the cool cotton sheets.

Elizabeth hadn't realized how the tension had been building until it was finally broken. She hadn't wanted to acknowledge the strong pull that lay between them. She snuggled against Donovan's side, more relaxed than she had been in months—years.

There were things that needed to be said, but right now, she couldn't think what they were. This changed everything, but she didn't want to think about the changes. She didn't want to think about anything except the delicious peace that filled her and the warmth of Donovan next to her. She drifted to sleep, aware of Donovan shifting her into a more comfortable position, his hand stroking the tangled hair back off her forehead.

She couldn't remember the last time she'd felt so safe and protected. Perhaps it had been the last time she'd gone to sleep in Donovan's arms.

It was not long past dawn when Donovan awoke. Sunlight streamed in through the lightweight curtains, spilling across the bed, promising a beautiful day. He didn't have to wonder why the sunlight was coming in at the wrong angle. Elizabeth's body was a warm, welcome weight along him. He knew exactly where he was.

For the first time in months, he was home. If Elizabeth was in his arms, that was home. It didn't matter in whose bed. It wouldn't matter if it was another state, another country or another planet. She snuggled closer to his side, one leg thrown across his thighs, one arm sprawled over his chest.

His smile held an element of pain. It had been so long. How could he have been such a fool to let this slip through his fingers, even for an instant? Having come so close to losing her forever, he'd never lose sight of just how precious she was. Without her, his life was only half-complete. She was what made everything worthwhile. His arms tightened around her. Now that he had her back, he'd never let go.

She'd been so sweetly responsive last night, demanding and giving, taking everything he had to offer and returning it to him ten times over. He nuzzled his face into her hair, inhaling all the remembered scents, refreshing his memory, savoring the peace of the moment.

These past few months had been miserable. But it was going to be all right now. They belonged together, and last night had shown that they both knew it. He kissed her forehead, kissing his way across each delicate eyebrow.

Elizabeth stirred. Donovan planted soft kisses down her nose before settling on her mouth. Her lips were soft and sleepy. She came awake under his mouth, her fingers flexing against his chest, reminding him of a cat kneading its paws with contentment. He pulled her closer, feeling himself growing hard beneath the weight of her leg. She felt it too, shifting her thigh to rub against him.

Their lovemaking was slow. Last night's driving pressure had been eased, and they took their time rediscovering each other. The pleasure was no less intense, but it was not the shattering force of the night before. Afterward, they lay silent for a while, savoring the delight in not waking up alone.

Donovan dropped a kiss on her temple, tasting the gentle pulse that beat there. "Let's go home. I want you back in our bed, in our home." He murmured the words against her ear, his contentment so deep that it took him a moment to sense her sudden stiffening.

He went still, feeling all the contentment drain away. Elizabeth pushed against him and he released her, watching as she sat up, the sheet drawn over her breasts. His heart was beating a little too hard and a little too fast. He had the sinking feeling that things were not going quite as he'd thought.

"Beth? What is it? You're coming back to me, aren't you?"

She looked away, but he'd seen the answer in her eyes. He swung his legs to the floor, sitting on the edge of the bed with his back to her, not wanting her to see the shattered look that must be in his eyes. Behind him, he felt her get out of bed, heard her open her closet door and knew she was putting something on.

"Donovan?" Her voice was hesitant, and he winced at the concern he heard. He wanted and needed her, but he was damned if he'd beg for her. He didn't want her pity. He stood up and walked around the bed, magnificently naked. He stooped to pick up his jeans, and stepped into them, keeping his expression rigidly under control.

"Donovan, don't be angry with me. Please."

He jerked the zipper up and shrugged. "I'm not angry. I shouldn't have assumed that last night meant you'd be coming back. I suppose these days, a night in bed together is no big deal." He reached for his shirt, but she got to it before he did, holding on to it when he would have pulled it away.

"Please. I don't want you to think it didn't mean anything to me. It's just too soon."

The catch in her voice made him look at her face, even though he only wanted to take his hurt and walk away. He wanted to go somewhere and beat his fists against a wall until that pain took away the ache in his chest.

But there was pain in her eyes, too, and he couldn't just walk away. With an effort, he shrugged, forcing a half smile.

"Don't worry about it. I assumed too much. You've probably got things to do, so if you'll give me my shirt, I'll get out of your way."

She shook her head, and his ache intensified. Did she know how gorgeous she was? Standing there in a peacock-blue silk robe, her hair like a tangled, golden curtain on her shoulders, his shirt clutched to her breasts.

"I don't want you to leave until we've talked this out."

"What's to talk about? We made love, I made some assumptions."

"Don't be so damned pigheaded!" Anger flashed in her eyes. "Talk to me. I don't want to hear all this macho claptrap. I want you to talk to me, and I want you to listen to what I have to say. This is exactly the garbage that got us in trouble in the first place. If you won't talk to me, how can I know what you're feeling?"

"If I have to tell you what I'm feeling, then what's the sense? If two people are close enough, they should know what the other feels."

"It doesn't always work that way. If it did, you would have realized a long time ago how unhappy I was."

He stared at her, his gut full of turmoil. He couldn't answer her because she was right. He should have known and have done something, changed something, become something else. Only he'd been blind to her needs—so blind that he'd lost her.

"What do you want me to say?" If the question was sullen, he couldn't help it. A man didn't go around laying his soul bare, not even to the woman he loved more than life itself.

She took a deep breath, and her fingers tightened around his shirt. "I don't want you to say anything. I just want you to listen. Last night meant a great deal to me. But I'm not ready to just pack up and move back in with you. I've never lived alone. If I give this all up and move back in with you, I'll never know if I can make it on my own."

He threw his hand out in an impatient gesture. "Don't give me that stuff about finding yourself."

"It's not 'stuff.' It's something that's very important to me. If you care about me, then you'll want me to do this."

She stood there, dignified despite her tangled hair and bare feet. Her eyes met his evenly, demanding his support.

Donovan stared at her for a long time without saying anything. If he had any hopes of winning her back to him, he had to give her this chance—not grudgingly as if he were doing her a favor but openly and generously. He had to give her honest support in finding her dreams. Perhaps if he did that, she'd realize that *he* was one of her dreams.

"All right." He reached out to touch her cheek. "I really want you to be happy, Beth. I guess I'm just not sure where we go from here."

Her smile was shaky, but she leaned her face into his hand. "Couldn't we just go on as we have been? Dating and things."

"After last night, I don't think I could go back to leaving you at your door at night. There isn't enough cold water in the whole state of Indiana to keep me cool enough."

She flushed. "I didn't mean to go back to being platonic."

He widened his eyes, his expression shocked. "Are you suggesting that we have an affair, Ms. Sinclair? How thoroughly risqué of you."

"Wouldn't you like to have an affair with me? We haven't had one in twenty years." Her eyes coaxed him, and Donovan felt himself melting. His hand slid from her cheek to the back of her neck, pulling her closer until her bare feet were tucked between his, the silk of her robe brushing his jeans.

"I can't imagine anything that would give me more pleasure."

If all their problems weren't solved by their talk, at least some of them were eased. The summer days spun by in a haze of Indiana heat. The farmers talked about it being one of the best summers they'd had in years, but Elizabeth and Donovan wouldn't have noticed if a tornado had flattened every cornfield in a hundred-mile radius.

Michael spent his time going to or returning from camping trips, but when he was home, he seemed pleased with the direction his parents were heading. Elizabeth hadn't been sure how he'd feel about the two of them being together yet not together, but he seemed to take it in stride. He was more concerned with how often he could talk his father into letting him borrow the motorcycle.

That motorcycle was another worry of Elizabeth's. She acknowledged the exhilarating thrill of riding down the highway with the wind in your face, but she was still uneasy with the idea of Donovan riding it, let alone their son. She also knew it would be foolish to forbid Michael. He was nineteen, and there was nothing more natural in the world than that he should be excited by such a nifty toy. She had to trust in helmets, good sense and luck to keep both her men safe.

Luck, at least, seemed to be running on her side these days. She was doing so well with the interior decorating service at Mason's that the owner had moved her into a bigger office, increased her salary, and was giving her a percentage of the sales she made. Remembrance was growing. There were several small developments going up on the edge of town. Donovan had designed three of them, and he freely admitted to pulling some strings to get her hired to decorate the model homes.

At first, Elizabeth was uneasy with the idea of Donovan using his influence to get her work, but he pointed out that she still had to prove herself. If she did a lousy job, the blame would fall on her head. He laughed when she slugged him with a pillow and announced that she never did a lousy job. The resulting pillow fight ended with her pinned deliciously beneath him, paying a forfeit in kisses, a penalty she didn't mind a bit.

That was the best part of summer. If there were still subjects that she and Donovan didn't discuss, there were a million others to talk about. The recent past was taboo, as was the more distant future. Neither one of them wanted to rock the careful balance they'd achieved.

She and Donovan spent time together three or four times a week. Sometimes he took her out; sometimes she cooked dinner at her apartment. Once or twice he insisted on cooking dinner for her at their old home, but there were too many memories there for either of them to be entirely comfortable. Everything had changed too much. By unspoken consent, they didn't make love in their old bed. Elizabeth couldn't have said why, but it just didn't feel right.

As far as she was concerned, things were going well. She had her job, her son and her relationship with Donovan was getting stronger.

But the one constant in life is change, and nothing stays the same for long. While Elizabeth was enjoying her life, Donovan was marking time, waiting for the moment when they could get on with the real business of living. It was inevitable that their two goals were on a collision course.

Chapter 13

Donovan paced across the apartment, his movements restless, the expression in his eyes abstract. Elizabeth sat cross-legged on the sofa, a small pile of mending on her lap, her fingers weaving the needle through a button, stitching it onto a blue chambray shirt.

"I told you the laundry would do that." There was an edge to his voice, and he took a deep breath before going on. "There's no reason for you to mend my shirt."

"I don't mind. I have to do some of my own things, anyway, and this is lousy weather for a picnic but great weather for mending." She glanced out the window at the rain and shrugged.

"Yeah." Donovan moved to the window and stared out. A distance away, lightning cracked. On the street below, the rain washed the pavement clean and made even the oldest car look shiny and new. Behind him, the small living room was the picture of tranquillity. When the rain had made a picnic in the country impossible, they'd spread a sheet on Beth's floor and eaten their picnic there.

He hadn't minded, because any time spent with Elizabeth was time well spent. After the meal, they sat on the floor and talked—about a new project he was designing, about a house she was decorating, about Michael's second year at college, which lay just around the corner. He'd felt well fed and content. So why was he so restless now?

He didn't have to look far for the answer. Glancing at Elizabeth, he could feel the tension tightening in the pit of his stomach. She sat with his shirt spread across her lap, cheerfully sewing a button on. She looked the very picture of wifely devotion. It was infuriating.

He didn't want her to play at being wife. He didn't care if she mended or cooked or cleaned house—he could hire someone to do any or all of those things. He wanted her back in his home—*their* home, dammit! He didn't want to pick her up for dates and then come back to her place for wonderful, semi-illicit sex.

He was kicking forty in the teeth, and he was too old for these games. He wanted a home again, a wife, and the support and love that went with commitment. He'd made a lot of mistakes before, but he wouldn't repeat them. From now on his marriage came first.

The words hadn't been spoken but there could be no doubt that they loved each other. Maybe their love would be even stronger than before. He'd tried his best to be supportive—he wanted Elizabeth to be happy, he was proud of her career. She certainly didn't have to give it up if she moved back where she belonged. They'd hire a housekeeper, a cook, anything. He just wanted her home again.

"Is something wrong?" The quiet question made him realize how long he'd been staring out at the rain. He turned and looked at her.

She'd finished his shirt, and it lay neatly across the arm of the sofa. A silk negligee lay across her lap, the needle suspended over a delicate strap, torn loose from the bodice. He'd done that when she'd been in a teasing mood. She'd tantalized him, stripping off his clothes and then letting her fingers stroke his heated skin until he thought he'd go mad. He had a dim memory of reaching for her, of hearing the fragile silk tear, but then she'd been sprawled across the bed and he'd been over her, within her.

She'd played the mistress that night, driving him wild with need. Now she sat there playing wife, her fingers deft with the needle, her concern for how he was feeling. He was tired of playing at marriage. He wanted a real marriage, a commitment, promises.

"Donovan?" She looked at him, sensing his mood but uncertain of the cause.

The thought that if he pressed the issue he might lose her slipped in, but he pushed it away. They couldn't keep straddling the fence. *He* couldn't straddle the fence anymore. One of them had to take the first step.

"You've been staring out that window for the past twenty minutes. Are you watching for floodwaters?" He didn't even hear her mild joke. Shoving his hands in his pockets, he leaned back against the wall.

"Do you ever think about what we're doing?"

"At the moment, we're not doing much of anything. I'm mending and you're staring. Not much to think about." Her attention returned to the negligee.

"I don't mean right this minute." His tone was impatient and he saw her fingers still as if she was beginning to realize that something was truly wrong. "Do you ever think about what we're doing overall?"

"Well, I'm not sure we're making great contributions to history, if that's what you mean."

He pulled his hands out of his pockets and strode across the room to sit next to her. She didn't look at him as he set aside her mending before taking her hands.

"Beth, look at me." Her eyes came to his reluctantly, and it didn't take a genius to read the wariness in her face. "Do you ever think about our relationship? Where it's been, where it's going?"

"Of course I do. It's going very well, don't you think?" Her eyes pleaded with him to agree. *Don't rock the boat.*

"No." Hurt flared in her eyes and he sought to soften the blunt denial. "It isn't that I don't love spending time with you, Beth. You know I do. But I want something more. We can't just drift along like this forever."

"I never said anything about forever."

"How long, Beth? We've been playing this game for two months. How much longer?"

"I don't know." She turned her head away, tugging on her hands, but he refused to release her. "I can't give you a schedule!" The quick flare of anger faded as quickly as it had come, and she looked at him, her eyes pleading.

His fingers tightened over hers, trying to convey how important this was to him. "I want a commitment. We're married, we've got a grown son. I don't want to play at having an affair anymore. I want to have you in my home, in my bed. Our home. Our bed. I want your clothes next to mine in the closet and your underwear drying in the shower. I want to live with you again. I want a marriage again."

"Let's give it some more time."

"I don't want to give it some more time. I've been without you for almost a year. I don't want to live without you another day. Dammit, Beth! You love me. I know you do. Why are you so reluctant to come home again?"

She pulled her hands away and twisted them together in her lap, staring down at them. "I'm afraid that if I move back in, things might go back to what they were, with you gone all the time and me filling my days with committees and tea parties. I don't want that again."

"Neither do I, and I promise it won't be that way. I admit I lost track of priorities for a while. I *wasn't* spending enough time at home. But I wouldn't risk losing you again. Don't you want a home with me? Maybe…maybe even another child? We're not too old to think about it. We used to talk about having another baby."

"We always decided to wait until everything was right before having another child." Her voice was thick with tears.

"That was another mistake, but it's not too late to change things now. If you want, we could try. And if you don't want another baby, that's okay, too. *You're* the most important thing. Please, Beth, say you'll come home with me."

He stared at her down-bent head, feeling each beat of his heart, hearing every drop of rain that fell outside. Everything depended on her answer. She *had* to come home. Anything else was unbearable. The silence stretched, and Donovan's nerves stretched along with it. Why didn't she say something?

"I can't." A solitary tear fell onto her clasped hands.

Donovan stared at her, feeling the world rock beneath him. Hurt and rage stirred inside, but he swallowed hard, reminding himself that anger never did any good.

"Why not?" Despite his best efforts, the question sounded cold and angry.

Beth lifted her head, tears sparkling on her cheeks as she reached out to him, laying her palm on his arm, feeling the iron-hard muscles there.

"I'm just not ready, Donovan."

"I see." The anger in his eyes told her that he didn't see at all. "Moving back in with me would entail sacrificing too much, is that it?"

"No."

"That's what you're implying."

"No, it isn't!" She stopped and drew a deep breath, trying to find the words to describe the confusion she felt when she thought about being his wife again. "I met you when I was sixteen. By the time I turned seventeen, we were married and I was expecting Michael. Even when you were in Vietnam, I wasn't alone because there was Michael depending on me and I had to hold things together for him and for you. You came home and I didn't have to be strong anymore. I quit work and devoted myself to being a wife and mother. I'm not ashamed of that, but now I've got something different. I'm really living alone. No one depends on me for anything."

"The problem with that is that no one is there to care if you don't come home some night. And there's no one to take care of you if you hurt yourself and no one to be excited for you if you get a big job. There's no one, Beth. Is that really what you want?"

The picture he painted was bleak, and she felt anger flare up, putting her on the defensive. "There's also no one to tell me what to do, or to read the paper at the breakfast table or to expect me to pick up dry cleaning without even thanking me. I can do what I want, when I want, without answering to anyone else."

He stood up and she followed suit, unwilling to let him tower over her. Not that he didn't tower quite a bit even when she was on her feet, but she felt a little less overwhelmed. His eyes were cold.

"Fine. You stay here, without any responsibilities to anyone but yourself. I hope you'll be happy. But I can't play that game anymore. I want a commitment, Beth. I want a wife and a family, someone to share things with. If you change your mind, you know where to find me."

She watched in shock as he pulled on his jacket and picked up his gloves and helmet.

"Where are you going?"

"Home. I can't play anymore."

"I'm not playing."

"No?" He shrugged, drawing on his gloves, not looking at her. "Call it what you want. I want you to be happy, but I can't live on the fringes of your life. If this is what you need to be happy, I wish you luck. Count me out."

"You're not going to bully me into making a decision like this."

"I'm not trying to. Goodbye, Elizabeth."

The door shut behind him. The quiet snick of the latch sounded more final than if he'd slammed it. *Elizabeth.* He'd called her Elizabeth. For the past few weeks she'd been Beth again. But just now he'd called her Elizabeth. *Goodbye, Elizabeth.* As if Beth wasn't someone he'd say goodbye to.

Outside, she heard the faint roar of the motorcycle engine and then it faded away, leaving only the rain. She turned slowly, feeling very old, and walked to the window. She saw shiny trees, shiny street, shiny cars, but he was gone. She let the curtain fall and crossed to the sofa, reaching down to pick up his shirt. It felt soft and supple in her hands. If she drew a deep breath, she could catch a whiff of his after-shave. She blinked against the tears that threatened to fall.

"Bull pucky." Carol spooned sugar into her cup of tea and stirred it vigorously.

Elizabeth blinked, startled by her friend's emphatic opinion. "Well, that's succinct. Would you mind telling me what you mean? What, precisely, do you think is bull pucky?"

"All of it." Carol set her spoon down with a thump. "Your whole line of reasoning."

"You think I'm wrong to want a little more time alone?" Elizabeth's voice was stiff. She'd been so sure that Carol would understand.

"I didn't say you were wrong. I said your reasoning was—"

"Yes, I know. Bull pucky." She rubbed her forehead, fighting the urge to put her head on the table and cry like a baby. It had been almost two weeks since Donovan had walked so quietly out of her apartment and out of her life. The first few days, she'd been angry, then she'd been hurt. Now, the anger and the hurt were all tangled up together in a big ball that had settled at the bottom of her stomach.

"I didn't think I was asking for all that much. A few more months, maybe. Is that so bad?"

"With some men and some relationships that would be just fine, but Donovan isn't some men. You're asking for more than he can give."

"If he loves me, he should be able to understand. I'm so afraid he'll take me for granted again—that things will go back to the way they were."

"If *you* love *him*, you should be able to understand what he needs. Loving somebody doesn't automatically make a person omniscient."

"I know that. But after all these years, you'd think he could trust me, that he'd know I wanted this time because it was important."

"Beth, almost a year ago, you walked out on him. Even if he understands why now, even if he's willing to admit that you had good cause, it's bound to shake a man's faith a little."

"But—"

"But nothing. You expect too much of him, Beth. Donovan may be the best thing I've seen in pants in the past twenty years, but he's human. You don't make many allowances for that."

"What do you mean? I don't expect him to be more than human."

Carol took a swallow of her tea, her thin face calm despite Elizabeth's anger. "Don't you?"

"No. I just expect him to be fair."

"Right away you're asking more than most people ever get. Life isn't always fair, and both you and I know it. If life was fair, you'd have my metabolism so you could eat another cookie without looking like the Goodyear blimp, and I'd have your looks." Carol crunched into a cookie to emphasize her point.

"This has got nothing to do with metabolism or looks. This has to do with loving someone and wanting what's best for them."

"Donovan does love you. The problem here is that you think you need something he can't give you: the time you need. But he *needs* a commitment from you. He needs to know you love him enough to be his wife again. Quite frankly, I don't see what the problem is. Do you think he's going to ask you to give up your job?"

"No, he wouldn't do that. He knows how much I enjoy it."

"Is it the house? You don't want to live in the old place again?"

"No. Besides, I'm sure he wouldn't mind selling it if it bothered me."

"Then what's the big deal?"

Elizabeth ran the tip of her finger through some spilled sugar, creating small pathways and then destroying them. What *was* the big deal?

"Don't try and tell me you don't love him. I've seen the way you look at him," Carol continued.

"I love him. It's just that he's so strong. I guess I'm afraid of getting lost in that strength again—of forgetting to be someone besides his wife." She swept her hand across the table, scattering the fine grains of sugar. "It sounds stupid."

"No, it doesn't, but you're stronger than you give yourself credit for, Beth. I watched you when you found out you were pregnant. You were scared but you coped. And when Donovan went to 'Nam and left you alone with Michael, you became Supermom before anyone knew what the term meant."

"And as soon as Donovan came home, I let him take over. I *wanted* him to take over."

"So what's wrong with that? You were tired. You'd been going it alone for quite a while, and Donovan needed to know that he was needed at home. He needed to know that he had something to offer you."

"So I wimped out and he played Mr. Macho."

"It wasn't like that. I was there, remember?" Carol's voice was gentle, but there was no getting away from the truth in what she was saying. "You were hardly a wimp. You helped put Donovan through college. You were one hell of a mom to Michael. When Donovan got his degree and started trying to get clients, you stretched money and worked like a dog to help him in every way possible. Don't be ashamed of that, Beth."

"I'm not ashamed of it. But, somewhere along the way, I forgot to look at *my* dreams."

"So, you got off the track. You're still young. You're working for your dreams now. Donovan has been supportive, hasn't he? He's helped get you some great jobs, hasn't he?"

"Yes. But, what if I went back with him and then decided to give it all up?"

"That's your *choice*, Beth. Dreams don't get handed to you on a silver platter. You've got to work to make them come true. If you want your career bad enough, you'll stick with it, and you know Donovan will do everything he can to help you."

Elizabeth rubbed her fingers across her forehead. The headache that had been lurking behind her eyes all day had become a reality, but the throbbing pain was nothing compared to the ache in her heart.

"I just get scared. It wasn't easy to walk out, and I'm so afraid I'll have to do it again."

"You won't have to. If things get bad, you'll talk to him this time. Donovan would lay down his life for you."

"Then why can't he give me more time?"

"He needs you." Carol's mouth twisted, her eyes half-wistful. "I'd give just about anything to have what the two of you have. You two almost make me believe in destiny."

She didn't have to say anything more. Elizabeth had more than enough to think about. The idea of Donovan needing her stuck in her mind. She'd always thought of it as the other way around. He'd been the one to take care of her, he'd been the strong one. She'd never doubted that he loved her, but she'd never thought of him as needing her.

She loved him. She didn't deny that, not to Carol, not to herself. But, if she went back to him, would she let herself get swallowed up in his strength again? The past year had taught her the value of independence. It had also taught her something of its loneliness. Donovan had hit the nail on the head when he pointed out that there was no one to care whether she came home at all.

If she kept saying it loud enough and often enough that she liked living alone, it might sound completely sincere. She missed hearing someone else stirring around. She missed— She missed Donovan. And Michael.

She'd deliberately avoided thinking about Donovan's suggestion that they might have another baby. Now, the thought slipped in, surprisingly appealing. It had been a long time since she'd had a child to cuddle. Michael had grown out of the cuddly stage early. A baby. Donovan's baby. Yes, the idea had definite appeal.

As Elizabeth crawled into bed that night she decided that Carol was right. Maybe she was crazy to worry about anything beyond the fact that she and Donovan loved each other. Surely they'd learned from their mistakes. It would be a risk, but if she didn't make a commitment now, it might be too late.

The thought sent a shiver up her spine. *Too late.* Awful words. She turned over in bed and stared at the moonlight pouring in through a crack in the curtains. It couldn't be too late for her and Donovan. She'd go to him first thing in the morning and tell him she loved him and wanted to be with him.

The thought brought a wave of contentment. Morning couldn't come soon enough.

It seemed as if she'd just closed her eyes when the alarm went off. Moaning, she groped for the clock, her face still buried in the pillow. She pushed the alarm button but the ringing didn't stop. Groggy, she opened her eyes and stared at the clock. The first thing that registered was that it said two o'clock in the morning. The second thing was that the room was dark. And the third and most frightening was that it wasn't the alarm making that awful noise, it was the phone.

She stumbled out of bed, her feet half tangled in the covers. By the time she'd covered the few short feet to the living room, the ringing seemed to have gotten ten times louder. She found the phone by instinct, snatching the receiver, her heart pounding so hard she could hardly breathe. Phone calls at two in the morning were one of two things: wrong numbers or emergencies. She prayed it was someone looking for an all-night pizza parlor.

"Hello?"

"Mom?" She forgot how to breathe at the sound of Michael's voice.

"Michael? What's wrong? Are you all right?" *Please God, let him be all right.* "Where are you?"

"I'm at the hospital."

The hospital. A thousand nightmares flashed through her mind. "Are you badly hurt?" Amazing how calm her voice sounded. You couldn't even hear the panic that was screaming inside her.

"I'm fine, just a few scrapes and some bruises."

"Thank God." She swallowed tears, knowing he wouldn't welcome hearing her sob over the phone. "What happened? Never mind. You can tell me about it later. I'll be down as soon as I get some clothes on."

"It was the motorcycle. I think it's totaled. This car came from out of nowhere."

His voice was shaky. He was not at all the calm, young man who sometimes seemed too adult to have ever been a child.

"Don't worry about the motorcycle. As long as you're okay."

"I'm fine."

"I'm going to call your father and we'll both be there as soon as we can."

"Mom?"

Elizabeth's fingers knotted over the receiver, hearing the fear in his voice. There was more. "What is it, Michael?"

"Dad was with me. He tried to avoid the car, but the guy came out of nowhere. There was nothing he could do."

Elizabeth stared at the dark room, feeling the bottom of her stomach dissolve. She swallowed hard, fighting to stay calm.

"Is he . . . is he badly hurt?"

"I don't know. They won't tell me anything. He...he looked awful when they put him in the ambulance. They just keep telling me not to worry, but no one will tell me what's going on. He was bleeding a lot. I'm scared, Mom." His voice cracked.

"Stay calm, darling. He's strong. You stay right there and don't worry about anything. I'll be there in twenty minutes."

She set down the phone, making a conscious effort to uncurl her fingers from the receiver. In all the years they'd been together, she'd never seen Donovan seriously ill or hurt. He'd always been so strong, so invincible. Maybe Michael was wrong. Maybe he wasn't that badly hurt. After all, a lot of blood didn't have to be serious. Everyone knew that head wounds always bled out of proportion to their seriousness.

Head wounds. Oh God, what if he hadn't been wearing his helmet? She swallowed the bile that threatened to choke her. Donovan always wore his helmet. He was adamant about it. There was no sense in giving herself nightmares until she knew there was something to worry about. She wasn't going to worry about anything until she got to the hospital.

Chapter 14

The hospital smelled of antiseptic and fear. The lights seemed far too bright for two-thirty in the morning. Elizabeth forced herself to look calm and controlled as she approached the desk in the emergency room.

"Excuse me. I'm Elizabeth Sinclair. My son just called me. He and his father were in an accident."

The nurse looked up, her expression professionally sympathetic. "The motorcycle-car collision."

Elizabeth shuddered at the description. "Could you tell me how they are? My son said he was all right, but he didn't know about my husband."

"I'm afraid you'll have to speak to a doctor for an official report, but I can tell you that your son seems to be just fine. Very stubborn. He's refused to allow us to sedate him. He won't even lie down."

"I'd like to see him, please."

"Go right through that door and turn right. A nurse will direct you from there."

Elizabeth followed her instructions, but she didn't need anyone to direct her once through the doors. Michael was huddled on a plastic chair in the hallway. His face was pale in the revealing light, dark bruises showing up here and there. He was wearing torn and dirty jeans and a denim jacket in much the same condition.

Elizabeth paused, assessing the damage. He looked young, frightened and a bit battered but otherwise whole. She swallowed a sob, offering up a prayer of thanks.

"Michael."

"Mom!" He stood up, wavering a bit, and then she had her arms around him. She held him close, savoring the feel of his strong, young body, miraculously whole. He hugged her, burying his face against her neck, not an adult but a boy again, frightened and in need of comfort.

"It's going to be all right. I'm here now." She offered him the assurance, as mothers have since the beginning of time. It was senseless. He was old enough to know that she couldn't make everything all right with a wave of some maternal wand, but the old ritual was a comfort to them both. They stood there for a few minutes, holding each other, drawing strength for whatever was to come.

After a moment Elizabeth drew back, easing Michael down into a chair and sitting next to him, keeping hold of his hand. She reached up to brush a lock of hair off his forehead.

"You shouldn't be out here. The nurse says you wouldn't let them do anything for you."

"It's Dad I'm worried about. No one will tell me anything."

"They're probably still examining him. You know how cautious doctors are. Any minute now he'll probably walk through those doors with nothing more than a few bruises. He was...he was wearing his helmet, wasn't he?"

"We both were."

Elizabeth closed her eyes for a moment, letting the images of hideous head injuries fade back into the land of nightmares.

"The car just came right at us. There was nothing Dad could do." Michael's hands clenched into fists. "Dad swerved and the bike went out of control. I was thrown clear when it went over, but Dad's leg was caught under it. I couldn't do anything. The bike just slid and slid, dragging him with it. I could hear the metal screaming on the pavement. At first I thought it was Dad screaming. It kept sliding. I thought it was going to go on forever. I ran to him. The bike had stopped, but he was still trapped under it. I started to lift it, but he stopped me."

"He was conscious?"

"Yes, and his face was all white and funny. He told me to set up flares and flag down a car. I asked him what was wrong, and he said his leg was trapped but that he was going to be all right. I wasn't to worry. And then he passed out."

"Did he regain consciousness?"

"He was in and out. He was awake when the ambulance guys came. I heard him say something about his leg to them."

He stared at the opposite wall, his face white and set and looking too worn for his nineteen years. "The damn bike just wouldn't stop sliding."

Elizabeth knew he was seeing the accident again in his mind. She'd have given anything to be able to wipe the memory clean.

"Your father is very strong. I'm sure he's going to be fine."

"There was so much blood. And no one would tell me anything. They kept wanting to poke and prod at me. I told them it was Dad I was worried about."

"I know. But as soon as we find out your Dad is okay, you're going to let the doctors examine you."

He might have argued with her but the door of the examining room opened just then. Michael and Elizabeth were both on their feet before the doctor was halfway through the door. With his grizzled gray hair and lean face wrinkled by too many years squinting into the sun he looked the very picture of a country doctor. His white coat might have looked reassuring if it hadn't been for the blood—Donovan's blood—streaked across it. Elizabeth swallowed hard. He stopped, seeing their anxious faces.

"I see you haven't let anyone take a look at you yet." His eyes skimmed over Michael's dusty clothes and bruised face. "Could have a concussion, you know, or a cracked rib or two. Be a miracle if you came off completely scot-free." He didn't wait for a reply, turning his attention to Elizabeth. "Are you Mrs. Sinclair? You look too young."

"How is he?"

His eyes were as gray as his hair, shrewd and not unkind. "He's a strong man. I think he'll pull through this."

"You think?" Elizabeth clutched at Michael's arm, not sure who was steadying whom. "You think?"

The doctor frowned at her from under bushy gray eyebrows. "Come into the lounge, the both of you. I could use some coffee, and I'm sure you could, too."

Elizabeth followed him dazedly. He *thought* Donovan would pull through? He had to pull through. It wasn't possible to imagine the world without him.

Dr. Carson, as he introduced himself, set cups of coffee on the plastic surface of the table, settling wearily into a chair across from Elizabeth and Michael.

"I'm going to be as straight with you as I can—partly because you look strong enough to take it and partly because I'm too damn tired to remember all the medicalese that doctors like to use to confuse people."

"What's wrong with my husband?"

"He's been pretty badly banged up. That's the bad news. The good news is that he's damned lucky to be alive. And you're even luckier, son."

Dr. Carson took another swallow of coffee, gathering his thoughts. "Mr. Sinclair sustained some bad bruising. Several ribs are broken. Luckily, none of them punctured a lung. He was wearing a leather jacket, which saved him from a lot of upper-body injuries. From the description I've been given of the accident, the jacket kept the pavement from removing half his skin. The helmet undoubtedly saved his life. Even with it, he's bound to have a pretty nasty concussion."

Elizabeth allowed herself to breathe. From the sounds of it, Donovan was hurt, but it was nothing that wouldn't heal. "So he's going to pull through?"

"Don't get ahead of me. That takes care of his simple injuries. From what you told us, son, your dad was trapped under the bike, and it slid quite a ways with him."

Michael nodded. "I couldn't get to him before it stopped. I tried to lift the bike off of him, but he said to leave it."

The doctor nodded. "Probably kept him alive. The leg that was trapped under the bike is badly damaged. An artery was cut, and the weight of the bike kept enough pressure on it to keep your dad from bleeding to death."

Elizabeth felt herself grow pale, and she clenched her fingers on the edge of the table, forcing herself to breathe steadily. "How bad is it?"

"We stitched up the artery. He's lost a lot of blood, but transfusions should help that situation." He stared down at his coffee, his eyebrows hooked together in a bushy frown. "That leg is in bad shape." He paused and then drew a deep breath before looking up, his eyes meeting hers. "He may lose it."

Elizabeth heard the words from a long way away. She stared at him, unable to absorb their meaning. "Lose it?"

"I'm sorry. I don't want to frighten you unnecessarily. We're doing everything we can to save it. We're arranging for a helicopter to fly him to Indianapolis, their facilities are more sophisticated than ours. Medicine can still work miracles sometimes."

Elizabeth barely listened. Her fingers locked with Michael's, offering comfort when she had none to give herself. "Will he live?"

"Barring any complications. He's a strong, healthy man. Even if... even if he does lose the leg, there's no reason he shouldn't have a fine, productive life. I know that may not be much consolation if it comes to that."

"All that matters is that he's alive. We'll deal with whatever else comes along. Can we see him?"

"We're readying him for the move. I think it might be better if you and your son had a friend drive you to the city. I'll give you the name of the hospital."

It had started to rain—a cool, late-summer rain that carried a promise of fall. Carol's big station wagon swished down the highway, unperturbed by a little moisture. Inside, no one had much to say. Elizabeth had given Carol the bare facts when she called from the hospital and Carol, who knew when to ask questions and when to stay silent, hadn't asked for any details. Michael sat next to the door, his face white in the occasional passing headlights. In the east, there was the faintest hint of gray, promising daylight.

"It's my fault." Michael's voice was raw with pain.

Elizabeth looked at him, dragging her mind from Donovan. She put her hand on his arm, feeling the rigid muscles there, reminding her that he wasn't a little boy anymore to be distracted and coaxed out of his fears.

"It's not your fault. You weren't driving the car or the bike. There was nothing you could do."

"Dad wouldn't have been out tonight at all if my stupid car hadn't broken down. I called him and he came out to pick me up."

"It's not your fault your car broke down."

"Yes, it is. I should have taken better care of it. Dad warned me. He said I couldn't expect it to be dependable if I didn't take care of it."

"Michael, you can't blame something like this on your car. Your father shouldn't have come to pick you up on the motorcycle. Are you going to blame it on that?"

"His car is in the shop. I should have just spent the night in my car and then called in the morning. It's my fault."

"Michael, sometimes things just happen and no one's to blame. The only person at fault here is whoever was driving the car that almost hit you."

"What happened to the car?" Carol asked the question quietly.

Michael's face tightened, looking eerily like his father in anger. "They didn't even bother to stop. They just drove off and left Dad lying there in the road."

"Seems to me like your mom is right. The blame lies with them. Your dad doesn't need your guilt right now. It's not going to do him any good."

"Maybe."

Elizabeth glanced helplessly at Carol, who shrugged. Michael was going to have to work through his feelings. All she could do was be there for him. She couldn't lift the burden entirely, no matter how much she wanted to.

Carol pulled the car to a stop outside the hospital. The sun had come up enough to cast a gloomy light on the big building. The rain still fell, a soft drizzle that did nothing to lift the spirits.

Michael opened his door and stepped out into the rain, hunching his shoulders a bit as he waited for his mother. Elizabeth gave him a worried look. She wanted to take his pain away. It hurt her that she couldn't.

"Are you sure you don't want me to wait with you?"

"No, that's okay. You've got a business to run. If you wouldn't mind calling Mrs. Tancredi for me, and you'd better call Donovan's office and—"

"I know who to call, Beth. Don't worry about anything. I'll bring you some clothes tonight and something for Michael. I suppose you two are going to stay around here for a few days. Have you got money?"

"Money?" Elizabeth hadn't thought of anything yet beyond her family's welfare.

"You know, the green, crinkly stuff. You'll need it to buy food, etc." Carol reached into the pocket of her jacket and pulled out a wad of bills. "I robbed the register at the nursery."

"Oh Carol, you shouldn't have."

"Don't be an idiot, Beth. You can pay me back when everything is straightened out. I've got an exact tally of every dollar. I'll also figure the going interest rate, if it'll make you feel better."

"Thank you." Elizabeth blinked back tears, knowing Carol hadn't the least idea of how much money she'd handed her. "I'll call you as soon as there's any news."

"You do that. He's going to be fine, Beth. Donovan is too tough to do anything else."

"I know." Her hands were shaking as she stuffed the money into her purse. "I . . . I was going to tell him I loved him."

"You're still going to tell him. He's going to make it, Beth. You've got to believe it."

"I do."

"You'd better get out of here before Michael melts." Carol hugged her, her slim arms offering comfort. "You call me if you need anything. Anything at all."

"I will."

She slid out of the car and walked over to Michael. When she set her hand on his arm, he jumped. She wondered if he'd even been aware that he was standing in the rain. She had to tilt her head to see his face as they walked toward the hospital. He looked so much like his father. She looked away, blinking back tears. Donovan was going to be all right. He just had to be.

It was almost thirty-six hours before she was allowed to see her husband. Every hour seemed like ten. The nurses were kind and gave her what information they could. She knew when he went into surgery and she knew when he came out. Those were the worst hours. She and Michael could only sit and wonder if they would be able to save his leg. She told herself it didn't matter. As long as he was alive, anything else was secondary. But she knew it did matter. Nothing could change the way she felt about him, but it would matter to Donovan, and it frightened her to think how it might change him.

When the doctor at last came out of surgery, he told them they hadn't removed the leg. That wasn't a guarantee that they wouldn't have to yet, but he was cautiously optimistic. The damage had been extensive, but they'd managed to put things back in more or less the right order. Now, everything depended on Donovan's recuperative powers—whether or not the bones and blood vessels would knit themselves back together.

Michael's grasp left bruises on her forearm, but Elizabeth barely noticed. Donovan was alive and he wasn't going to lose his leg. She refused to believe anything else. She wasn't going to lose him. Once the doctor left, she put her arms around her son's waist and wept with relief.

After that, it was still almost another full day before they let anyone in to see Donovan. By then, the doctor's cautious optimism had been upgraded to not-so-cautious optimism. Things seemed to be going well. They weren't making any promises, but Elizabeth didn't care. All she wanted now was to see Donovan.

They warned her that he looked worse than he actually was, and she braced herself. But nothing could have prepared her for seeing him lying there, almost as pale as the sheets. Tubes ran everywhere, like some hideous, modern art sculpture. She bit her lip, hesitating in the doorway.

She'd never seen him so helpless. Donovan had always been larger than life, full of strength. This didn't even look like him. She crept closer, swallowing hard. Seeing him like this made her realize that she'd almost lost him. She grasped the side railings that fenced him into the bed and stared down at him. Reaching down, she brushed a lock of thick, black hair off his forehead, her fingers trembling.

"I love you, Donovan Sinclair." Her hushed voice was almost drowned in the quiet hum of the machinery they had him attached to. His eyelids fluttered. She held her breath as he opened his eyes slowly.

He stared up at her, his eyes a muddy green. "Beth." Her name formed on his lips though no sound came out.

"Don't try to talk, love. You're in the hospital but you're all right. Everything is going to be all right."

"Michael?" This time the name was distinguishable.

"He's fine. A few bruises and a scrape or two, but that's all."

"Worried." He closed his eyes as if the small effort had exhausted him.

"You don't have to worry about anything but getting better." She stroked her fingers over his cheek, feeling the faint rasp of stubble. She thought he'd gone back to sleep, but his lashes lifted again. This time his eyes were a little brighter, a little more urgent.

"My leg? Heard talking. Ambulance."

"Your leg is fine. It's going to be just as good as new," she promised recklessly.

Some of the urgency faded from his eyes. His hand lifted an inch or so and then fell back against the covers. Beth took his fingers in hers. "Go back to sleep, love. I'll stay with you."

"Don' worry." The words were slurred, his lashes already dropping against his cheeks. Beth sat until the nurse came and insisted she leave. They told her that they didn't need another patient on their hands, which was exactly what she'd be if she didn't get some rest.

From then on, Donovan progressed faster than the doctors had dared to hope. Elizabeth spent as much time with him as the hospital would allow. Neither of them spoke of the future or of what had happened between them before the accident. Future and past had been put on hold for now, but it couldn't be left that way forever.

"I want to know exactly what condition my leg is in. I'm tired of all this tap dancing around the subject."

Dr. Marin studied her patient over the top of her glasses. His impatience was easy to read. Overall, he'd been a good patient, better than most strong, healthy men ever were. She was well pleased with his recovery, but she had a feeling he might not quite share her enthusiasm when he knew the full truth.

"What, exactly, do you want to know?"

Donovan glared at her. "I want to know exactly what condition my leg is in." He spoke each word distinctly.

"Medically speaking, you're lucky you have a leg at all. Ten, even five years ago, damage like that would have resulted in amputation."

"I know that and I'm grateful. Believe me, I'm grateful." Gratitude, however, was hardly the emotion that filled his voice. "Now, I want to know the extent of the damage."

"You'll walk, if that's what's worrying you. You'll have a limp, but you'll walk."

"How much of a limp?" His tone was even, but she could see the lump his fist made under the sheet.

"Probably a fairly extensive one."

"Fairly extensive. What's fairly extensive? Am I going to be dragging my leg behind me like Quasimodo?"

"It shouldn't be that bad." She caught the rising irritation in his eyes. "Mr. Sinclair, I'm not trying to be difficult, though I know it sounds that way. The truth is I can't tell you just how much you will or won't limp. The damage your knee sustained was, quite frankly, horrendous. The joint is never going to work like it did before the accident. That's putting it as bluntly as I know how. You'll limp. You'll have pain if you overextend. You'll be on crutches for quite a while, but there's no reason to think you'll have to be on them permanently.

"As for running or going one-on-one on a basketball court, to a certain extent that will depend on you. You're certainly never going to have the speed you may have had in the past, and the knee is going to be prone to injury. You'll tire more quickly and you'll have to learn to gauge yourself."

"In other words, I'm never going to be normal again."

"That's a harsh way to put it. *Normal* is a relative term."

"It doesn't seem relative when it doesn't apply to you anymore. Don't worry, Doctor. I'm aware of how lucky I am. I could have lost my leg. I could have been killed. I'm grateful. Really I am. I just need to start preparing for what my life is going to be like once you guys turn me loose."

Elizabeth hurried down the corridor. The quiet bustle of the hospital had become familiar during the past few weeks. She smiled at a nurse whose name she didn't know but whose face was part of the daily routine. She should have been here when the doctor had told Donovan the extent of the damage to his leg. She didn't care whether he'd ever run a four-minute mile—all that mattered was that he was alive and going to stay that way. But she knew that Donovan wasn't going to feel the same. For a man who'd never been ill a day in his life, limited mobility was going to be a painful and difficult reality.

She stopped outside his door and smoothed her hands over the full skirt of her pale blue dress. Donovan liked her in blue, and he liked her in dresses. He'd always said it was a crime to cover legs like hers. She wasn't sure she agreed, but it was a small thing, a simple effort to cheer him.

She pushed open the door and stepped into the room. It was always a shock to see him lying in the hospital bed, though most of the tubes and machinery were gone now.

"Hi."

He'd been staring at the wall opposite the door but, at her soft greeting, he rolled his head to look at her. For just an instant, she thought she saw pain in his eyes, but then the expression was gone so quickly she might have imagined it.

"Hi. Nice dress." His smile seemed a little tight at the edges, and the lines in his face appeared a little deeper.

"That's what you said last time I wore it." She bent to kiss him and wondered if it was her imagination that made his response seem lukewarm.

"At least you know I wasn't lying."

"True." She sat in the chair beside his bed, her eyes betraying a touch of anxiety.

"How's Michael?"

"Fine. School starts next week. He said to tell you he'd be in this weekend."

"The doctors said I might be able to come home by then." His tone didn't indicate any excitement about this major step in his recovery.

"That would be wonderful! We'll have to do something to celebrate."

"No!" Elizabeth's eyes widened at the harsh refusal, and Donovan seemed to realize he'd been too strong. His smile was strained but coaxing. "I don't want any fuss. I just want to come home and settle in without having to be polite to people for a while. I'll probably be beat, anyway."

"Of course. I should have thought of that. Well, we'll have a celebration later, when you're feeling up to it."

"Fine." Silence settled between them. Elizabeth looked at him, trying to read his expression, but there was nothing there. He stared absently at the foot of his bed.

"Dr. Marin said she talked with you today. About your leg."

"Yeah. It was sort of a good news-bad news situation."

She waited, but he didn't seem inclined to say anything more. "I'm sorry. I know you must be pretty upset." *Talk to me Donovan. Tell me what you're feeling. Let me comfort you.*

"I don't know. It isn't that bad." His smile was twisted. "I could have lost the leg. Basically, I'm pretty lucky."

He didn't sound like he felt lucky, but the tone put up walls saying he didn't want her sympathy and didn't want her getting too close right now. Elizabeth swallowed her hurt. He had to deal with this in his own way. Maybe he needed some time to come to terms with his injury before he could talk about it.

"Well then, I'll go by the house and get it cleaned up and stock up on food for your homecoming. I have a feeling that's not really Michael's forte."

"You don't have to do that." Again, the tone put walls between them, shutting him on one side with his pain and closing her out. She wanted to scream and demand that he let her inside, but she couldn't.

"It's no problem. Is there anything I can—" She broke off as he stirred restlessly.

"Look, I hate to be rude, but I'm really beat. I'd like to get some sleep. The way this place is run, they get you up at dawn to take blood samples and poke needles in you." His mouth smiled but he didn't look at her, and his words made the dismissal clear. Polite, gentle but still a dismissal.

Elizabeth stared at him a moment and then got up. She didn't believe for a minute that he was going to go to sleep, but she didn't say anything. If he needed time alone, she'd give it to him.

"I'll come back this evening."

"Sure, that'll be great. I'm sorry I'm so exhausted."

"That's okay." She hesitated. She usually kissed him goodbye when she left, but he didn't look at her and didn't give any indication that a kiss would be welcome. She hovered awkwardly for a moment and then turned away. It was silly to feel hurt. He just needed a little time.

Donovan watched her leave, his hands clenched into fists, the knuckles aching with the pressure. His chest hurt, a burning ache that threatened to eat right through him and leave him bleeding. The door shut behind her, and the room seemed suddenly darker.

He wanted to call her back. He wanted to feel her arms around him and smell the sweet scent of her perfume. But he couldn't do that. Not now. Maybe not ever.

Chapter 15

I swear, these potholes are life threatening. Are you sure they're not bothering your leg too much?'' Elizabeth glanced anxiously at Donovan.

"I'm fine. If my leg was that fragile, they wouldn't have let me out of the hospital.'' The tightness of his smile reminded her not to fuss, and she quelled her concern. She had to keep in mind that Donovan wasn't going to welcome too much fussing. She was almost surprised he hadn't insisted on trying to drive himself home.

Neither of them said anything more until she pulled the car into the driveway. It could have been a comfortable silence, but it wasn't. It seemed as if there were things that no one was saying. Donovan was shutting her out as clearly as if he'd slammed a door in her face. He was pushing away her concern, telling her without words that he didn't need her help. Not hers, not anybody's.

"Well, here we are."

"Here we are." Donovan's agreement held no enthusiasm.

Elizabeth opened her door and circled the front of the car to his side. He was already halfway out the door, maneuvering crutches and a heavily bandaged leg.

"Here, let me help." Her move forward was checked by the ferocity of the look he threw her.

"I don't need any help." The words were accompanied by a smile that would have made a strong man cower. She stood back, her hands at her sides as she watched him struggle to get the crutches solidly under him.

When he was at last upright and more or less on his own two feet, he looked at her again, his smile less threatening but still cool. "I didn't mean to snap at you, but I've got to learn to manage things on my own."

"I understand." She didn't understand at all. Why did he keep her at arm's length? Why did he treat her as if she were a distant relation, someone he didn't know very well and didn't want to know any better?

The front door opened as Donovan reached the bottom of the steps, and Michael rushed out.

"Dad!" Donovan loosened his grip on one crutch enough to return his son's hug. Elizabeth swallowed hard. It hurt to see the warmth of his smile. She loved Donovan, too. Why was he pushing her away?

"How are you feeling?"

"Not bad. It's good to be home."

"It's great to have you back. Here, let me help you up the stairs."

"Thanks." Michael wrapped one arm around his father's waist. Elizabeth trailed behind them, knowing that if she'd made the same offer, Donovan would have thrown it back in her teeth. She couldn't even convince herself that it was because she didn't have the physical strength Michael did.

They made it into the house without incident, though Elizabeth held her breath with every step Donovan took. She didn't even want to think about the kind of damage a fall might do to his knee. Once inside, Donovan leaned on his crutches and drew in a deep breath.

"God, it's nice not to smell antiseptic."

"I made it a point not to clean anything. I figured a little dirt would be a nice change for you."

"Thanks, Michael." Donovan grinned at his son, and Elizabeth fought back her tears. He hadn't smiled at her like that in days. In fact, he'd barely even looked at her.

"Hi, Mom. I didn't mean to ignore you." Elizabeth smiled and returned Michael's hug.

"That's okay."

"You look tired."

"Thanks, Michael. I know I can always depend on you for an ego boost." She smoothed her hand over her hair, aware of Donovan looking at her, his eyes cool and watchful.

"Is there a reason we're all standing in the hall? I don't think it's a good idea for you to be on your feet for too long."

"Are you staying? I thought you'd probably want to get home right away. After spending all that time in the city, you must have a lot of things to catch up on."

Elizabeth stared at Donovan, wondering if it was possible to feel your heart actually break. The words weren't rude. The tone was light, even friendly. But the intent was clear. He didn't want her here. How could she tell him that her apartment wasn't home? *He* was home. She was aware of Michael drawing in a quick breath and knew that he'd caught his father's meaning as clearly as she had.

"I thought you might need some help with dinner and things...." Her voice trailed off, her eyes pleading with him. *I love you. Please, don't push me away.* If Donovan saw the plea, he chose to ignore it.

"I think Michael and I can manage okay. We did before."

"Of course. Silly of me." She smiled, hoping the light was dim enough to conceal the glint of tears in her eyes. "I'll give you a call tomorrow—maybe."

"Don't worry about me, Elizabeth. I'm fine. I really appreciate all the time you've spent on me. I hope it hasn't caused you too many problems."

"No problem. No problem at all." She backed toward the door, hoping he'd change his mind. "I'll see you both later, I guess."

"Sure, Mom. I'll come by tomorrow." Michael hugged her, and she wondered if it was her imagination that his arms held her a little tighter than usual. Maybe he sensed his father's coldness and was trying to make up for it. She blinked rapidly and managed a tight smile.

"Bye." She lifted her hand, hardly able to see Donovan through her tears, and slipped out the door, closing it quietly behind her.

Donovan watched her go without moving, his expression blank. Only the muscle that twitched in his jaw gave any indication of his feeling. He wanted to run after her and take her in his arms and tell her that he hadn't meant to hurt her. His fingers tightened around the crutches. He wasn't going to be running after anyone. Not now, not ever.

"You could have asked her to stay for dinner."

Donovan blinked and looked at Michael. It wasn't hard to see the disapproval in his son's eyes. "I'm sure your mother has a lot of things to do." He turned and thumped his way into the living room, lowering himself into a chair, painfully aware of the awkwardness of his movements.

"She was practically in tears." Michael stood in the doorway, his jaw tight.

"Probably tears of relief that she can get home again." Donovan kept his voice light.

"I don't think that was it. I think you hurt her."

"Well, I didn't mean to."

"I think you did."

Donovan's eyes jerked upward to meet Michael's angry gaze. "Leave it alone, Michael."

"Why?"

"This is between your mother and me. If I hurt her, then I'm sorry, and I'll tell her so myself."

"I don't understand you two at all. You love each other. Any idiot can see that. I thought you were going to get back together. I thought—"

"Drop it!" Donovan swallowed hard, aware that the words had been too loud, too harsh. "There are a lot of things between your mother and me that you can't possibly understand. I said that if I hurt her feelings, then I'll apologize. Satisfied?"

Michael looked far from satisfied, but he knew when to stop pushing. He didn't mention Elizabeth again that evening. It was a pity that Donovan's mind couldn't drop the subject as neatly. He knew that he'd hurt her. It hadn't been his intention, but it had been the result anyway.

Donovan stirred restlessly, the sheets rustling beneath him. His knee ached with a steady, throbbing pain that was beginning to seem almost normal. The doctors had warned him to expect that. It wasn't the pain in his knee that was keeping him awake. It was the gnawing feeling of loss eating into his gut that made sleep impossible.

He hadn't hurt this bad when she left him. Then, he'd had anger and righteous indignation to smother the pain. Now he had nothing. He stirred again, drawing a stabbing pain from his knee that warned him not to forget it was there—as if he could forget.

He didn't have to close his eyes to see the car bearing down on them, the headlights blinding him. He remembered swerving, trying desperately to keep the bike upright and then feeling it going over and knowing there was nothing he could do. And then he'd been sliding down the road, the weight of the bike pinning his leg to the unforgiving macadam even as it dragged him along.

He shuddered, staring up at the dark ceiling, beads of sweat coating his forehead. He didn't need the doctors to tell him he was lucky to be alive. He'd known it from the moment he opened his eyes to see Michael's terrified face staring down at him. And he knew he was lucky he hadn't lost his leg. He was truly grateful for that.

But it didn't change anything. He still had his leg, but it would never be right again. The doctors could talk about him living a full, healthy life, but they weren't the ones with a bent and twisted joint that would never be right again.

And there was nothing in the world he wanted more than to have Beth with him right now, but he didn't want her pity. He didn't need anyone's pity. If she could have come to him out of love, it would have made his

world whole again. But he'd rather do without her forever than know that she'd only come back because she
felt sorry for him.

He closed his eyes, forcing her image from his mind,
willing his body to relax. Sleep. In sleep, he didn't have
to think about what had happened or how things might
have been.

Elizabeth took a deep breath and tightened her grip
on the bag in her left hand. The door in front of her was
familiar, but she couldn't have been more nervous if
she'd been facing a firing squad. Her hand was shaking so badly that she had to try twice before she could
get her finger on the doorbell. She could hear the quiet
chime ringing inside the house.

The early October weather was blustery, hinting at
winter cold. The chill she felt had nothing to do with the
weather. It had to do with what lay behind the door. It
felt strange to be standing on the doorstep, a visitor to
a house that had been her home for more than ten years.

She heard the quiet thump of Donovan's crutches and
shoved her hands into the pockets of her jacket, cross-
ing her fingers in a childish prayer for luck. It had been
almost two weeks since she'd brought him home. Two
weeks that she'd forced herself to stay away. If he
needed time to adjust, she'd given it to him.

None of her silent self-encouragement helped when
the door swung open and she was face-to-face with
Donovan. Her gaze met his, and all her carefully re-
hearsed, cheerful speeches flew out the window. She
could only stare at him, drinking him in. He looked
well. He'd lost some of the hospital pallor and gained a
few pounds. His hair fell in a heavy, black wave onto his
forehead, giving his face a boyishness that softened the

strength of his chin. He was wearing a flannel shirt and a pair of worn jeans, the leg cut open at the seam to make room for the bulk of his cast. The lines around his mouth were too deep and his eyes were too tired, but he'd never looked better to her.

"Elizabeth." If he felt any emotion on seeing her, she couldn't tell. His expression revealed nothing.

"Hi. I thought you might be able to use a good cook. What with Michael in school and all and I know cooking isn't your favorite thing to do and I didn't have any plans for tonight. They had some great steaks at the market and it seemed a pity to waste them. Steak just doesn't taste right if you eat it alone."

She stopped, looking at him with what she hoped was a casually friendly expression. Donovan seemed to hesitate, as if weighing her words, his eyes searching her face.

"Can I come in?"

"Sure. Sorry. I didn't mean to keep you standing on the doorstep." He backed away, the crutches making his movements awkward. She looked away. It hurt to see him shackled. She didn't have to close her eyes to remember the graceful, swinging stride she'd always loved.

Donovan saw her look away and his jaw tightened. He shut the door with more force than was necessary and turned toward the kitchen. He felt clumsy and gawky on the crutches, but he'd grown accustomed to them and had actually begun to take some pride in his ability to maneuver. Seeing them through someone else's eyes, however, made him realize how awkward they must look.

"I was hoping you wouldn't mind if I just dropped in. I brought some wine and I thought maybe I'd throw some potatoes in to bake and we could relax over some wine until it was time to start the steaks." She set the sack on the counter and began to unload it, not looking at Donovan, talking too much.

"That sounds fine." He sounded doubtful, but she pretended not to hear it. She'd determined to make this a wonderful evening, and she was going to do just that, even if she had to drag him along with her.

"I bought a cabernet. I thought it would be nice with the steaks." She set the bottle on the counter and threw him a quick smile.

"Great. You know me. I don't know a cabernet from a Chardonnay." He opened a drawer and took out a corkscrew. Balancing on the crutches, he reached for the bottle. Elizabeth turned away from the oven and saw him preparing to twist the corkscrew into the cork.

"Here. Let me do that." She reached for the bottle, but Donovan's hand tightened, refusing to release the bottle.

"I can do it." The words were quiet but held anger firmly in check. Her eyes jerked to his face. "It's my leg that's crippled, not my hands."

She stepped back, flushing. "I'm sorry. I guess I just got used to worrying about you while you were in the hospital. I guess a wine bottle isn't a real threat, is it?"

"Not unless I drop it on my good foot." His smile was tight, the humor not reaching his eyes.

She turned away, cursing herself. She had to remember that he could manage and he didn't need her to fuss over him.

She scrubbed the potatoes more vigorously than was really necessary. Behind her, there was a subdued pop as the cork left the bottle. She deliberately didn't move to get the wineglasses or offer to pour the wine. Donovan wasn't helpless, and she had to make sure he knew that she realized that. Once the potatoes were in the oven, she turned to him. The wine was sitting on the counter, catching the light and refracting it into deep red patterns on the countertop.

"If you'd bring the wine, we can go into the living room." It obviously galled him to have to ask even that much, but there was no way he could carry a glass of wine and manage his crutches at the same time. Once in the living room, the silence threatened to grow awkward.

"How have you been managing?" She made the question casual, one any friend might ask.

"Fine."

"Have you been into the office?"

"Only once, but Donna brings work out to me."

He was really doing his part to keep up the conversation. How was she going to lead around to the subject of their relationship when he was acting as though they'd never had one?

Donovan swirled his wine, staring down into it. Did she have any idea how beautiful she looked? She was wearing a bright blue sweater that made her skin look milky white. Her hair was caught back in a loose twist, a few strands falling free around her face. He'd never seen her look more beautiful, more desirable. He took a swallow of his wine and glanced at her again. Why was she here?

"How are things at the store? You didn't have any problems because of all the time you spent at the hospital, did you?"

"No, they were very understanding."

"Good."

The room was so quiet they could hear the wind stirring the leaves outside.

"How's your leg?"

"I can't complain. It aches once in a while but nothing major. I'd rather have it there and aching than not there at all."

"We were so scared that you were going to lose it."

He stirred restlessly. "It's all over and done now, so you don't have to worry."

"I can't help but worry about you. A person always worries about someone they care about." *Great.* She sounded like a high school grammar book. *A person.* Why didn't she just come right out and say that she'd been worried about him? She stole a look at his face and then looked away. He didn't look as if he'd welcome her concern.

"That's nice of you, Elizabeth, but I'm fine."

His tone was so cool, pushing her away. She blinked against tears. "You know, for a while there, you called me Beth again."

"I did? Sorry."

"I...kind of liked it. It made me feel like I did when we were kids, when Michael was just a baby."

He stirred restlessly, and she knew it was only the weight of his cast that kept him from getting up and pacing the floor.

"That was a long time ago, Elizabeth."

He used the name deliberately, pushing her away.

"Not all that long." He didn't say anything, and she swallowed hard. "Do you know what day this is?"

Donovan threw her a quick look from under his lashes, his jaw tightening. Did she think he could forget?

"I have no idea." His voice was cool, as if whatever it was, it couldn't possibly be important.

"It's our anniversary."

"I don't think divorced people celebrate anniversaries."

She drew a quick, hurt breath. "We're not divorced."

"Only a matter of time." He took a swallow of his wine, not looking at her.

"Is that what you want? A divorce?"

"Seems the logical step. When two people don't live together anymore, there doesn't seem to be much reason to stay married."

"Donovan, before the accident, you said you wanted me to move back in with you."

"That was before the accident." The icy tone of his words might have stopped her, but she'd come too close to losing him forever to stop now.

"Why should that change the way you feel?"

"When you come that close to dying, it makes you think about a lot of things."

"Don't you . . . don't you want me anymore?"

He swallowed the last of his wine, wishing it was whiskey so that it might burn away some of his pain. She sat there looking like a dream come true and asked if he still wanted her. It was like asking a man dying of thirst. But he wanted her on his terms, not because she thought he needed her.

"Look, you've built a life you like. I've got a life of my own."

"We could combine the two. You thought we could."

"That was before the accident."

"I don't see why that changes anything. I . . . I want to move back in."

The stem of his wineglass snapped. Beth was beside him in an instant, reaching for his hand, but he jerked it away from her, the movement so full of rage that she couldn't move. She knelt next to his chair, staring up at him, watching the cool facade melt into seething anger.

"I don't need your help. I don't need anyone's help. I don't need you."

She sucked in a breath, her eyes shimmering with tears. There was deliberate cruelty in his words. He'd never been deliberately cruel to her.

"Donovan, please. I love you."

He outstretched his uninjured hand as if physically pushing her away. "Stop it. I'm not a fool. It's my leg that's crippled, not my brain. You think I can't manage on my own. That's pity, Beth. Not love. I don't need your pity."

A small kernel of healthy anger stirred beneath her hurt. "I was going to tell you before the accident. In fact, I made up my mind the night it happened. I was going to call you the next morning."

"Bull. I appreciate what you're trying to do, but no thanks. I can manage just fine. I don't want your damned pity."

The anger grew. She had just laid her soul bare to him.

She stood up, dashing her hand impatiently over the tears on her cheeks. "Fine. You don't want my pity, you don't have it. Why should I bother to pity you? You're doing a fine job of feeling sorry for yourself. You just go ahead and sit there and think of yourself as a cripple, but it's not your leg that's keeping you there. It's your thinking. I love you, Donovan Sinclair, and I think you love me. You almost let me go once and you're a damned fool if you let me go again."

She was almost to the door when she heard him call her name.

"Elizabeth." She hesitated. "Beth." She stopped but didn't turn. The tears that flooded her eyes blurred the hallway.

"What?"

"Don't go." She didn't turn, still poised for flight. "I can't chase you." The words held pain, and she turned to find him struggling out of the chair, half balanced on his good leg. His face was white but, looking into his eyes, she knew it wasn't pain. It was fear. Fear of losing her?

"What?" *Please. Please say that you love me.*

"Beth, I…are you…" He stopped and looked at her, and she felt some of the chill fade. "Are you sure it's not just pity?" His eyes showed his fears, his vulnerability.

She swallowed hard, taking a step toward him. "I'm sure."

"I don't know if I believe you but, God, I want to."

"Donovan." She crossed the short distance and put her arms around him. He wavered and then found his balance, his arms coming around her, holding her tightly, his face buried in her hair.

"God, I love you. I love you, but I can't stand it if it's pity."

She drew away, easing him back into the chair and kneeling in front of him. "Don't be an idiot. Who could pity you? You're too stubborn to pity."

His hands cupped her face, drinking in the love in her eyes. "Be sure, Beth. I can watch you leave now, but I don't know if I could later. Don't stay if you aren't sure."

"I'm sure. I've been sure for a long time. I'd have told you sooner, but you had to go and have this stupid accident. And then I thought I was going to lose you."

His thumbs brushed the tears from her cheeks, feeling their healing power. She was crying for him. Not because she felt sorry for him but because she'd almost lost him. The hard knot that had lain in his chest began to dissolve. She loved him. The knowledge held more healing power than all the medicine in the world.

"You're never going to lose me, Beth. I lost you once but never again. I'll never lose sight of the most important thing in the world. You are my world, and without you, everything is gray."

He leaned forward, kissing the dampness from her cheeks. His mouth settled on hers in a kiss full of promise, full of love.

"I love you, Donovan. I'll love you forever."

And he knew it was true.

*   *   *   *   *

SET SAIL FOR THE SOUTH SEAS
with
BESTSELLING AUTHOR
EMILIE RICHARDS

Next month Silhouette Intimate Moments begins a very special miniseries by a very special author. *Tales of the Pacific*, by Emilie Richards, will take you to Hawaii, New Zealand and Australia and introduce you to a group of men and women you will never forget.

In Book One, FROM GLOWING EMBERS, share laughter and tears with Julianna Mason and Gray Sheridan as they overcome the pain of the past and rekindle the love that had brought them together in marriage ten years ago and now, amidst the destructive force of a tropical storm, drives them once more into an embrace without end.

FROM GLOWING EMBERS (Intimate Moments #249) will be available next month. And in coming months look for the rest of the series: SMOKESCREEN (November 1988), RAINBOW FIRE (February 1989) and OUT OF THE ASHES (May 1989). They're all coming your way—only in Silhouette Intimate Moments.

IM249

Silhouette Intimate Moments

COMING NEXT MONTH

#249 FROM GLOWING EMBERS—Emilie Richards

Years ago Julianna had been a poor girl from the wrong side of the tracks who had loved—and married—Gray Sheridan, the richest kid in town. Their life together hadn't worked, but when they met again they were different people except for one thing—the love they shared.

#250 THE SILVER SWAN—Andrea Parnell

Regina Lawton needed a holiday. Too many strange people had been appearing in her life recently: prowlers, detectives and a mysterious man named Pierce Buchannan. But once she got to her vacation paradise, she found Pierce waiting for her—posing a very potent danger to her heart.

#251 SUSPICIOUS MINDS—Paula Detmer Riggs

Naval investigator Roarke McKinley had trusted a woman once, and it had almost cost him his life. Never again, he vowed—and then he met Juliet Prentice. Though she was a suspected spy, his resolve weakened. How could he serve his country if it meant betraying the woman he loved?

#252 BETTER THAN EVER—
Marion Smith Collins

Ryan O'Hara had never brought Bree Fleming anything but trouble. It was just too frightening to fall in love with a cop. This time it wasn't love that brought them together, it was business, but Bree found herself losing her heart all over again.

AVAILABLE THIS MONTH:

#245 HEARTBEATS
Lucy Hamilton

#246 MUSTANG MAN
Lee Magner

#247 DONOVAN'S PROMISE
Dallas Schulze

#248 ANGEL OF MERCY
Heather Graham Pozzessere

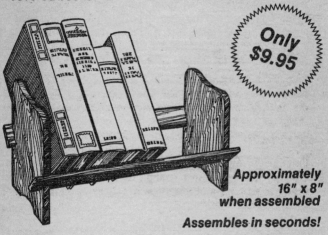

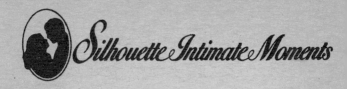

Silhouette Intimate Moments

At Dodd Memorial Hospital, Love is the Best Medicine

When temperatures are rising and pulses are racing, Dodd Memorial Hospital is the place to be. Every doctor, nurse and patient is a heart specialist, and their favorite prescription is a little romance. This month, finish Lucy Hamilton's Dodd Memorial Hospital Trilogy with HEARTBEATS, IM #245.

Nurse Vanessa Rice thought police sergeant Clay Williams was the most annoying man she knew. Then he showed up at Dodd Memorial with a gunshot wound, and the least she could do was be friends with him—if he'd let her. But Clay was interested in something more, and Vanessa didn't want that kind of commitment. She had a career that was important to her, and there was no room in her life for any man. But Clay was determined to show her that they could have a future together—and that there are times when the patient knows best.

Himouto (干物妹)

A lazy little sister who never lifts a finger around the house.
"At home, Umaru is a himouto."
Origin: a portmanteau of imouto (little sister) and himono (a woman who is elegant and polished in public, but secretly a slob at home).

From Shueisha's *Imouto Dictionary*.

Characters

Inside

Blob
Inside Umaru

Master →

Taihei's little sister. Once she steps through the front door, she turns into an irresponsible slob whose motto is, "Eat, sleep (Zzz...), play!" ♪

Siblings

Taihei

Umaru's big brother. He has an office job, but he also works a second job doing chores and generally being a "house-husband."

Story

In the outside world, Taihei's sis Umaru is the perfect high school girl, ♥ beloved and envied by all. But this beautiful little sister has a big secret!! Once she steps across the threshold into their home, she indulges in the himouto lifestyle of lazing around, ♪ here, there, and everywhere!! ♪ When Umaru's classmate Kirie accidentally witnesses her "inside face," Umaru avoids trouble by claiming to be "Komaru, Umaru's little sister"... With a new friend thrown into the mix, Umaru's self-indulgent lifestyle and himouto world is slowly but surely expanding...!

UMR

Umaru's second secret persona: a genius gamer who dominates the arcades. Nabs crane game prizes in a single shot!!

Beauty
Outside Umaru

Drop-dead gorgeous. Smart, talented, and athletic. A perfect beauty admired by all. But actually, she's...?

Outside

Idolizes

Tachibana Sylphynford

Umaru's classmate. A biracial rich girl who is smart and athletic but a bit of a spazz. Sees Umaru as a rival.

Motoba Kirie

Umaru's classmate. A lone wolf who doesn't fit in. People think she's scary because she glares a lot and hardly ever talks. Apparently, she has some interest in Umaru, as well as her "little sister"...

Ebina Nana

Umaru's classmate and apartment neighbor. She's from a farming family in Akita, and sometimes her accent slips out. Very polite and kind of shy.

Siblings

Alex

Taihei's junior at work.

Bomba

Taihei's coworker and Kirie's big bro.

Section Chief Kanau

Taihei's boss.

HIMOUTO! UMARU-CHAN 3

CONTENTS

I'LL NEVER GET TIRED OF WATCHING THIS GUY.

NICA NICA VIDEO (Z)

NASSU ALWAYS CRACKS ME UP.

HURR HA HA HA!

AH HA HA!

I'M CONNECTED TO THE **WHOLE WORLD** RIGHT NOW!

LOUNGE
LOUNGE

GETTING TO WATCH AWESOME FUNNY STUFF FOR **FREE**... THE NET IS **AMAZING**.

Tilt~

OUCH! WHACK

THUNK

SLOOSH

SLIIIDE

GOTTA SAVE IIIIT!!

SHE'S GONNA BLOOOOW!!

IT EVEN GOT UNDER THE DESK...

SCRUB SCRUB

JEEEEEZ... I SPILLED MY COLA... WHAT A WASTE!

fzzzz—

FLICKER
FLICKER

SST

Scrub scrub

WHAT'RE ALL THESE BLINKY LIGHTS...?

WHAT'S THIS BOX THINGY? WHAT'S IT DOING UNDER HERE...?

V W M

⚠

Unable to connect to the Internet.

ドキ ドキ ドキ ドキ
BADUM BADUM BADUM BADUM

Klika
Klika

7

NET PC

MODEM

AND I SPILLED COLA ON IT... IT'S DEAD FOR SURE!!

TH...THIS IS BAD...!! THAT BOX MUST BE THE THINGY THAT CONNECTS US TO THE INTERNET !!!

NWAAAAHHH!!

AH!!

ROLL ROLL ROLL

I KNOW!! I'LL ASK YAPOO QUESTIONS!!

what do I do?! I can't use the internet!!

Wh wh...

WHOOM

I HAVE THIS TABLET I NAGGED ONIICHAN INTO BUYING FOR ME... THE NET SHOULD WORK ON I--

AHA!

DUH!! I CAN'T LOOK IT UP BECAUSE I CAN'T GET ON-LINE!!

VWM

e to connect he Internet.

NUAAAH!!

8

WITHOUT THE INTERNET, I'M CUT OFF FROM THE WORLD...

I DON'T... I DON'T HAVE MY INTERNETS...

UUUGH...

Unable to connect to Wi-fi.

NET
PC
mog pad
wifi
MODEM

CRAP, IT'S ON WI-FI!!

SOOB

mog Pad

Cannot install updates because there is no Internet connection.

THWUD

TO THINK ONE LITTLE COLA SPILL COULD CREATE SUCH CHAOS...

CRAWL CRAWL

I GUESS I'LL CALM MYSELF DOWN WITH SOME VIDEO GAMES...

chk

WHRRR...

AND I'M HERE TO CHILL!!

Rattle rattle

I'M HOME...

IS CUT OFF FROM THE WORLD!!

⚠

Unable to connect to the Internet.

UMA-RU...

CLAA-

NG

THE MO- DEM'S BUSTED?

OHHH ...

DOOOOOM

WHAT THE--?!

GLOOM

IT SAYS GETTING IT WET WHILE IT'S ON CAN DAMAGE IT, SO IT'LL NEED REPAIRS.

SHAKE SHAKE SHAKE SHAKE

NASSU- UUU!!

HUH?

HEY, TANU- KICHI.

10

C'MON, TAIHEI. YOUR TURN.

WHAT'S SO FUNNY ABOUT THAT?

TUMBLE TUMBLE

BWAH HA HA HA HA HA!!

HEH HEH HEH!

WON IT AT PACHINKO.

SERIOUSLY, WHAT'S WITH THE MASK?

HURR HA HA HA!! IT'S SUCH A GREAT FACE... BUT SO PATHETIC ...!!

ROLL ROLL ROLL—

. . . . . RABBLE— RABBLE—

DUDE, THESE ARE NOT THE RULES I KNOW!!

HUH?! WHAT HAPPENS WHEN YOU HAVE A JOKER REVOLUTION, TANUKICHI?!

THREE IS THE STRONGEST!

DUDE! ARE YOU KIDDIN' ME?!

TA-DAAA

READ 'EM AND WEEP, BOYS!!

IT'S A HAMSTER HOOD.

'CAUSE OF HER TANUKI HOOD.

YUP.

BY THE WAY...IS "TANUKICHI" SUPPOSED TO REFER TO UMARU?

JUST GO TO A MANGA CAFÉ OR SOMETHING.

POUT

NEWS

WHEN I WHINED ABOUT THE NET BEING OUT AT HOME, ONIICHAN GAVE ME MONEY!

The reason the net is out.

?

BEEEAM

MY FIRST MANGA CAFÉ!!

14

THREE...

HMMM...

NO...

PACKAGES

7 HOURS: 1,4

5 HOURS: 1,00

3 HOURS: 680円

1 HOUR: 400円

HOW MANY HOURS WOULD YOU LIKE?

PHEW...

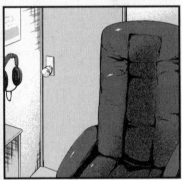

I WENT AND RENTED THIS SPACE FOR SEVEN WHOLE HOURS...

BADUM

BADUM

UH-OH...

LIKE I MADE MYSELF A SECRET BASE...!!

IT ALMOST FEELS...

AND NOT JUST THIS BOOTH. THEY'RE ALL LIKE THIS!

SO TINY!!

PEEK

Shonen Jumpu

uhyoohh! ✨

IT'S LIKE THE WORLD'S MOST COMFORTABLE SECRET BASE!

PLUS, THERE'S ALL THE INTERNET I CAN BROWSE, ALL THE MANGA I CAN READ, AND ALL THE DRINKS I CAN DRINK!!

TIP-TOE

TIP-TOE

→ Sneaking for some reason.

There's ice cream, too?!

PLUS, SINCE I'M ALONE...

NFU FU...

RUMMAGE RUMMAGE

I'M GONNA BINGE READ THREE LONG-RUNNING MANGA SERIES TODAY.

HEH HEH HEH...

16

HUH? WHAT'S THIS THING?

YUP, IT DON'T GET MORE COMFY THAN THIS.

I CAN TOTALLY WEAR MY HAMSTER HOOD!!

EVEN THOUGH I'M AWAY FROM HOME...

THIS IS...

TH...

THIS BASE IS BETTER THAN MY OWN HOME!!

A... A MASSAGE!! I EVEN HAVE A MASSAGE CHAIR...?!

WH...

WHAAAAT?!

HEH HEH HEH...

BRYNHILDR IN THE LIGHTNESS 9

17

I NEVER WANNA LEAVE.

だっらああ LOUUUNGE

THIS IS THE LIFE.

TIK TOK

Time Remaining

4:00

SILENCE...

GOTTA MAKE 'EM THE BEST SIX HOURS EVAH!

I STILL HAVE SIX HOURS LEFT...

TAKA TAKA

· · · · · · ·

· · · · · · ·

IF YOU LEAVE NOW, YOU'LL LOSE YOUR REMAIN-ING FOUR HOURS. ARE YOU SURE?

I SEE HERE THAT YOU PUR-CHASED THE SEVEN-HOUR PACK-AGE...

CASHE

IT'S FINE.

WHAT...? WE JUST HAD PIZZA THE OTHER DAY.

OOH, OOH-- ONII-- CHAN! LET'S GET A **PIZZA** FOR LUNCH!

ブー WHFFR

ブー WHFFR

SUN- DAY.

. . . .

WHO COULD THAT BE?

DING DOOONG

HUH?

YOU NEED TO EAT BET- TER--

PIZZA

AH! UMARU-CHAN! HELLO!

UMARUUUUN

GOOD AFTERNOON, EBINA-CHAN!

OH!

G...good afternoon, Onii-san...

EBINA-CHAN!

Ah!

Erm... No...

DID YOU WANT TO GO OUT WITH UMARU?

J'R R R

M B L オ オ

REALLY? THAT'S HIGH-QUALITY RICE! THANKS!

M...my family sent me a bunch of Akita Komachi rice...! I'd like you to have some!

Akita Komachi

HEAVE

G Y U R F R

E L G R

22

URGGG...

BLUUUSH

To thank you for this awesome gift.

Eh?!

Would you like to stay for lunch?

...

!

WHIRL

I'm s-s-s...so sorry... my stomach...

Akita Komachi

Heh heh heh...

This is perfect...

Akita Komachi

10k

!

GLANCE

?

23

CHARCOAL TAKES A LONG TIME... BUT THIS IS SPECIAL RICE, SO...

FSSHI

LET'S DO THIS RIGHT AND COOK IT IN A TRADITIONAL EARTHENWARE POT!

I'LL SHOW HER HOW GOOD A PROPER MEAL CAN BE...!!!

UMARU'S ALWAYS STUFFING HER FACE WITH JUNK FOOD...

RRRRR

UMBL

AH... BUT...

AS IN PIZZA!

IT WOULD REALLY BE BETTER IF WE ALL WENT OUT TO EAT TOGETHER, THOUGH.

WIPE WIPE

IT'S OKAY! I'M GLAD I GET TO EAT WITH YOU.

FSSHH

SORRY. LOOKS LIKE ONII-CHAN'S IN THE ZONE.

EBINA-CHAN...

． ． ． ． ． ． ．

GETTING TO SHARE A REAL HOME-COOKED MEAL WITH FRIENDS MAKES ME HAPPY...

I...

I ALWAYS EAT ALONE, SO...

LUNCH IS SERVED.

Rattle rattle

?

!

FIDGET

FIDGET

FIDGET

....

OKAY! LET'S DIG IN.

UGH... SO MANY VEGGIES...

WAAAH—

AND I PICKED SIDES THAT I THOUGHT WOULD COMPLEMENT IT BEST.

I COOKED THE RICE IN A CLAY POT.

MUNCH

!

STREEETCH

WHY COULDN'T THIS BE PIZZA...?

LET'S EAT!

MRRRN...

?

BEEAM

THIS IS DELI-CIOUS!

OH! IT'S FINE!

PANIC PANIC PANIC

Ah...! Excuse me... My accent slipped...

ERR-RM ...

So gol durn tasty...

26

THANK YOU FOR THE FOOD!

THAT AKITA RICE WAS FANTAS-TIC.

AH...!

AYUP!

"AYUP"?!

THAT MEANS "RE-ALLY GOOD," RIGHT?

"GOL DURN TASTY."

Waaah—

GYURRGLGL...

SURE THING. COME AGAIN SOME-TIME.

UM...
THANK YOU SO MUCH FOR ASKING ME TO STAY FOR LUNCH.

がああああああ
FLUUUAAH

IS SHE TRYING TO SUPPRESS HUNGER PANGS...?

SQUIRM

SQUIRM

SQUIRM

THE WAY SHE'S HOLDING HERSELF...

Oh, n-n-no!! I-It was plenty!

FIDGET

YOU STILL HUNGRY?

NOT YOU TOO, EBINA?!

UM... THEN...

MAYBE A SMALL ONE...?

PIZZA...?! I DON'T KNOW...THAT WOULD BE A LOT AFTER A WHOLE MEAL...

HUH?!

ONII-CHAN.

WHY DON'T WE ORDER A PIZZA?

Meoww——

Meoww——

Meoww——

FWAP

ONII-CHAN! IT'S SNOW-ING!!

LOOKS LIKE I'D BE BET-TER OFF STAYING IN.

I WAS GOING TO GO TO THE SUPER-MARKET, BUT...

IT'S SO WHITE OUT-SIDE! THINK IT'S GONNA STICK?

SNOW, HUH...? NO WONDER IT'S SO COLD.

BUST OUT? WHAT?

YOU KNOW, THERE'S SOMETHING I WAS GOING TO BUST OUT AFTER SHOPPING.

YEAH, RIGHT. YOU'RE ONLY GOING TO PLAY VIDEO GAMES!

Expert, huh?

C'mon! Sit your butt down!

PLEASE ALLOW YOUR FRIENDLY NEIGH-BORHOOD SHUT-IN EXPERT TO PLAN YOUR BUSY AND PRODUCTIVE DAY IN!

S W E E T !!

SMAK
SMAK

THE KOTA...!

THE KO-TATSU.

UMARUOOON

SO, THIS IS WHAT IT TAKES TO GET HER UP OFF HER BUTT...

HOW MAY I BE OF ASSIS-TANCE, ONII-CHAN?

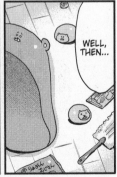

WELL, THEN...

DON'T JUST SHOVE IT INTO A PILE!!

shuv shuv shuv—

THERE WE GO!

AWWW...

FIRST, YOU CAN PICK UP YOUR MESS!

I'LL TURN OVER A NEW LEAF NEXT YEAR.

CHAOS

SHEESH... WHERE WOULD SHE BE WITHOUT ME...?

EEEK!

WHFFF

SHP
SHP
SHP
SHP
SHP

Burnable

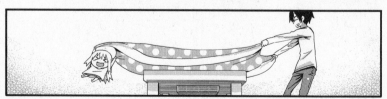

DIVE—

HAAAA!

GET OUT OF THERE!!

IT'S READY!!

じんわーーーり

SHIVERRRR

NWOP

SUCH ENERGY...

byuun

AH!! SINCE WE'VE GOT THE KOTATSU OUT, I GOTTA GRAB A BUNCH OF STUFF!

IT FEELS LIKE... HEAVEN. HOW IS THIS POSSIBLE?

SUCH A TINY SQUARE SPACE, AND YET...

NOW THIS...

IS PARADISE!!

SILENCE...

Z Z Z...

TOO BAD WE DON'T HAVE MANDA-RINS. MAYBE I'LL GET SOME TOMOR-ROW.

TOASTY WARM

AHHH...

YOU'RE GONNA CATCH A COLD!

HEY, UMARU! WAKE UP!

LEAN

I'D BETTER WAKE HER UP... IT CAN'T BE HEALTHY TO SLEEP IN SUCH UNEVEN HEAT...

WELL... SO MUCH FOR ALL THAT ENERGY...

Umaru Thermal Image

36

I GUESS ONE HOUR WON'T KILL HER.

SLOP
SLOP SLOP SLOP
SLOP

SLOP

BAM

AH! I GOT IT!

YOU'RE MAKIN' SWEETS, AREN'T YA?

H... HÄÄH ?!

I'M NOT DOING ANY-THING!!

JOLT

WAZZAT? YOU WHIPPIN' UP A CURSE OR SOME-THIN'?

QU... QUIT IT!!

IT...

C'MON, tell yer big bro!

WHAT'S UP WITH THAT? NOT LIKE YOU HAVE ANY FRIENDS TO GIVE 'EM TO. SO WHAT GIVES?!

IT'S...

NOTH-ING. REALLY...

? SHUP

THEN I SEE DO YOUR BEST. ...

WHMM...

"Let's bake them together sometime!"

"I'd sure like to eat your cookies again."

"Kirie-chan, you're so skilled!"

BLUSH BLUSH GRIN GRIN

Become Better at

"THANK YOU!"

"EH? KIRIE-CHAN, YOU MADE THESE COOKIES FOR ME?"

GACK!!

もわわわ
SMOKE SMOKE SMOKE

Become Better at speaking to People

Break the Ice with Homemade Sweets

For instance, during breaks.

You should get a conversation rolling!

Introduce Topics Proactiv

AND BAKE A NEW BATCH.

I'LL PUT THEM ASIDE...

GROSS...

UGH...

I CAN'T GIVE THESE TO UMARU-SAN.

CRUNCH!!

CRUNCH

"WELL DONE, MY LOYAL HENCH-WOMAN!!"

I HOPE SHE LIKES THEM.

PATTER

THE COOKIES FOR MASTER TURNED OUT GREAT!

YO.

I'LL PUT THEM IN THIS.

rattle

♪

LEAVIN' 'EM SITTIN' AROUND WITHOUT A WORD.

SHEESH. NO NEED TO BE ALL TIMID.

CRUUNCH

CRUNCH CRRRNCH

USE MORE SUGAR NEXT TIME, THOUGH.

YOU COULDA JUST SAID SO!

YOU BAKED THESE COOKIES FOR ME, RIGHT?

BEAM

YOWCH!!

SMACK

HUH?! WHAT?! WHAT'RE YOU DOIN', KIDDO?!

JOLT

DOOOM...

Tra la la!♪
Tra la la!♪

....

DUUN

Um! These are for...!

WHACK

HM?

U...

Umaru-san!!

44

ズザァァ SK チチ

THANK YOU!

YOU MADE COOKIES FOR ME?

ARE YOU ALL RIGHT ?!

KIRIE-CHAN!

MURMUR   MURMUR

KIRIE-CHAN...

CRAP! CRAP!

CRAP!

Ex...

excuse me...!!

GRIIIN

YUM-MY!!

MNCH MNCH

REALLY?

THANKS! CHOCOLATE, HUH?

SHE SAID THOSE ARE FOR YOU.

Guest Illustrator: Hiroyuki Shoji

GUESS WE NEED TO GET A NEW SET OF GLASSES...

CLINK

CLINK

FSSH

IT'S CRACKED.

AH!

THE EVERYTHING STORE

ISN'T THIS AMAZING, UMARU?! YOU CAN BUY ANYTHING HERE FOR A HUNDRED YEN!! ANYTHING!!

RAH!

Everything 100 yen

Everything 100 yen

Everything 100 yen

WHOA!! THIS SECTION'S NEW!

UH-HUH, SURE...

. . . . . .

BUT THERE REALLY ISN'T MUCH HERE THAT I'M INTERESTED IN...

ONII-CHAN SURE IS EXCITED...

I CAN'T BELIEVE WE TOOK THE TRAIN TO A HUNDRED-YEN SHOP...

fidget fidget

HMPH... HE SAID HE WAS TAKING ME SOMEPLACE FUN!...

MRR GRR GRR...

PARTY GOODS

Balding Wig

Whoops! My Ear Got Big!!

Funny Glasses

Afro

49

THAT MEANS I COULD BUY A NEW TOY EVERY DAY!

WOW... THEY'RE EVEN SELLING *DOLLS* FOR 100 YEN...!

WAIT, WHAT THE WHAT?!

Only loo yen?!

oniichaaan!

TOY SNAKE.

SQUIRT GUN.

oniichaaan!

okay, maybe not...

ONII-CHAA-AN!!

PINCHI

BUT FORGET CUPS-- NOW THEY'VE GOT TEA SETS AND EVEN MUGS!

I ALWAYS THOUGHT IT WOULD BE NICE IF THEY HAD A BIGGER SELECTION OF CUPS...

AH.

AH! ONII-CHAN! *THERE YOU ARE!*

PWOP

YOU CAN EVEN STAND THE LID UP?! THAT'S SO USEFUL!!

KAHH!

WHAT THE...?! A LID HANDLE FOR ONLY 100 YEN?!

STANDARD POT LID 100円

YOU CAN USE IT TO SQUIRT SOY SAUCE, CHILI SAUCE, AND VINEGAR ON YOUR GYOZA ALL AT THE SAME TIME...!

Super-convenient!!

LOOK AT THIS!!

Gyoza

BEAM

OH, OH! SINCE IT'S ONLY 100 YEN, CAN WE GET THIS, TOO?

ALL RIGHT! I'M GONNA GET A BASKET!!

GO FOR IT! IT'S ONLY 100 YEN, AFTER ALL!

verything Store

TWING

THAT'S SO USEFUL!!

FAGH!

FFT

CHK

CHIRP... CHIRP...

Good morning.

CHIRP... CHIRP...

LOOKS LIKE I IMPULSE-BOUGHT A BUNCH OF USELESS JUNK, TOO...

I BOUGHT SO MUCH STUFF SINCE IT WAS ALL JUST 100 YEN...

TWEET TWEET TWEET...

TWEET TWEET...

World Clocks

Useful! REMOTE Holder-kun

I GUESS I GOT A LITTLE CARRIED AWAY...

NOW THAT I THINK BACK ON IT, UMARU SEEMED BORED...

Rattle rattle

"Uh-huh, sure."

AH!

ONIICHAN, G'MORNING!

NOTH-ING...

THAT WAS REALLY FUNNY!

ONII-CHAN!!

MY EAR GOT HUGE!!

SHOOP

HUH? WHAT'S WRONG?

．．．．．．．．

OOH!!

GREAT IDEA!

WHY DON'T YOU HAVE KIRIE-CHAN COME OVER AND SHOW HER THAT?

STICK

MERRY Christmas

Xmas

DECEMBER 24TH.

TONIGHT IS CHRISTMAS EVE.

MERR-RRY...

CHRIST-MAS!!

Merrry Christ-maaas!

4ND-BACK

NOPE! IT'LL BE A PERFECT, LAZY CHRISTMAS NIGHT AT HOME, SCARFING COOKIES AND WATCHING TV!

BUT UMARU'S NOT GONNA SET ONE FOOT OUT THE DOOR!!

YASS!! TONIGHT, EVERYONE WILL BE RUNNING AROUND CHECKING OUT THE CHRISTMAS LIGHTS...

JUST HAVE TO WAIT FOR ONIICHAN TO GET HOME FROM WORK.

LOUNGE LOUNGE

NOW, THEN...

OVERTIME ON CHRISTMAS EVE...

TAKA TAKA TAKA TAKA TAKA TAKA TAKA

HEY, TAIHEI. LET'S BOTH DITCH THIS STUPID COMPANY.

THERE'S NOT MUCH LEFT. HANG IN THERE.

PILED HIGH

WHOA! DON'T SAY STUFF LIKE THAT OUT LOUD.

THIS IS MESSED UP!! THE HECK IS WRONG WITH THIS PLACE?!

ACK.

GOOD POINT...

IF YOU ORDER IT ON CHRISTMAS, IT WON'T GET DELIVERED IN TIME, IDIOT.

SANTA COSTUMES.

YOU WANNA WEAR ONE, TOO?

WHAT ARE YOU LOOKING AT, ANYWAY?

Santa Costume

3,980 yen free Shipping

Add to Cart

In Stock   Favorite

Reviews ★★★★★

500 points

DON'T LET THE DOOR HIT YOU IN THE BUTT, AFRO.

GRIN

Ah...! Section Chief Kanau! We were just taking a little break...

NRRRL

ジロっ

HOW ARE THOSE CHECKS COMING ALONG?

I- IT'S NO PROB- LEM.

SORRY YOU HAVE TO WORK ON CHRIST- MAS, TAIHEI.

Um...

I, ah, can't see my screen.

SAY, TAIHEI... DO YOU HAVE ANY **PLANS** FOR TO- NIGHT?

O-oh... thank you very much.

YOUR LAST PROJECT PROPOSAL WAS GREAT. UPPER MAN- AGEMENT SUCKS FOR REJECTING IT.

KIRIE-CHAN ISN'T TWEETING TODAY...

tmetter

HRRRM...

Kirierin

355 Tweets 30 Following 1 Followers [Following]

Tweets

Who to Follow

......

I WONDER IF THEY'RE ALL DOING STUFF TOGETHER.

AND EBINA-CHAN WENT TO VISIT HER FAMILY...

TIK

TOK

JINGLE

JINGLE

JINGLE

Live Christmas Concert

59

FIDGET

FIDGET

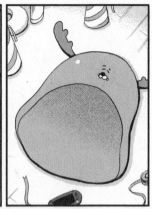

DING DOOONG

JOLT

U-UM... NO... I...

We just ran into each other.

?

HUH? DIDN'T YOU HAVE ANY CHRISTMAS PLANS, KIRIE-SAN?

ONII-CHAN!! KIRIE-CHAN!!

!

Shwup!!

I BOUGHT A CHRISTMAS GIFT FOR MASTER... SO...

K.has

ERR... I PICKED THIS UP WITH MY COWORKER. HE SAID WE SHOULD WEAR THEM HOME SINCE IT'S CHRISTMAS AND ALL...

O... ONIISAN, WHY ARE YOU DRESSED AS SANTA?

PING

SO SHE IS.

AH!! M-MASTER, YOU'RE A REIN-DEER TODAY!!

Merry Christmas, Umaru-chan! Akita is a winter wonderland~!

YUP, I SURE AM!

HEH HEH HEH...

MERRY CHRIST-MAS!

HUH?

WASSUP, *KIRIEEE?!* SANTA IS IN DA HOUSE!!

On nights when the moon appears reflected in the water, the curious flying fish appear. So, too, does umaru-chan now pitch her tent in anticipation.

I wanna play video games!

I have knitting to do.

Hey!! Let's go on a family drive!!

L A A A A Z E

YAAAAY!!

Take your whole house for a drive in a Dekan-tea!!

NEW DEKANTEA

is a Dekan-tea!!

No prob-lem!!

Because our car...

♪ Bigger is Better!

Test drive one today at your local Doyota dealer!

....

WHAT AM I GOING TO DO WITH YOU...?

Groggy groggy groggy

'm still sleepy...

Whaaaat ...? Ten more minutes ...

SNOOZE SNOOZE

UMARU! WAKE UP! YOU'LL BE LATE FOR SCHOOL!

SHAKE SHAKE

Twing

Skreek?

Senbei rice crackers

WAKE ME UP WHEN WE'RE CLOSE TO THE SCHOOL.

WHAMMM

FINE, YOU CAN SLEEP IN THE CAR!

64

W-WELL, YEAH... I DO...

How'd you know that?

YOU *DO* HAVE A DRIVER'S LICENSE, RIGHT?

A... A CAR?

Fssh—

WAIT... HOLD ON...!!

I TAKE THE TRAIN TO WORK, SO I DON'T NEED A...

THAT GUY NEEDS TO LEARN TO KEEP HIS MOUTH SHUT...

We got our licenses together.

BOMBER SAID YOU GOT A PERFECT SCORE AT DRIVING SCHOOL.

WHUUUH?! FOR REALZ?!

OKAY... WE CAN GO, BUT WE'RE ONLY GOING TO LOOK...

Hmmmm...

I DON'T KNOW WHAT BROUGHT THIS ON, BUT I PROBABLY SHOULDN'T LET THIS CHANCE SLIP AWAY...

?

UMARU ALMOST NEVER SHOWS INTEREST IN ANYTHING OUTSIDE THE HOUSE...

APPARENTLY, YOU CAN RENT A SPOT FOR 4,000 YEN A MONTH.

I DIDN'T KNOW OUR BUILDING EVEN *HAD A* PARKING LOT.

W O O O W...

THERE'S A **TAX BREAK** ON HYBRIDS ...?

I SEE...

I GUESS THE LOWER GAS MILEAGE MAKES A REAL DIFFERENCE, TOO?

THEY MAKE THESE ECO-FRIENDLY CARS A GREAT DEAL!

YES, SIR!!

CAR

HM?

ONII-CHAN! ONII-CHAN!

AND I THOUGHT MY JOB WAS ROUGH...

Relentless sales pitch

GRAAAH

OH, OF COURSE!! EVEN WITHIN THE SAME MODEL, GASOLINE MILEAGE IS...

System support tech.

URGH...!

Kantea (・・・・)

2,000,000 円

AH, CRAP-- SHE GOT INTO IT...!!

HONK HOOONK

LOOK! IT'S THE DEKAN-TEA! IT'S GINOR-MOUS!

DEKANTEA

!

IT'S... BETTER TO HAVE A BIGGER ONE, IN CASE WE EVER WANT TO GO OUT WITH EBINA-CHAN AND KIRIE-CHAN! DUH!

You could fit eight people in this thing!

EH? WH... WHY?

WHY WOULD WE NEED SUCH A BIG CAR WHEN THERE'S ONLY TWO OF US?

CARE TO TAKE IT FOR A SPIN?

WHAT DO YOU THINK?

SO MUCH SPACE

HUHN... SO, SHE WAS THINKING OF HER FRIENDS ...?

IT'S THE COM- MERCIAL FOR THIS CAR!

AH! THE TV'S ON!

DEKAXTER

WHY DID YOU BRING YOUR HOOD HERE?

FLOP

FLOP

WOO- HOO! IT'S HUGE!

YAAAAY!!

Take your whole house for a drive in a Dekan-tea!!

HUGE CAR

UMARU IN THE HOSPITAL

OPEN ROADS

LIVES AT STAKE

KIDS RUNNING OUT

TERRIBLE ACCIDENT

ACCIDENT DURING TEST DRIVE

ACTUAL TRAFFIC

Inch...

inch...

inch...

Inch...

Inch...

iiinch...

WHOA!!

A cat!!

SCREECH

THEY DIDN'T GET A CAR.

BADUM

BADUM

BADUM

Umaru & New Year's Eve

EHH... ACTUALLY, IT WAS PRETTY AWFUL, SINCE I GOT SICK AND STUFF...

HOW 'BOUT YOU, TAIHEI?

All you viewers out there, how was your 2013?

New Year's Eve Around the World

The year's almost over!

LIVE

I WANT TO EAT SUKIYAKI AGAIN!

NEXT YEAR...

THAT WAS LITERALLY DAYS AGO.

MY GREATEST 2013 MEMORY IS... GETTING TO BE SANTA.

I WANNA GO TO THAT RAMEN PLACE AGAIN, TOO!

LIKE HOW WE ATE IT THAT ONE TIME.

OH YEAH...

SUKIYAKI? YOU MEAN KANSAI-STYLE?

DECEMBER 31ST.

73

OH, RE-ALLY...? AKITA, HUH...?

SHE'S MY FRIEND. SHE'S VISITING HER FAMILY IN AKITA RIGHT NOW.

Ayup.

WHO'S EBINA-CHAN?

NYOOP

WE SHOULD GO WHEN EBINA-CHAN GETS BACK.

Masterrr!!

OH YEAH... I MADE FRIENDS WITH KIRIE-CHAN THIS YEAR, TOO.

THE PAST TWELVE MONTHS HAVE BEEN PRETTY EVENTFUL, NOW THAT I THINK ABOUT IT.

SPEAKING OF EBINA-CHAN, SHE CAME TO LIVE IN THIS BUILDING JUST THIS YEAR, DIDN'T SHE?

LIVE

BOOONG

LIVE

SHOULD WE GO ON OUR NEW YEAR'S SHRINE VISIT LATER, AS A GROUP?

WHOA! THAT SHRINE IS PACKED.

MY LITTLE SIS IS LIKE THIS TOTAL SPITFIRE, YA KNOW? I BET SHE'S JUST TRYIN' TO HIDE HOW SHE'S SHY AROUND ME, THOUGH.

oh yeah...?

MAYBE I SHOULD'VE INVITED HER OVER TODAY...

WELL, *DUH!* I WANNA SEE THE FIRST SUNRISE OF THE NEW YEAR, TOO!

UMARU, ARE YOU SERIOUSLY STAYING UP FOR THE MIDNIGHT COUNTDOWN?

....

MIND IF WE WATCH *YOU LAUGH YOU LOSE?*

You Laugh You Lose, New Year's Eve Special

Tanaka: Out

THAT'S CRAZY TALK, ONIICHAN! WE GOTTA BE IN THE KOTATSU FOR THE COUNTDOWN!!

HEH HEH HEH...

WHAT KIND OF NEW YEAR'S PARTY IS *THAT?*

¡Arriba, arriba!

WHAT'S IT GONNA BE, ONIICHAN? THE SAMBA?

WHEE!

WHEE!

PM 11:30
12/31 | Tues

HUH?

CLATTER

SO, TAIHEI-- SHALL WE GET THIS PARTY STARTED?

Zaaaa

Kaki no

KAKI NO TANE (SOY RICE CRISPS AND PEANUTS SNACK).

CHIIING

EDAM- AME.

CHIING

SKEWERED CHICKEN.

ON NEW YEAR'S EVE...

YOU GOTTA DRINK, BRAH!!

PATTER

SINCE UMARU'S STAYING UP THIS YEAR, I FIGURED I'D KEEP IT DRY...

"BUT"?!

UH, BOM-BA... THANKS FOR BRINGING ALL THIS, BUT...

SHWAAA

ICE CREAM.

MELON BREAD

SNACK BREAD.

PLOP

PRING-LEZ.

Crispy

TAM

THIS IS ALL SODA?!

ド ド Dun-duun い？

NO PROPER FEAST IS COMPLETE WITHOUT SODA!!

SHE'S DEVELOPED A COLA THEORY!!

☆ Umarun Ranking ☠

☆	Cola	☠
☆	Melon Soda	☠
☆	Lemon Soda	☠
☆	Plain Old Soda	☠
☆	Ginger Ale	☠

CLASSIC COLA IS THE BEST DRINK TO GO WITH SNACKS! THE NEXT BEST THING IS MELON SODA. ITS SWEETNESS BRINGS OUT THE SALTINESS OF THE SNACKS.

HEH HEH HEH... NOTHING BUT THE BEST FOR NEW YEAR'S!

WHOA, WHOA, WHOA... THIS IS REAL COLA, NOT THE GENERIC STUFF!!

SIGH...

ACK!

WOW, BOMBER. YOUR SNACKS ARE LIKE A MEAL.

HEY, THERE'S MORE TO FINGER FOOD THAN JUST JUNK FOOD.

WHEN DID I DO THAT?!

Party is a go!!

YASS!! PERMISSION GRANTED!!

YUP, 'CAUSE IT'S CHOCOLATE! THAT GIVES IT A DIFFERENT TEXTURE, TOO!

WAH!! THE TASTE OF ICE CREAM AFTER KAKI NO TANE IS TO DIE FOR!!

MMMM... THE MEAT AND THE CHIPS ARE MELTING TOGETHER IN MY MOUTH.

CHEW CRUNCH CHEW

SWEET!! THIS IS THE FIRST TIME I'VE EATEN CHICKEN SKEWERS AND CHIPS AT ONCE!!

Hey! Eat the onion, too!

CHUUUG

PW

OP

SSST

SIP

AH.

SHE'S OUT COLD, HUH?

YEP.

NAH, LET HER SLEEP.

I'll get out the futon.

AREN'T WE GONNA WAKE HER UP FOR THE COUNT-DOWN?

POTATO CHIPS

GOONG...

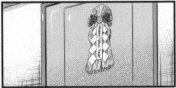

AH!

ONII-CHAN!

KLAK

I WANNA LIVE IN A WORLD THAT'S CAUGHT IN A NEW YEAR'S TIME LOOP.

ROLL ROLL

MMM... NEW YEAR'S IS GREAT. IT'S THE ONE DAY THAT WAS **MADE** FOR LAZING AROUND.

UMA-RU.

FWMP...

......

HUH?

DO YOU REMEM-BER THAT **PROMISE** YOU MADE ME?

?

Faaah!—

YES, DEAR BROTHER OF MINE...?

......

82

I'D RATHER YOU DID IT NOW!

IT'S ALMOST NEW YEAR'S. LEMME WAIT UNTIL THEN, AND I'LL PICK IT ALL UP.

MESSY

What is up with that seat?

fwoo

WHAAA?

UMARU! THE APARTMENT'S A MESS!

THAT WAS FOREVER AGO.

IT WAS IN LATE NOVEMBER.

WELL... I GUESS I DID SAY THAT, BUT...

DAAAZE——

DO YOU REMEMBER NOW?

GASP!

NEXT YEAR'S WHEN I TURN OVER A NEW LEAF!

FLASH

NO WORRIES, ONII-CHAN!

IS ALREADY HERE!!

September 2013
October 2013
November 2013
December 2013
borderline
January 2014

THE "NEXT YEAR" WHEN I HAVE TO TURN OVER THAT NEW LEAF...

CUT THE CRAP!

Zawawa..

I DID INDEED SAY THOSE WORDS--HOWEVER....!

ONII-CHAN, YOU MUST REMEMBER THAT I DID NOT SPECIFY A PLACE OR DATE.

LOOOM

OH, YOU TOTALLY REMEMBER...YOU WOULDN'T LIE TO ME, *WOULD* YOU~?

LET'S GO ON OUR NEW YEAR'S SHRINE VISIT.

HUH? THEN WHAT'RE WE DOING NOW?

YOU CAN START AFTER ALL THE NEW YEAR'S FESTIVI-TIES.

AHH...

FINE, FINE... I'LL CLEAN THE STUPID APART-MENT.

Baked Potatoes

A peace sign? Really?

Woo!

PRETTY BIG CROWD FOR THE SECOND DAY, HUH?

YUP.

DOON DOON

JINGLE JINGLE

DID YOU WANT TO DRESS UP IN A FORMAL KIMONO FOR THIS, TOO?

CLAMOR CLAMOR

UMA-RU...

TRUST HER TO FIND THE ONE THING HERE THAT'S LIKE GAMBLING...

OOH! DRAWING FORTUNES! LET'S SEE WHO GETS BETTER LUCK!

F... FOR- GET I ASKED...

?

NOT EVEN A LITTLE.

They're a pain in the butt.

One thousand reads

Good Luck to Come

NO CLUE.

WHICH IS BETTER, "A LITTLE LUCK" OR "GOOD LUCK TO COME"?

"A LITTLE LUCK."

WHAT'S YOURS SAY, ONII-CHAN?

Fortunes

HERE. FOR AN OFFER-ING.

5yen coin   CLINK

HEY!

Offerings

Offerings

oh yeah?

Then mine's a secret, too!

OH, RE-ALLY?

IT WON'T COME TRUE IF YOU TELL ANY-ONE.

WHAT DID YOU WISH FOR, ONII-CHAN?

OH YEAH.

ONII-CHAN...

I WONDER WHAT THIS YEAR WILL HOLD FOR US...?

AND SO, IN LAZI-NESS...

THE NEW YEAR BEGINS.

PLEASE AND THANK YOU!

HERE'S TO ANOTHER YEAR TOGETHER...

RIGHT BACK AT YA.

YEAH!

·······

!

YOU'RE NOT GONNA TURN OVER A NEW LEAF AT ALL, ARE YOU?!

WH-- HEY!

STUFF LIKE CLEANING-- OH, AND TONIGHT'S DINNER AND STUFF!

OH, YOU KNOW ...

BY THE WAY, WHAT'S UP WITH THE "PLEASE AND THANK YOU"?

I want meat!

I WONDER WHERE SHE KEEPS GOING...

SHE WENT OUT AGAIN...?

rattle

HUH?

SUNDAY.

.....

HEEEY! KIRIEEEE!

LAAAAZE だら り

YES, MASTER!! THIS IS LIKE PARADISE ON EARTH!!

HOO BOY... IT'S ALREADY FEBRUARY, AND WE'RE STILL IN THE KOTATSU, HUH?

ANY-THING YOU SUG-GEST!!

YES, MASTER!!

GRAA

RAWR

WANNA PLAY VIDEO GAMES?!!

THAT GIVES ME AN IDEA!! KIRIE-CHAN...

ZONBI PARADISE
START OPTION

WE'LL MOVE ALONG FASTER THAT WA...

FLOP

LET'S PLAY IN CO-OP MODE!

FLOP

ZONBI PARADISE
► START
OPTION

Huh?!

Wha?! Wh... why would anything be the matter?!

WHAT'S THE MATTER, KIRIE-CHAN?

DRIP

DRIP

DRIP

CHA- CHK...

YEAH!!

THEN LET'S TURN OFF THE LIGHT FOR AMBIENCE!!

WHIRL

N-n-nothing's the matter!! Z-zombies? Ha! They're not scary enough!!

ARE YOU **SCARED** OF ZOMBIES AND STUFF?

※Don't play with the lights off at home, folks!

F F T

PLAYER 2 KIRIE

BADUM BADUM BADUM

Choose your character!!

I'm scared!

It's dark!

Little Kirie's memories.

91

M... MAS- TER!!

PLAYER 1 KOMARU

OKAY, KIRIE-CHAN! LEMME TEACH YOU THE CON-TROLS!!

PERK

FLASH

Bawawawawawawawa!

QUIVER

QUIVER

QUIVER

WAIT! YOU NEED TO FIND A BETTER WEAPON, OR...

GLASSES

SHOT GUN

BADUM BADUM

BADUM BADUM

OMEN

Y-Y-YOU CAN COUNT ON ME!! I-I'LL P-P-PROTECT YOU...!

DEA...

LURCH

D... LIIINE...

I...I'M SORRY, MAS-TER!!

PANIC PANIC

SLIIIDE

blam

KIRIE-CHAN, LOOK OUT!!

92

EON MOLL

CLAMOR

NOW I'M JUST BUMMING AROUND DRINKING FRUITY MILK.

HAD NOTHIN' BETTER TO DO, SO I PLAYED SOME PACHINKO...

CHATTER

WHAT ARE YOU DOING?

CHATTER

I SEE...

HUH?

THAT YOU, TAIHEI?

B

ZELLERS
Zellers puts the zest in life

'SUP?

SLURP—

OH. WEIRD RUNNING INTO YOU HERE.

SALE   SALE   SALE

LE   SALE

HUH?

IS IT A GIRL? I'D BETTER INTRODUCE MYSELF!

WHY...?

CLAMOR

CLAMOR

CLAMOR

OH, HEY.

CAN I COME HANG AT YOUR PLACE?

SURE, BUT... UMARU HAS A FRIEND OVER.

I'm shopping for dinner.

DOOOOM

DROOL

93

WE'RE GONNA BE TOAST IN NO TIME!

SUPER HARD MODE

ACK! WHOOPSIE! GUESS I SET IT ON NIGHTMARE MODE OUT OF HABIT!!

SALE

SA

CASE

NENDORO

MATRYOSHKA

SHOT GUN (TAMAGIRE)

Eeeep!!

Aiegh!

Aiegh!

Aiegh!

YAWARAKA SWORD

Ngyah!

HMM...

I KINDA FEEL LIKE THE ZOMBIES SHOULDN'T BE THIS STRONG...

H-HO-KAY... THANK OO THO MUCH.

600

SHWEEEM

WE'RE ALMOST TO THE BOSS, KIRIE-CHAN! LET'S HEAL UP WITH THESE HERBS.

It's chewy.

ONCE WE CLEAR THIS LEVEL, I'LL SWITCH TO ANOTHER GAME...

Hrrm...

oh god oh god oh god...

KIRIE-CHAN LOOKS PRETTY FREAKED OUT, TOO...

GROARRR!!

NWAAAAH!! IT'S THE BOSS ZOMBIE!!

BA-KOOM

RRRMBL

KRAK

KRIK

94

Kirieeee! You hooome?

Nwaah!! Stay awayy!!

SWING SWING SWING

WH... WHAT'S THE MATTER, KIRIE-CHAN?!

QUAKE QUAKE QUAKE

NGYAAAAH!!

シャキィィン!!
SHCLINK

YASS! SE-CRET COMBO WEAP-ON!!

PIPE + CASE

WAH!

SHINE

COULD IT BE...?!

Ba-chk

HEY, THIS IS...A KNIFE SET!

95

NWAAAH!

SHLK

Mission Complete !!

I... I think it's that fruity milk I drank earlier...

HUH? WHAT'S WRONG ?!

My... my stom-ach...

HRNNGH!

Augh!

GURGLGL

Waaah!

THAT WAS AMAZING, KIRIE-CHAN! YOU RAWK!!

duh-duuun

W...WE DID IT, MAS-TER!!

Rank S

YOU GONNA BE OKAY?

Arrgh—

Y'know, I think I'm gonna go home... I'm too embar-rassed to use the bathroom in front of girls...

96

YOU HAVEN'T BUDGED FROM THAT KOTATSU.

Since last year.

BOY... I CAN'T BELIEVE IT'S STILL THIS COLD, CAN YOU?

TOASTY

WARM

Potato chips

EXERCISE WILL WARM YOU UP. MOVE YOUR BUTT!

IT'S COLD... UMARU DOESN'T WANNA...

Geh!

AH. IT'S ALMOST TIME FOR SPORTS DAY AT SCHOOL, RIGHT?

Handout

AHEM...

IN TODAY'S PHYS ED CLASS, WE'LL BE PLAYING TENNIS.

I WANNA GO HOME!!

OH, I'M NOT ALL THAT...

FWOO=

WOW, UMARU-CHAN... YOU LOOK GREAT EVEN WHEN IT'S THIS COLD OUT...

SHIVER

SHIVER

Brrr!

LET'S BEGIN BY GETTING FAMILIAR WITH THE TENNIS BALL.

I DON'T WANT TO RUN AROUND LIKE AN IDIOT IN THIS COLD...

Eep!

POING

POING

THIS IS SO EASY. IT'S KINDA FUN!

POING

POING

FLINCH

UMARU-SAN!!

NOT TO WORRY!! I TOOK THE LIBERTY OF RESERVING ONE FOR US!!

OH, BUT... THERE AREN'T MANY COURTS, SO...

I CHALLENGE YOU TO A MATCH!! I WILL NOT LOSE IN TENNIS, OH NO I WON'T!!

T... TACHIBANA-SAN...

TEAM
Team Umaru & Kirie

H... HOW DID I GET MYSELF INTO THIS...?

Chatter chatter

CHATTER

CHATTER

UMARU-CHAN'S PLAYING A MATCH!

WHAT'S GOING ON?

HUH?

DON'T YOU WORRY YOUR LITTLE HEAD! I'LL TAKE CARE OF ALL THE HARD STUFF!

UM...I'M TERRIBLE AT TENNIS. ARE YOU SURE YOU WANT ME?

TEAM
Team Sylphyn & Ebina

99

BUT SHE DOESN'T STAND OUT.

H...HOW IS THIS HAPPENING?!

KIRIE-CHAN IS UNEXPECTEDLY ATHLETIC...

Love Fifteen!! (0-15)

BAAAN

Yah!

SWISH

BONK

YOU JUST TOSS THE BALL UP AND HIT IT... RIGHT...?

Serve!!

Team Sylphyn and Ebina!

EBINA-CHAN'S GOT HER EYES CLOSED. I'LL MAKE THIS A GENTLE SERVE.

SERVE SWITCH.

PoM

POOR EBINA-CHAN...

I'M SORRY...! ALSO, IT'S EBINA!

EBIHARA-SAN!! WHY ARE YOUR EYES CLOSED?!

Love Thirty!! (0-30)

oh mah gosh!

Seriously!

THAT BALL IS MINE!!

WHY'S SHE TAKING IT TO THIS LEVEL?!

CRASH

Miiiine!

SHOOM

!

SHUPAA

AN EXQUISITE SERVE, JUST AS I'D EXPECT OF MY RIVAL UMARU-SAN!

YOU ARE A WORTHY OPPONENT FOR ME!

THIS IS OF NO CONSEQUENCE, INDEED IT IS NOT.

SYLPHYN-SAN, ARE YOU OKAY?!

GRIP

Waaaaah!

Switch courts!

Waaaah

"Th...there're a lot of people watching, but...it's just a friendly game, right?

"Su...

"Ebina-chan's got her eyes closed. I'll make this a gentle serve."

"serve switch"

PON

WELL,
I'M NOT
COLD
ANY-
MORE!

. . . . .

THEN,
SINCE
UMARU-
CHAN
PUSHED
HERSELF
TOO HARD,
SHE HAD
NO CHOICE
BUT TO LAZE
AROUND FOR
THE NEXT
WEEK TO
RECOVER.

FIZZLE ――――...

. . . . . .

WHAT'S
UP
WITH
YOU?

JEEEZ...
WHAT ARE YOU, MY MOM?

HERE'S YOUR LUNCH! NOW GO GET READY FOR SCHOOL!

UMARU! DON'T EAT POTATO CHIPS FIRST THING IN THE MORNING!

WHEW...

ANOTHER EXHAUSTING DAY...

WELL, AT LEAST I'M OUT OF THE OFFICE EARLIER THAN USUAL...

I'LL DROP BY THE SUPERMARKET, THEN COOK DINNER...

HUH?

SCRITCH

SCRITCH

MEOW?

WHERE AM I...?

KAW

KAW

KAW

KAW

108

HUH?

Nyankoro Canning Factory

Meownderful

IT'S EASY TO GET LOST IN RESIDENTIAL AREAS...

SHOULD I GO BACK THE WAY I CAME OR KEEP MOVING FORWARD...?

Meownderful!

I REMEMBER SEEING THIS POSTER WITH UMARU. I'VE BEEN DOWN THIS STREET BEFORE.

THAT'S RIGHT.

Look! It says "meownderful"!

IF I WAS WITH UMARU, IT MUST HAVE BEEN RECENT...

I DON'T REMEMBER HAVING BEEN HERE AT ALL, THOUGH...

I'LL JUST KEEP GOING...

SO, IT SHOULD COME OUT ON A STREET I KNOW...

NAH, IT CAN'T HAVE BEEN RECENT.

uhyohhh!

Chipo

BUT SHE BARELY EVER LEAVES THE APARTMENT, SO...

NO, I'D REMEMBER IT THEN.

AFTER I GOT MY JOB...?

NO... MAYBE WHEN I WAS IN HIGH SCHOOL?

WHEN I WAS IN JUNIOR HIGH?

URK...

IT'S ALREADY DINNERTIME?

Dinner smells

WHEN YOU FOLLOW THE SAME ROUTINE EVERY DAY, IT ALL BLURS TOGETHER...

IT'S ALREADY BEEN ABOUT FIVE YEARS SINCE I JOINED THE WORKING WORLD...

BUT IF THAT WERE THE CASE, UMARU'D HAVE BEEN THROWING A TANTRUM...

No no no!

KICK KICK

KICK KICK

I WAS HUNGRY... I WANTED TO GET HOME FAST.

WHEN I TOOK THIS STREET BEFORE, IT WAS ABOUT THE SAME TIME OF DAY...

I FEEL LIKE...

are you hungry?

Taihei-kun...

WHUH?! SOMETHING'S OFF HERE!!

?! ?!

?! ?!

WHAT THE HECK?! WHY'S UMARU CALLING ME "TAIHEI-KUN"?!

HUH?!

111

GUESS I'LL ASK UMARU WHEN I GET HOME...

. . . .

MEOW?

THEN I'LL KNOW WHERE I AM.

FIRST, I SHOULD GET BACK ON A MAIN ROAD.

YOU'RE THAT CAT FROM BEFORE, RIGHT? ARE YOU HERE BE- CAUSE THE CANNING FACTORY IS CLOSE BY?

LICK
LICK

IT WASN'T UMARU, AFTER ALL...

I REMEM-BER...

AHHH ...

I love cats, too!

Isn't it cute?

Ah! A cat!

Hmm ?

What is it, Taihei-kun?

Nyankoru Canning Factory

Yeah, Mom!

SO HOME IS *THIS* WAY.

SCHOOL IS THAT WAY...

ALL RIGHT.

WHEN I GET HOME, I'LL MAKE UMARU SOMETHING BETTER THAN POTATO CHIPS.

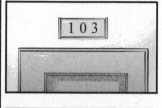

UMARU

UN

103

IT SHOULD BE SIMPLE, SO I'LL JUST WHIP SOME UP AND...

uhyohhh!

HEH HEH HEH... AND I'VE BEEN HAVING WICKED CHOCOLATE CRAVINGS, TOO!

WELL, I SAW CHOCOLATE AT THE STORE... BUT I WANTED TO MAKE IT MYSELF...

YOU DON'T USUALLY INVITE ME OVER, EBINA-CHAN.

EH?

O-OKAY.

I'LL... BE RIGHT BACK, EBINA-CHAN...

SHFF

How to Make Homemade Chocolate

WHAT'S THIS ABOUT?

HEY, LOOKEE WHO I FOUND.

RE-ALLY?!

N-n-no!! please, stay!!

WELL, I DON'T WANT TO MAKE EBINA-CHAN UNCOM-FORT-ABLE...

But making chocolate is hard. C'mon, help us out for a bit!

LOOK, YOU... I WAS IN THE MIDDLE OF DOING THE LAUNDRY.

WHISPER WHISPER WHISPER

ISN'T THIS USUALLY GIRL STUFF...?

CHOCO-LATE, HUH...? I DON'T HAVE MUCH EXPERI-ENCE MAKING IT...

WH...
WH...?

BA-

THUMP

FLASH

SHE HAS...

TWO REFRIGER-ATORS!!

Umaru Conference

I'LL PUT KAKI NO TANE IN MY CHOCO-LATE!

What could possibly go wrong?!

I KNOW!

Fidget

Fidget

GAMA

?
? ? ? ?
? ? ? ?
?

AND HER KITCHEN'S SO TIDY!!

CUT IT UP.

MELT IT.

Nom nom!

POUR IT INTO A MOLD.

CHOCOLATE'S QUICK AND EASY TO MAKE AS LONG AS YOU AREN'T DOING ANYTHING FANCY WITH DECORATION OR FLAVOR.

WOOOW...

oh mah gosh!

FIDGET

DROOL

YADDA YADDA

FOR TRUFFLES, YOU MIX IN FRESH CREAM.

FOR GANACHE, MALT SYRUP.

WHEN IT'S MELTED, YOU CAN PLAY WITH IT IN ANY NUMBER OF WAYS.

WOW, THAT'S FAST!!

AND YOU'RE DONE.

OH, AND REMEMBER...

・・・・・・

121

YOU'RE MIXING IN YOUR **FEELINGS** FOR THE CHOCOLATE'S RECIPIENT, TOO.

THERE'S MORE TO IT THAN JUST MIXING INGREDIENTS INTO THE CHOCOLATE.

WITH VALENTINE'S DAY CHOCOLATE, YOU'RE DOING ALL THIS WORK TO GIVE IT TO SOMEONE SPECIAL...

DANG IT, HE'S IN LECTURE MODE...

IN THE FIRST PLACE, CHOCOLATE ORIGINATED WHEN PEOPLE GROUND UP CACAO BEANS AND ATE THEM. IT CAME TO JAPAN FROM SPAIN. THE MILK CHOCOLATE WE KNOW TODAY RESULTED FROM...

YADDA YADDA YADDA

"I saw chocolate at the store...but I wanted to make it myself..."

FOR THE CHOCOLATE'S RECIPIENT...

MIX IN YOUR FEELINGS...

....

122

GAH, I ACCIDENTALLY WROTE...

FIZZLE

"DEAR" ON IT!!

Dear

What the heck did you put in that?

GLANCE

A secret ingredient!

AH WAH WAH WAH WAH WAH...

O-O-OH NO... NOW I HAVE TO WRITE A **NAME** AFTER THAT...

IT'S FOR HER- SELF?!

Dear EBINA

UH... CAN I GO HANG UP OUR LAUNDRY TO DRY NOW?

Y...

YUP!

CHOCOLATE YOU MADE YOURSELF IS DELI- CIOUS. RIGHT, EBINA- CHAN?

REWARDS FOR GOOD GRADES, AS A HIGH SCHOOL-ER...?

YOU MUST GET HEAPS OF REWARDS FOR GRADES LIKE THAT.

I'M SO JEAL-OUS.

OH MY GOSH!

100

UMARU-CHAN, YOU GOT ANOTHER 100?!

SEE? TOLD YA!

OH... I DON'T REALLY...

I WANNA REWARD!! I WANT ONE, I WANT ONE, I WANT ONE!!

COULDA FOOLED ME...

COME OOON. I'M WORKING SO HARD!

UGH, HE'S TALKING LIKE AN OLD FART AGAIN...

YOU SHOULDN'T BE WORKING HARD JUST TO GET MATERIAL REWARDS.

I GUESS IT'S TRUE --IT NEVER HURTS TO TRY!!

EH?!

RE-ALLY?!

OKAY, YOU WIN THIS ROUND.

RRRUMBL...

WELL, I SUP-POSE THIS MEANS SHE'S BEING RESPON-SIBLE AT SCHOOL, AT LEAST...

DUH-DUNNN

Thanks for your business!

ONII-CHAN, C'MON! LET'S EAT!!

WOW, THIS STUFF ISN'T CHEAP...

SUSHIII!!

SNAP

COME TO THINK OF IT, WE DON'T EAT SUSHI MUCH...

WE DON'T GO OUT TO EAT OFTEN... AND WE DON'T MAKE IT AT HOME...

SNAP

① Begin with white-fleshed fish.

② Move on to battleship sushi, rolls, egg sushi, etc.

③ The main event: red sushi!

④ Finish off with lemon aburi (partially grilled) sushi to cleanse the palate.

HEH HEH HEH... OH, ONII-CHAN. SO IGNO-RANT.

BUT YEAH--I'VE HEARD THAT, TOO. YOU START WITH THE LIGHTEST-TASTING SUSHI, RIGHT?

Industry Insider

WHY ARE YOU TALKING IN CODE?

Which is obviously pig latin.

AH-AH-AH! NOT SO FAST, ONIICHAN! WHEN YOU EAT-WAY USHI-SAY, THERE ARE ULES-RAY!

TSK TSK TSK TSK

SO FAR SO GOOD ...

SLURRRP——...

1. First, drink some tea and relax.

♪ The Correct Way to Eat Sushi, Brought to You by Umaru! ♪

3. As for the eating order...

It'll ruin the experience if you end up with a big honking mouthful of unexpected wasabi!

Does that ever even happen?

HEY, THAT'S BAD MAN-NERS!!

SHP   SHP

2. Even if the label says, "No Wasabi," check anyway, just in case.

※It does happen once in a while.

128

WHAAAAAT?!

YUMMM!

SOPPING WET

PICK YOUR FAVORITE, DROWN IT IN SOY SAUCE, AND GO TO TOWN!!

CHEW   CHEW

NOM

BUT YOU GOTTA USE THAT MUCH, OR YOU WON'T TASTE ITS DELICIOUS FLAVOR~!

TOO MUCH SOY SAUCE IS BAD FOR YOU!

SPIS.

MEDIUM FATTY TUNAAAA~!!

M...

WE DON'T EAT SUSHI OFTEN. I GUESS I UNDERSTAND WHY SHE'D GO FOR HER FAVORITE FIRST.

BUT YEAH...

order up!

Got another order!

Comin right up!

YOU ADDED THAT RULE IN JUST NOW!!

4. While eating sushi, don't think about what's unhealthy and stuff like that.

5. Pay attention to what your dining partner takes.

HIS FAVORITE SUSHI IS FLUKE FIN...?

SWIP

STARE

NOM

WELL, IT *DID* COME WITH CHOPSTICKS... IF IT WERE ON A COUNTER, THEN MAYBE I WOULD.

YOINK

I THOUGHT YOU WERE GONNA EAT WITH YOUR HANDS, ONII-CHAN.

SPKKS

F...

FLUKE FIIIIN~!!

SHH

SHRIIIMP~!!

GLY~

JIG~

SALT-
WATER
EEL...!!

EEEEL

SALMON
ROOOE~!!

POP

THNK
THNK
THNK

SEA
URCHIN...!!

AMBER-
JACK!!

SALMON!!

TUNA
ROLL!!

PAH

E!!
G!!
G!!

SPIN
SPIN
SPIN

TEA...!!

FIZZZZ—

......

COLA GOES WITH SUSHI, TOO!

WHY ARE YOU DRINKING COLA?

Some sushi restaurants even serve cola.

HMM? SIIIGH—

WHY DOES TEA TASTE SO GOOD AFTER EATING SUSHI, ANYWAY...?

5. Pay attention to what your dining partner takes.

......

YOU ATE A MEDIUM FATTY TUNA AT THE START... YOU DIDN'T EAT *BOTH* OF THEM, DID YOU?

BY THE WAY, UMA-RU...

SO *THAT'S* WHAT SHE MEANT BY THAT.

4. While eating sushi, don't think about what's unhealthy and stuff like that.

⭐ No. 50 The Absence of Umaru

Guest Illustrator: Haruno Tomoya

HM?

DON'T BE GONE TOO LONG.

TP

BYE, ONII-CHAN! I'M GOIN' OUT!!

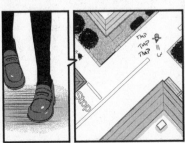

TMP TMP TMP

DID YOU TWO HAVE PLANS? I'M SURE SHE'LL BE BACK SOON.

UMA-- AHEM, KOMARU JUST WENT OUT...

HUH?

· · · · · ·

THANKS FOR THOSE COOKIES. THEY WERE GOOD.

OKAY, SO THEY WERE A LITTLE BURNT.

AH.

SORRY I FORGOT TO SAY THIS BEFORE, BUT...

Ha ha ha...

DROP- PING BY UNIN- VITED?!

RATTLE RATTLE RATTLE
RATTLE RATTLE RATTLE

W-- W... we didn't.

SPLAT

134

SWUP

WHAAAAT?!

DON'T HUMOR ME.

GLAAA-

RE

GLAARE

GLAARE

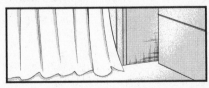

UMARU...

THUNK

Huh?!

THIS IS SERIOUSLY AWKWARD...

HURRY UP AND COME HOME ALREADY ...!

SWUP

AH... OH YEAH. I WAS IN THE MIDDLE OF LAUN-DRY...

MAYBE IT'S BECAUSE UMARU'S NOT AROUND...?

I THOUGHT SHE'D GOTTEN MORE COMFORTABLE WITH ME RECENTLY...

SHTMP

LEAP

ROLL ROLL ROLL

TMP

STRUT

STRUT

. . . .
. . . .
. . . . . .

KIRIE-CHAN DIDN'T GET TO PLAY WITH UMARU AFTER ALL. POOR KID.

IT'S EVENING ALREADY...

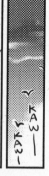

KAW—

KAW—

ABOUT THE COOKIES...

I'M SORRY...

UH...

UM...

I'M SORRY...

ERM...

I GAVE HER...

THE WRONG BATCH...

UM...

Oh...

THOSE ONES WERE BURNT...

138

TO TELL ME THAT...?

DID SHE COME HERE TODAY...

I HOPE ONII-CHAN ISN'T MAD...

I GOT ON A REAL HOT WINNING STREAK AT THE ARCADE AND LOST TRACK OF TIME...

SNEAK SNEAK

TAIPO

TAIPO STATION

....

!

PEER

YOU'RE BACK.

OH.

BWUH?!

AW, JEEZ... I-IT'S OKAY-- RIGHT, KIRIE-CHAN?!

SWIP

BUT SOMEONE TOOK HER OWN SWEET TIME COMING HOME.

SHE DROPPED BY IN THE AFTER- NOON TO PLAY WITH YOU.

HUH?

WHAT'S KIRIE- CHAN DOING HERE?

HWUH?!

I SHOULD BE HEAD- ING HOME.

MAS- TER...

OH, IS THAT ONE OF THOSE LAID-BACK MASCOTS?

AH! LOOK AT THIS! IT'S SO CUTE!

UMARUUUUN

WHEN YOU OPEN IT, HE WAKES UP!

Sleepy Seal! Bag

IT'S A "SLEEPY SEAL" LUNCH BOX BAG!

That's what makes it cute!

That is so weird!

· · · · · ·

NO.

ONII-CHAN? ♥

PRETTY PLEASE ...♥

BEE-

AAM

BUT THESE ARE ALL OLD.

CRAMMED...

IF YOU WANT WEIRD MASCOT MERCHANDISE, YOU HAVE PLENTY OF THAT IN THE CLOSET!

BUT I WANT A SLEEPY SEAL BAG!!

YOU ALREADY HAVE A BAG, DON'T YOU?

NO!

SWITCH

C'MOOON. BUY IT FOR ME, ONII-CHAAAN.

NO!

ONII-CHAN... I'M... LONELY...

SNIFFLE...

144

THIS IS HER FINISHING MOVE...?

FLAIL FLAIL

BUY IT, BUY IT, BUY IT!!

FLAIL FLAIL

SWITCH

STOP TRYING OUT DIFFERENT PERSONAS!!

BUY IT, ONII-CHAN!

ᵁᵁ

SHP

I'LL PUT THAT MONEY TOWARDS YOUR BAG.

BUT YOU HAVE TO GIVE UP COLA AND POTATO CHIPS FOR A WHOLE WEEK!

KAA

SWEET!

:

OKAY, OKAY...

WHAAAAAAT?!

WH...

BNNNT

Potato Chips

Paradise

Cola

Potato Chips

Paradise

Cola

Onii-chaaan!

IS THE IDEA REALLY THAT HORRIFY-ING...?

FOOOM

AND SO BEGAN UMARU'S LIFE WITHOUT COLA.

Three days! C'mon, have a little mercy!

No! One week!

BISH

THAT'S NOT WHAT "AT LEAST" MEANS!

MAKE IT AT LEAST TWO DAYS!!

NOW SHE'LL HAVE TO STOP DRINK-ING COLA, AT LEAST FOR A WHILE.

PSSH

KA-KLAK

HEH HEH... THAT WAS A STROKE OF GENIUS, IF I DO SAY SO MYSELF.

IF I'M GOING TO KEEP HER FROM DRINKING COLA, I'LL HAVE TO TAKE THINGS UP A NOTCH...

SHOCK

IT'S BECOME MINDLESS INSTINCT FOR HER...

GASP!! MY HANDS ARE OPENING A COLA BOTTLE OF THEIR OWN VOLITION!!

THIS PREVENTS UMARU FROM INDULGING OUT OF SHEER HABIT.

TAIHEI'S FIRST STEP IS TO BOX UP ALL OF THE COLA AND POTATO CHIPS IN THE HOUSE.

KEEP OUT KEEP OUT KEEP OUT KEEP OUT

THE NO-COLA WEEK BEGINS... NOW! (AFTER THIS ONE.)

Fine, but that's the last one.

Oniichan, okay if I drink this one? Wouldn't want it to go to waste!

BUT ON THE FOURTH DAY... SOMETHING WENT WRONG...

THE SECOND AND THIRD DAYS PASSED SMOOTHLY.

HE CHECKS HER RECEIPTS AND LIMITS HER POCKET CASH.

NEXT, AN ALLOWANCE CHECK SO SHE DOESN'T BUY ANY COLA OUTSIDE OF THE HOME.

CONVENIENCE K

SUPERMARKET

147

OH, NOTH-ING.

WHAT'S THE MAT-TER? YOU LOOK GUILTY AS HECK.

SIZZZZ

CHOMP

CHOMP

CHOMP

GURRRGLE

CRAP. NOW THAT SHE'S GIVEN UP COLA, SHE'S TRANS-FERRED HER APPETITE TO MEAT.

I NEED **MEAT**, ONII-CHAN. ANY KIND OF MEAT.

NOTHING BEATS THE TINGLY FEELING OF CAR-BONATION GOING DOWN MY THROAT!!!

FIZZZZ

KAAAH!!

GULP GULP

GLANCE

It's Tea

DON'T DISRESPECT THE TEA.

SIIIIIIGH—

IT'S SO FLAT...!!

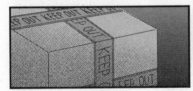

NWOP

IT'S NO GOOD TRYING TO BE SNEAKY. I KNOW HOW MANY BOTTLES ARE IN THERE.

UMARU.

FLICK

FREEZE

QUIVER
QUIVER
QUIVER

OH! YOUR BAG! IS THAT SLEEPY SEAL?!

ACK!! S-SLOW DOWN!! YOU'LL MAKE YOUR-SELF SICK!!

GLUG GLUG GLUG

I DON'T NEED THAT STUPID OLD BAG!!

NWAAAAH!!

I SURE DID!

DID YOU GET YOUR FOLKS TO BUY IT FOR YOU?

I DIDN'T KNOW YOU HAD CHAR-ACTER GOODS LIKE THAT, UMARU-CHAN!

TOO LATE.

GOTTA WRAP THIS UP BEFORE ONII-CHAN GETS HOME.

I BETTER REVIEW THE PATTERNS ONE MORE TIME.

SCRIBL
SCRIBL

HMMM...

MY CONNECTION AFTER THE FIFTH COMBO IS STILL TOO SLOPPY...

I SEE... SO, YOU WANT TO GO WATCH IT?

NOM
NOM

THE ARCADE I ALWAYS GO TO IS HOLDING A FIGHTING GAME TOURNAMENT.

Plaza GAPCOM

MR-sama,

Thank you for registering to attend the upcoming Plaza GAPCOM tournament.

Please see the details below

at the arcade, we will

A GAME TOURNAMENT, HUH?

HUH?

I KNOW! YOU HAVE TOMORROW OFF, RIGHT? YOU SHOULD COME WITH ME!

YOUR IDEAS ABOUT ARCADES ARE WAY OUT OF DATE, ONII-CHAN.

Uhn!

Death

Arcade Kings

BE CAREFUL, OKAY? ARCADES ARE DANGEROUS PLACES.

Hrrm...

PLAZA GAPCOM

SERENE
へぃわぁ

COIN FEVER

Taiko

TREMBLE
TREMBLE

OH... OKAY.

I'M GONNA GO CHECK ON THE TOURNAMENT. YOU FIND SOMETHING FUN TO PLAY!

HUH?

EXCHANGE

GLANCE

GLANCE

GLANCE

WHERE DO I BUY TOKENS?

WOW, YOU WERE RIGHT. THERE'RE EVEN KIDS AND SENIOR CITIZENS HERE.

SEE? TOTALLY SAFE, RIGHT?

HA, YEAH... MY LITTLE SISTER DRAGGED ME HERE TODAY. SAID SOMETHING ABOUT A TOURNAMENT.

IT'S UNUSUAL TO RUN INTO YOU OUTSIDE OF WORK... LET ALONE IN AN ARCADE.

HUH?! ALEX-KUN?!

IS THAT YOU, TAIHEI-SENPAI?!

POP

VWUM

SPACE STREAM FIGHTER IV

!

FFT

WHOA, WHAT A COINCIDENCE. I'M--

the battle for the title of S.S.F. 4's #1 player!!

We will now begin...

ROAR

DUUN

I'm your host, GAPCOM employee Hado Ryuichi.

May I have your attention... Thank you for your patience, everyone...

HUH? YOU DIDN'T KNOW?

TH-THE MOOD JUST COMPLETELY CHANGED IN HERE...

YEEEAAHH!!

THEY HOLD RANKING MATCHES AT ARCADES ACROSS JAPAN.

SPACE STREAM FIGHTER 4 IS A POPULAR FIGHTING GAME ALL OVER THE WORLD.

I-I SEE...

NO TRUE VIDEO GAME FAN WOULD MISS IT FOR THE WORLD.

ALL THE BEST PLAYERS IN THE COUNTRY ARE GATHERED HERE TODAY, IN THIS VERY ARCADE, TO DETERMINE WHO AMONG THEM IS THE BEST.

RECENTLY, EACH PLAZA GAPCOM ARCADE HAD A MATCH TO DETERMINE ITS NUMBER ONE PLAYER.

1	Q.Z.R		1	A.A.C		1	K.F.C
2	O.P.T		2	C.U.U		2	S.S.O
3	A.E.R		3	A.F.F		3	A.T.A
			4	P.P.R		4	O.J.P
			5	H.U.		5	E.L.T
			6	A.O		6	T.R.F
			7	u.s			

First, the champion who dominates this very arcade's rankings...

DUUN

And now, I'll introduce our contenders!!

155

156

Bonus Story:
The Oniichans' Christmas

Klak

klak

klak

WHAT'S SHE DOING HERE AT WORK, ON CHRISTMAS EVE?

SHE'S AS GORGEOUS AS EVER...

OH? GOOD WORK TODAY.

WE'LL BE LEAVING FOR THE NIGHT!

AH! SECTION CHIEF! GOOD WORK TODAY!

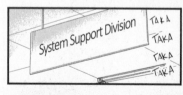

System Support Division

TAKA
TAKA
TAKA
TAKA

TAKA
TAKA
TAKA
TAKA

Klak klak klak

I'M SURE SHE'D ALWAYS PRIORITIZE WORK OVER THAT KIND OF THING.

162

OVERTIME ON CHRISTMAS...

Taka taka taka taka taka

SMIRK

WHAT ARE YOU LOOKING AT, ANYWAY?

HEY. NO ESCAPING INTO FANTASY.

THIS SUCKS, MAN...I WANNA GO BACK TO THE FREEDOM OF MY CAREFREE YOUTH...

GROAN—

SANTA COSTUMES. YOU WANNA WEAR ONE, TOO?

WE'RE MAKING GOOD PROGRESS.

IT'S NO PROBLEM.

UM...

S... SECTION CHIEF KANAU! WE WERE JUST TAKING A LITTLE BREAK...

HOW ARE THOSE CHECKS COMING ALONG?

NRRL

W... WELL, BETTER GET BACK TO IT!

NRRMBL

?

TAKA TAKA

....

!

NRRL

I, AH, CAN'T SEE MY SCREEN.

UM...

WHOA!

SAY...

TAIHEI... DO YOU HAVE ANY PLANS FOR TONIGHT?

NO...I WAS JUST GOING TO GO HOME...

WHAT?!

YOU DON'T?!

R-- RIGHT ...

I DON'T HAVE ANY...

SWIP

W... WELL, ERR... IF YOU *DID* HAVE SOMEONE TO MAKE PLANS WITH, YOU WOULDN'T WORK ALL THIS OVERTIME, RIGHT?

FREE... ON CHRISTMAS EVE...

ERM... SO YOU'RE ...

HMM...

THEN ...

RakuLchin

Big Christmas Sale in Progress!!

X'mas Tree (lights not included)

Super Sudu Suit

Ben9

I...

I SEE...

C'MON. WE'RE THE ONLY ONES LEFT HERE. IT'S OKAY TO SPEAK OUR MINDS, RIGHT?

BOMBA, DON'T TALK TO THE SECTION CHIEF LIKE THAT!!

PICK PICK

STAYIN' AT WORK 'CAUSE YOU GOT NOWHERE BETTER TO BE?

YOU'RE IN THE SAME BOAT, AREN'T YA?

SLUMP

165

OH MY. SO SORRY. MY HAND SLIPPED.

KEH KEH KEH

GAAH!! WHAT'S YOUR DAMAGE, KANAU?!!

DAAUGH!!

YES, BUT IT TICKS ME OFF!

...

!

WANT TO HANG OUT, THE THREE OF US...? FOR OLD TIME'S SAKE?

S-SO... KANAU...

NO THANKS.

I'LL PASS.

Klak
Klak
Klak

YOU BOTH GO HOME TO YOUR FAMILIES, TOO.

I HAVE A FAMILY DINNER TO ATTEND TONIGHT.

SWP

TSUTAYAN
VIDEO CD BOOK

TSUTAYAN

NIIICE!! DIDJA HEAR THAT?! WE'RE FREE!!

. . . . .

HMM? THOUGHT I'D GET SOMETHING FOR MY LIL' SIS.

SO, WHAT ARE YOU RENTING?

YA THINK? I BET IT WAS JUST A RANDOM THING.

IT'S PRETTY **UNUSUAL** FOR KANAU TO COME BY OUR OFFICE.

H U N H.

BETCHA *SHE'S* NOT DOIN' ANYTHING TONIGHT.

Ooh, this is a good one.

N-NO, UM...

Your membership card...?

WHAT? IS IT *THAT* ODD FOR A SINGLE PERSON TO RENT A DVD?

DOOOOOMU ゴゴゴゴゴゴ

UM... MISS ...?

¥ CASHIER

Through 19/25 1 Day 80円!

WAIT, YOU WERE *SERIOUS?*

Through 11/25!

¥mas Disco

AH!

OH, HEY! BET THEY SELL SANTA COSTUMES AT VILLAGE GANVARD, HUH?

THE ONIICHANS' CHRISTMAS (FIN)

168

Sankaku-sensei did badly in the surveys back in Part 2!! Is it game over?!

ALMOST TWO MONTHS HAD PASSED...

AND WITHOUT GETTING ANYTHING ELSE INTO A MAGAZINE...

LAAAZE

Chk Chk

Grenade!!

AFTER THE RESULTS OF THE READER SURVEYS...

FAAAH!

THE SECOND ONE-SHOT.

Young Jump's Okuma

Sankaku Head

VRRNZ

YJ
Okuma-san

VRRNZ

VRRZ

VRRRNZZ

HELLO?

BADUM
BADUM

BEEP

.....

YES?!

San-kaku-san...

On-the-phone pose.

SHRAM

HUH?! UH, NO!! NOTHING AT ALL!!

STOP

Were you in the middle of something?

D...

FWA

will be considered at the next serialization meeting!

Your idea, D.T. & Uniflash...

Faaah!

SAY WHA-AAT--?!

D.T...

AND IT SEEMED THAT OKUMA-SAN SAW POTENTIAL IN ONE OF THEM-- D.T. & UNIFLASH.

I CAME UP WITH THUMB-NAILS FOR THREE DIFFERENT IDEAS AND SENT THEM OVER...

Computer Granny

I Love Bread

D.T. & Uniflash

ENDED UP JUST BOUNC-ING A BUNCH OF IDEAS OFF EACH OTHER.

I'D PUT OUT TWO WORKS, BUT NEITHER ONE HAD BEEN VERY POPULAR... AND SO OKUMA-SAN AND I...

Cursed Student Council

Fujinto-n

Not that one. Not this one, either.

I DECIDED THE D.T. BOYS WOULD BE ASPIRING MANGA ARTISTS. ("UNIFLASH" IS WHAT WE CALL NARRA-TION BUBBLES DRAWN WITH ACTION LINES, BECAUSE THEY LOOK LIKE SPIKY UNI → SEA URCHINS←).

MANGA ARTISTS.

INK

BUT THAT CONCEPT ALONE WASN'T STRONG ENOUGH, SO I CAME UP WITH...

Thinking back on it now, maybe this came from Volume 1's unpopular student council guys.

Young Jump

"D.T." STANDS FOR DOUTEI (VIRGIN). I WANTED TO DRAW A STORY ABOUT SOME VIR-GIN GUYS GETTING ALL ROWDY.

D.T. & Uniflash

Created to be a series (so it's unfinished). Three unpopular boy's start high school. They're all super lame with zero special abilities, but they do all have one thing going for them: a very strong desire to get rid of their v-cards. So, they've been looking for a club that will get them the ladies when they happen to run into a super-hot upperclassman, "Unifura-senpai." She leads them along by the nose...and they end up joining her "Hardcore Manga Research Club," a club for people who are super serious about becoming manga artists!

A foursome of three D.T.s and Unifura-senpai.

Yessss!!!

Okay. Then let's do it lots!

We'll do it Senpai!!!

We'll do it!!

FLAASH

HERE ARE THUMB-NAILS AND CONCEPT ART FOR D.T. & UNIFLASH.

It came out a little...

Sample character art

It...

Would have serious manga jargon that ends up sounding like naughty talk.

erect.

It's...

RRRRMBL

THAT'S WHY THIS IS A SERIES THAT ONLY YOU, SANKAKU-SAN, CAN CREATE.

YOUR GAGS ARE TAILORED TO THE MAGAZINE'S TARGET AUDIENCE... YOU'VE HAD EXPERIENCE WITH SEVERAL MANGA MAGAZINES...

I GOT SO INTO THE GROOVE THAT I UP AND DREW ABOUT SIX CHAPTERS' WORTH.

I can draw something that doesn't end in one chapter!

I'D NEED THREE CHAPTERS' WORTH OF THUMBNAILS FOR THE SERIALIZATION MEETING.

OKUMA-SAN'S EXPRESSIONS ARE HARD TO READ.

FLASH!

IT MADE ME LAUGH QUITE A LOT!! I THINK THIS MAY BE THE ONE!!

NO, I MEAN THE GAP BETWEEN HER LOOKS AND ACTIONS. COMPARED TO YOUR LAST TWO SUBMISSIONS, YOU'VE GOTTEN BETTER AT CREATING CHARACTERS WITH SOME DEPTH.

Tee hee hee hee hee!

OH, WELL... SHE IS A PRETTY GIRL CHARACTER, AFTER ALL...

UNIFURA-SENPAI. SHE'S CUTE.

NOW, THIS CHARACTER...

TAP

FOUR PAGES ?!

VWOOOM

SO, THERE'S ONLY FOUR PAGES TO WORK WITH, BUT I'D LIKE YOU TO DRAW A SIDE STORY FOR THIS, TO RUN IN MIRACLE JUMP!!

OKUMA-SAN IS ACTUALLY PUTTING A LOT OF THOUGHT INTO THIS FOR ME.

Miracle Jump

HE'S COMPARING IT TO MY PREVIOUS WORK...

Three wired boys.

Special Feature: Hot Girls Who Aren't Wearing Any!!

phimos

#1 Technique!!

Has tiny jokes like this.

"The 3 D.T.s"
Miracle Jump No. 8
(April 2012 issue)
4 pages
A one-shot in which the three D.T.s do some dumb chatting. I only had four pages, but it's crammed full of D.T. & Uniflash-type jokes.

GRAA

Miracle Skuzze

R-18

500 bucks and going strong!!

AND SO, WE SUBMITTED D.T. & UNIFLASH TO THE SERIALIZATION MEETING, AND I DREW "THE THREE D.T.S" AS A FOUR-PAGE ONE-SHOT.

The "bring a naughty book to school" thing.

THE SERIALIZATION MEETING BEGAN.

DOOOOM

Shueisha

AND SO...

To be continued!!

ALL WE CAN DO NOW... IS HAVE FAITH.

Zaa

WE'VE DONE EVERYTHING IN OUR POWER.

Special Thanks My editor, Okuma-san; my assistant, Kitagawa-san; Masaoka-san; Kagetsu Suzu-san; Inagaki-san; my mom; Shoji Hiroyuki-san; Haruno Tomoya-san

START

UMR vs. TSF!
Who will win?!!

Sylphyn turns beet
red?! But why?

Ebina's walking
fashion unveiled!!

A tragedy so awful
that Umaru cries?!!

Kirie gets gloomier
than ever before?!!

SLIDE SLIIDE
SLIDE

BWRKM

AHH-HHH-HH...
I DON'T WANNA GET UUUP...

Taihei turns into a couch potato?!!

NUM NUM

Badum! A meeting full of Umarus? But what's it about?

And then, a summer full of fun begins!!!

Umaru the food buff! ♪
Umaru eats the king of junk food!!

LET'S GO!!
HIMOUTO
UMARU-CHAN
4

Coming Soon!!

SEVEN SEAS ENTERTAINMENT PRESENTS

HIMOUTO! UMARU-CHAN Volume 3

story and art by SANKAKUHEAD

TRANSLATION
Amanda Haley

ADAPTATION
Shanti Whitesides

LETTERING AND RETOUCH
Carolina Hernández Mendoza

COVER DESIGN
Nicky Lim

PROOFREADER
Janet Houck

EDITOR
Jenn Grunigen

PRODUCTION ASSISTANT
CK Russell

PRODUCTION MANAGER
Lissa Pattillo

EDITOR-IN-CHIEF
Adam Arnold

PUBLISHER
Jason DeAngelis

Seven Seas books may be purchased in bulk for promotional, educational, or
business use. Please contact your local bookseller or the Macmillan Corporate
and Premium Sales Department at 1-800-221-7945, extension 5442, or by
e-mail at MacmillanSpecialMarkets@macmillan.com.

Seven Seas and the Seven Seas logo are trademarks of
Seven Seas Entertainment, LLC. All rights reserved.

ISBN: 978-1-626929-32-6

Printed in Canada

First Printing: October 2018

10 9 8 7 6 5 4 3 2 1

FOLLOW US ONLINE: *www.sevenseasentertainment.com*

READING DIRECTIONS

This book reads from *right to left*, Japanese style.
If this is your first time reading manga, you start
reading from the top right panel on each page and
take it from there. If you get lost, just follow the
numbered diagram here. It may seem backwards at
first, but you'll get the hang of it! Have fun!!

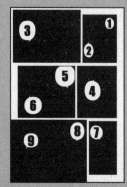